The Lancashire Witches

A Horror Bound Novel

by

Steve Woods

Author's Note

There has been volumes written about The Lancashire Witches, and their legacy and folklore is still evident today, not just in the Pendle area. I have taken a few liberties with names, locations and historical accuracy. It was never my intention to misrepresent any individual, their character or place in history. Equally my descriptions of Lytham Hall and Read Hall are loosely based on records of those country house estates.

This novel is a work of fiction.
The characters and events in this book are imaginary and not representative of any real person or actual event.

Steve Woods is a retired police officer and native of
Preston, Lancashire.
For the past thirty years he has been living in
Lytham St. Annes with his gorgeous wife Bev.

Also by Steve Woods

WHEN EVIL VISITS

PRIEST TOWN

Available through
horrorboundbooks.wordpress.com

Follow the blog via Facebook at
facebook.com/horrorboundbooks

Acknowledgements

My special thanks to Christine O'Hara, founder member of the *Book Club on the Fylde* and includes members Christine Russell, Christine Twistleton, Margaret Crowther, Joanne Livesey, Niamh O'Donaghue, Lesley Sumner and Bev Woods.
These erudite women, who meet every month over a glass of wine to discuss and dissect a particular book, individually proofread copies of my first draft manuscript and came back with uncompromising advice and suggestions.
Without Chris and the book club members, my many blunders in grammar, punctuation, spelling and content would have been embarrassingly exposed throughout this story.

Cover Art Design by Mick Tapper @
latcreative.co.uk

In 1612, nine witches from the Forest of Pendle were hung
at Gallows Hill near Lancaster Castle.
The location of the nine unmarked graves remained a secret
and there the witches lay for century after century,
like dormant seeds waiting to flourish.
A child of one of these sorceresses survived the witch-hunt,
and now the time is right for revenge, to put things right.

1

All Hallows' Eve, 1611.

Malkin Tower on the east side of Pendle Hill was a dilapidated timber building overlooking the Forest of Pendle. Visitors would have trouble finding it, but the local villagers knew where it was and who lived there.

It was home to the Demdikes.

A crowd of around fifty men and women had gathered outside The Lamb Inn at Newchurch, where the local magistrate Roger Nowell addressed them. He was unarmed, but others brandished axes and pitchforks, a few carried shotguns and there were plenty of blazing peat torches, candle lanterns and oil-lamps. The 'vigilance committee' organised by the self proclaimed witch finder, Roger Nowell, had come from Sabden, Roughlee, Barley and surrounding farms and they were eager to set off, like hounds on a fox hunt.

Old Mother Demdike was at the slop-stone, gutting a rabbit, when she looked through the broken pane and saw the bobbing torches and lanterns appear on the track further down the hill. Dropping the rabbit and a handful of viscera onto the stone, and wiping bloodied hands on her dress, she called to her daughter, "Elizabeth, get the child, they are coming. We must leave now".

It was eight o'clock in the evening and Elizabeth's nine year old daughter was asleep on a straw bed. She was roused by her mother and they moved quickly, gathering a few belongings. Mother Demdike threw a pan of water over the fire, contained within a circle of stones, heating a cast iron pot hanging above the flames from a heavy metal tripod. She deftly kicked the cauldron on to its side, the green warming liquid spilling on to the dirt floor, allowing unidentifiable creatures to crawl and flounder in the dissipating brew.

"What about the grimalkin, where is he? We can't leave him". The young girl asked, looking round the dismal hovel.

"Don't worry about him, he'll be fine. There's plenty of homes that will welcome a black cat over their threshold. But hurry, we must go, now", Old Mother Demdike urged her granddaughter.

It was a full moon, the clear sky foretelling an early autumn frost, when the three of them fled Malkin Tower by the back door, the building obscuring their escape. They avoided the track and trudged across country towards the top of the hill, but it was heavy going in the long grass and bracken. The eighty year old grandmother had to stop regularly, resting on her walking stick to catch her breath. She looked back and saw the mob had reached their home and already flames had taken hold of one side of Malkin Tower.

"Mother, we must carry on, we have to warn the others". Elizabeth said in between gasping breaths.

"Elizabeth, there are no others, we are the last, don't you realise that? They've saved the Demdikes till the end. I cannot go on, I'm too tired. You and the child keep going, they'll be happy to have me as the prize, they won't come after you".

Elizabeth turned to her daughter, "Pet, you must run from here. I am staying with your grandmother". She looked back and could see figures moving away from the burning building, some pointing towards them. She put her hands on the girl's shoulders, their faces only inches apart. "You don't have much time. I'll always love you pet, don't forget that, but you must go and one day put this right. Do you hear? You must put this right".

With tears streaming down her face the young girl hugged her mother, turned, hitched her dress and lunged barefoot through the damp undergrowth. She did not look back until she reached the top, near to the cairn marking the summit of Pendle Hill. The mob had found the two women and already they were dragging them down the hill. With all her strength the young girl shouted against the billowing smoke.

"Mother! I will put this right. I promise I will put this right".

2

October 1901.

A large cat, black as a raven, lay splayed across a cushion on the antique rocker by the fire. It stared expressionless at the old woman. His one green eye unblinking, the other long removed by Auntie Vena, the socket neatly stitched. The cat watched her every move, its head resting on front paws. The scene looked a picture of feline and domestic bliss, apart from the whimpering.

The plaintive crying came from beyond the kitchen cellar door under the stairs.

Auntie Vena was sat in her favourite armchair sipping a Scotch whisky from a chunky crystal tumbler. She wore a crisp white blouse under a black woollen cardigan, a knee length Abercrombie tartan skirt and well-polished stout black brogues. With her free hand she gently smoothed her short White hair and gave the cat a sigh. It was six 'clock in the morning and she had been sat awake by the fire through the night, the empty spirit bottle would testify to this. She arose from the chair with an effortless ease that belied her appearance and crossed the room. Still holding the glass tumbler she turned the key in the lock and opened the heavy cellar door.

"Stop snivelling you little wretches or I'll feed you to the rats". Her voice was loud and strong and seemed to bounce along the brick passageway and stone steps that disappeared into darkness.

She remained still, listening, and once satisfied with the silence, closed the door, locked it and returned to the armchair.

The room was small, but cosy and warm. The coal fire was always lit and well banked and not just on cold October mornings. The furniture and furnishings were sparse. Apart from the two occupied chairs, there was only a small table by the armchair and a dark solid sideboard bearing a large glowing oil-lamp. There were no ornaments, keepsakes, knick-knacks, photographs or mementoes and only a pendulum clock confidently counting every second was allowed wall space. Curtains hid the window that looked onto the garden and the outside world, blocking out the twilight.

Auntie Vena had much to think about, as it would soon be All Hallows' Eve.

3

The procession snaked along Friargate in true carnival style. The circus had come to town and Meadowbank looked on with great amusement. He was stood further down the street where the crowds were thinner, accompanied by his friend and colleague, Detective Sergeant Samuel Huggins. Both ate from a large paper-bag of roast potatoes, chomping against the scalding heat.

"Yer can't beat a good circus eh Sam?"

The hot potato in Huggins' mouth prevented him from replying, so instead he nodded his head in agreement, puffing out his cheeks.

The circus was heading for the market square, where a large crowd was eagerly waiting. They mingled with the assorted street sellers providing eatables and drinkables, including pickled whelks, parched peas, hot potatoes, penny pies, tea, coffee, ginger-beer and lemonade. They were all doing a roaring trade and of course the ale-houses were open for those not interested in the entertainment. Chinese acrobats, male and female, wearing sparkling leotards, tumbled and cart-wheeled. Painted clowns teetering on six-foot stilts hidden under long trousers distributed leaflets, Indian snake-charmers played their mystical punjis, jugglers and a marching band entertained the crowd. War painted white horses walked in unison and ridden bareback by North American Indians, in full feathered headdress. At the front of course, strode the ring master, complete with red jacket and top-hat, proclaiming 'the greatest show on earth has arrived'. An assortment of wagons and cages trundled over the cobbles. One wagon was painted gloss black, the red gothic lettering identifying the hidden passengers as 'A Living Freak Show'. Inside the wagon, in the swinging lamp-light the three midgets ignored the cheering, continuing to play cards with the bearded lady. The 'Melting Man' with horrific burn and scar tissue to his head, face and chest, somehow managed to doze as the wagon rocked and bucked.

The last wagon in the parade was a heavy cage containing a demented hyena.

The handler, representing a big game hunter was dressed in a safari hat, khaki jacket, breeches and calf-length boots, walked with the two horses, holding onto a bridle with one hand and waving to the crowd with the other.

The small signs fixed to the bars on both sides read, 'Striped Hyena. *(Hyaena hyaena)*. From Darkest Africa'. The sign did not say that the beast was caught as a pup many years ago in Ethiopia and transported across northern Africa and the Mediterranean into Spain, France and finally England. It had never set a foot out of its present cage for years, nor had it tasted warm blood or been part of a clan.

The hyena was laid on the sparse straw, its head continually swinging side to side like a metronome, which brought much amusement from the crowd. A large pack of hungry and excited stray dogs ran through the procession, barking at everyone and everything, in particular the old tiger in the cage at the head of the parade and the hyena at the rear. A huge wolfhound, which seemed to be the pack leader, snarled and snapped at the wretched hyena, which in its normal habitat would take down a wild boar and challenge a leopard or cheetah over a kill. The front left wheel of the wagon suddenly sank into a large pothole that had gone un-noticed by the 'big game hunter', the severe jolt snapping several of the wooden spokes and lifting the diagonal corner of the cage off the ground with a lurch, throwing the animal against the bars and within reach of the dogs. The wolfhound struck first and sank its teeth into the hyena's flank. The response as immediate. The caged animal snarling with rage, suddenly resembling the feared carnivore it was, turned to face its attacker. Undaunted, the wolfhound stood firm, growling with pure menace at the hyena, less than two feet away. A Jack Russell Terrier cross, roused to a state of manic excitement by the frenzied barking, managed to squeeze between the bars of the cage and attacked the hyena.

The crowd looked on, some in disbelief and others mistaking the furore as part of the carnival programme. The small brown and white terrier, bred to flush foxes from burrows, grabbed hold of the grey fluffy tail and began to rag it as if it was a rabbit. The hyena moved fast and took the terrier in its mouth, and with those powerful jaws quite capable of crushing buffalo and zebra bone snapped the little dog in two. The hyena, feeling alive, as it had never done so before, tossed the carcass to one side and charged around the sloping cage, yelping and barking as if calling to a mate. Lowering its head, the caged beast launched itself at the locked gate, those powerful shoulders smashing into the bars, snapping the latch and springing the gate open with a crash.

The hyena bounded onto the cobbles and the wolfhound continued the attack. The freed animal spun round to face the dog that was equal in height, but no match in strength, power and intelligence. The large hound flung itself towards the waiting hyena. Instinct took over and the beast, caged for far too long, grabbed the dog's powerful neck and shook it hard until the wolfhound was dead.

By the time the 'big game hunter' had reacted to the cries from the crowd, leaving the horses, and dashing to the rear of the cage, the hyena was sprinting along Friargate away from the town centre.

Meadowbank and Huggins craned their necks towards the screams and swelling crowd, then hurried towards the commotion.

A uniform constable with pencil and notebook to hand was already taking details from the 'big game hunter'. The two detectives saw the wolfhound with its throat ripped out and looked into the cage.

"What 'ave wi got 'ere Bill?" Meadowbank recognised the constable.

"Not sure at t' moment Inspector. Some sort o' wolf 'as escaped".

"It's not a wolf, it's a striped hyena", said the man wearing the safari helmet as if he was 'The Old Shekarrry', The Great White Hunter.

"An 'iyena. What's that then?" asked Huggins. "A large and powerful predator". The hunter did not seem too concerned about losing a large and powerful predator.

"Is it dangerous?" Huggins continued.

He nodded at the cage and said, "Very. That's why it was kept in there".

"Will it come back on its own?" Meadowbank asked.

Nodding to the cage again, he replied, "Would you come back to that? It needs to be shot and soon".

"Reet Bill. You carry on 'ere an' me an' Sergeant 'Uggins will return t' nick an' open t' gun cabinet. We'll 'ave an' armed search party on t' street wi'in th' hour".

4

The old woman strode along Moor Park Avenue, the thick leather soles of her shoes announcing her presence. She pulled along a bulky tartan shopping trolley on two wheels and was grateful her house was not that far away. The electric street lighting partly illuminated the houses on the north side, but failed to penetrate the darkness of Moor Park opposite and it was the street lighting that enabled her to see the two police constables enter the avenue from St. Paul's Road. She hesitated briefly in an effort to determine which direction they would take, either turn right or left towards her.

The constables both carried Lee-Enfield service rifles slung over their shoulders and stopped at the edge of the grassland to peer into the night. The old woman carried on walking, but now much slower and even though she appeared to have her head down, unconcerned, she watched them intently.

The officers, seemingly satisfied with the silence within the vast area of darkness before them, turned left to resume their patrol.

There was a moan from within the shopping trolley. The old woman stopped and bent down, unfastened the buckles securing the flap as if readjusting her shopping load, put her hand inside the trolley and gripped a thin exposed neck. She squeezed hard, her blue eyes seemed to blaze as a

21

shock wave of energy travelled along her arm and coursed through the small body, which was dangerously close to awakening. The shopping trolley rocked and pulsated briefly, as if caught by a sudden gust of wind and the bulky contents that a second ago pressed against the fabric, seemed to shrink until the shopping trolley appeared to be carrying a light load, if anything at all.

"Good evenin' Madam. Yer tekin' a chance bein' owt this late an' on yer todd", the older of the two constables said.

She turned slowly, fully aware of their presence.

"I would not call seven thirty in the evening late officer, unless a curfew has been imposed". Her voice was surprisingly soft, without any trace of a dialect and her enunciation distinct.

"Most folk are stayin' indoors 'cause o' t' beast that escaped from t' circus earlier".

Though irritated by their interference, her curiosity demanded more.

"Beast? What manner of beast is this?"

A low rumbling growl interrupted any answer and both constables exchanged a wide-eyed glance before turning towards the park.

And there it was.

A striped hyena, normally found in the deserts and savanna's of Africa, emerged from the night and stopped within the street lighting. Snarling with its hackle raised, it stared crazily at the two officers. A deep red tongue licking its drooling mouth and the beast noisily sniffed the air, as if savouring the feast to come.

There was a scramble as the officers attempted to bring their rifles into a firing position. Then the hyena struck.

In three mighty bounds it leapt at the policemen, crashing into them both, its jaws clamping round the older man's throat and knocking his colleague flailing backwards. In one bite the hyena had ripped out most of the neck from chest to chin. The younger police officer scrambled to his feet and one look at the circus beast devouring his mate, 'Tommy Ten Pints', sent him sprinting towards Garstang Road, leaving his rifle behind. The notion of using his whistle to summon assistance would not enter his mind until he had run at least a mile towards town.

The old woman walked past the hyena, which was now effortlessly dragging the body towards the park.

"Good boy. There's a good boy", she cooed, as if acknowledging a neighbour's dog with a bone. The hyena watched her with indifference as it readjusted its grip to a shoulder and with its head aloft it trotted into the night with its kill.

5

The Stanley Arms Hotel, re-built in 1854 and named after Frederick Arthur Stanley 16th Earl of Derby, stood on Lancaster Road in the town centre. It was Friday lunchtime on market day and the ale-house was busy with customers queuing for the bitter and mild, produced in the hotel's own brew-house in the rear yard.

As it was Friday, meat was off the menu, but the absence of pork, lamb or beef was more than compensated with the selection of fish dishes and assortment of potato pies; potato, butter and onion; potato and cheese; potato and carrot and the firm favourite, potato and vegetable stew with a pastry crust.

Detective Inspector Meadowbank was sitting with Detective Sergeant Huggins at their usual 'reserved' table, which gave a good view of the main door.

"Albert, I'll tell yer somert fer nowt, this veg pie is 'alf decent. A bit o' scrag end or well done brisket mixed wi' it an' it would bi unbeatable".

Meadowbank inspected his sergeant's plate.

"It's teken yer long enough t' work that owt. Yer've nearly cleaned pattern off yer plate. Lets face it Sam, you'll eat owt that's grows in, or shits on t' ground".

The inspector was enjoying several smoked Fleetwood kippers with a mound of buttered bread and seemed oblivious to the small bones in every forkful. Over the past few months it had become a tradition for them to have Friday lunch at The Stanley, an occasion they both looked forward to, particularly as the food was compliments of the landlord, William Walmsley. Drinks had to be paid for though. That was made clear by the landlord, as he knew to his cost what these two men could drink between them. Huggins reached over, and took a slice of his colleague's bread and mopped up the last of his gravy.

"Did yer know it's all t' cow an' horse an' pig shite they use fer muck spreadin' an' manurin' an' what 'ave yer, that gives veg it's taste?"

Meadowbank looked at Huggins to see if he actually believed that, as he watched him wipe the plate spotlessly clean, then decided to change the subject. He knew better than to get into a nonsensical argument with his sergeant that could rumble on and on, especially over food.

"'Ave yer sin t' 'eadlines in today's Evenin' Post?"

He unfolded the newspaper for his sergeant.

Child Snatcher Still At Large

"Bastards! That's really 'elpful". He fumed as he read the front page.

"They're only doin' their job Sam, t' sell more papers an' we need t' do ours. I'm off t' interview t' parents again shortly. We're missin' somert. There's got t' be a connection".

"It could just be three random abductions an' not necessarily by t' same person. Albert, we all know kids disappear an' never get reported to us. There's a lot o' sick people out there, child-molesters, devil worshippers, sadists an' we 'ave a town full of 'em".

"Yer reet, but three kids go missin' on three consecutive nights an' all from Moor Park. That's not random".

"There's a good possibility that t' hyena 'as 'ad 'em. We found poor ol' Tommy's remains on t' park an' that's where t' beast were last sin".

"Exactly! 'is remains were found. T' zoologist from t' Harris Museum reckons it will only eat t' fleshy parts of t' body: stomach, entrails an' neck, which is what it did wi Tommy. There's bin no trace of these kids or their remains whatsoever, so I'm discountin' an' hyena attack fer time bein', but I agree t' answer must be waitin' for us somewhere in t' park area".

The inspector was wearing a charcoal coloured three piece woollen suit, one the pawnbroker had put aside for him. It was a good fit and complimented his black Balmoral lace up boots, also from the pawnbrokers.

Their conversation was interrupted by a commotion at the door. Six men entered the ale-house, boisterous and aggressive as they barged the lunch-time customers to one side. Meadowbank and Huggins looked at each other and nodded. They knew trouble when they saw it, as did William Walmsley.

Meadowbank leant forward, "They're not navvies, look like stevedores or ships crew".

The sergeant nodded in agreement.

"Six pints of bitter", the smallest one said loudly. He wore a leather cap and leather jerkin over his jacket, his hands and face smeared with oil and dirt.

"Where are you lads from then, eh?" William Walmsley asked casually.

All six men were now spread along the bar as the other diners and drinkers either moved or were pushed away.

Meadowbank was correct, they were stevedores, from SS Ina Mactavish, a small Glasgow coaster that had recently docked for a few days in-between unloading lime and loading on cotton.

"I said six pints, are you deaf?". The other five laughed. The small man's Clyde accent of the Glasgow patter was unmistakable.

"Let's keep it friendly, eh?".

"I call six pints of bitter on the house friendly, so that's very decent of you".

His manner was anything but friendly.

A smartly dressed middle aged man, remained standing at the bar with a large gin and tonic in front of him. He was near to the smaller man with the leather cap.

"Landlord, I'll pay for these gentlemen's drinks".

"An' who the hell are you?"

"A friendly local".

"You're no friend of us, so fuck off an' you can leave the drink an' sandwich behind on your way out, if you know what's good for you".

His friends found this very amusing.

The small Scotsman, staring at the older man casually reached towards the cheese sandwich served up in front of the smartly dressed gentleman to claim it as his own, as if he had paid for it. The older man moved fast. He reached inside his jacket and whipped out a stiletto dagger, bringing it down in one movement, piercing the back of the extended hand, the needle like point embedding into the wooden bar top.

The Scotsman yelled in agony and stared in disbelief at his right hand spurting blood now pinned to the bar. His five fellow countrymen moved closer to see what the kerfuffle was all about.

The gentleman, wearing a dark tweed trilby hat, was not much taller than the screeching Scotsman, around 5'8". He wore a light grey two piece woollen suit and matching cravat. The jacket hid the close fitting sheath. His black mohair overcoat had in a specially designed pocket, a fully loaded Webley MK1 service revolver, a most powerful handgun.

But it was his walking cane he reached for and with a further quick hand movement that belied his age, he produced a long slender sword from within the malacca wood and held the point at the the throat of one of stevedores who was getting dangerously close.

"Gentlemen, I came here for a quiet lunch, but your thuggish behaviour has put paid to that. Take one step closer young man and I shall skewer your

28

neck good and proper. I am now going to take my leave. Do not be foolish enough to follow me".

His accent was of someone born and bred in the county.

With his left hand he took out the revolver and placed it on the bar for everyone see.

The three foot rapier remained pressing just above the Adam's apple, producing a trickle of blood. He kept his gaze fixed on the big and mean looking stevedore, as he reached for his gin and tonic, knocking it back in one.

The rest of the many customers watching, including Meadowbank and Huggins, had frozen, waiting for the charge, but it never came.

The gentleman returned the revolver to his overcoat pocket and deftly transferred the sword to his left hand and retrieved the dagger without much effort. The small Scotsman slumped forward with a groan, clutching his wounded right hand.

Now armed with the sword and the dagger he walked backwards towards the swing-doors, pushing them open.

"Your friend may have my sandwich now, if he is still hungry?" he said calmly, before disappearing through the door.

Meadowbank moved first. He had already slipped his brass knuckle-duster onto his right hand. He did not believe this had finished yet.

As he approached the bar, the stevedore with a trial of blood running down his neck produced a cutthroat razor and took a step towards the swing doors. Meadowbank did not hesitate and punched him hard on the forehead with his right fist.

"The man said don't follow 'im".

The labourer staggered backwards, his forehead split open. He was already unconscious as he fell onto the bar and into his companion who was still trying to stem the blood flow from his hand.

As Meadowbank left through the swing doors, Huggins remained inside watching his inspector's back and brandishing a lead tipped baton.

A hansom cab waited outside.

The driver was aiming a coach-gun at the inspector. The smartly dressed passenger stood by the open cab door with sword at the ready. He recognised the police officer and lowered the rapier to his side.

"Ah! Inspector, better late than never. I expected those louts through the door first".

"Do I know yer?"

"We have never met, but I know who you are Mr. Meadowbank and your colleague Sergeant Huggins. After you both stopped Jack the Ripper, your reputation precedes you. Allow me to introduce myself, I am Sir Roger Nowell, Lord Lieutenant of Lancashire".

Meadowbank was holding the malacca sword cover and tossed it towards Sir Roger.

"Yer may want this back".

He caught it adeptly.

"Thank you. And for the record I don't intend making any formal complaint against those ruffians. Good day Inspector". He touched his hat and stepped into the carriage, calling for the driver to move on.

Sergeant Huggins emerged from the public house. "That lot 'ave 'ad the stuffin' knocked out of them. I don't think we'll 'ave any more problems from them".

"Let's 'ave a quiet word just t' mek sure, eh Sam?" Meadowbank replied.

6

At the same time as the two detectives sent the Scottish stevedores back to their boat, one person remained near to the confessionals in Saint Wilfrid's church. She was kneeling at the end of a dark wooden pew waiting for the cubicle to become vacant. As she knelt on the cushioned rail she kept her head bowed, her hands pressed in prayer and partly covering her face in an attempt to stifle her sobbing.

The young woman was a domestic worker for a wealthy family on Winckley Square, and wore a black cape over her servant's uniform of a white blouse and long black skirt.

At last the cubicle door opened and an old man stepped out slowly and shuffled to another pew to say his penance.

The young woman nervously glanced around to make certain it was her turn, then stood and genuflected towards the altar, making the sign of the cross when leaving the pew. Her hat hid her red eyes as she stepped into the dark confessional, pulling the door closed before she lowered herself onto the bare wooden kneeler. Without lifting her head too much, she could see the shadow of the man sat behind the black mesh screen. She took a deep breath and said in hush tones, "*In nominee Patris et Fillii et Spiritus Sancti Amen*".

Once more she made the sign of the cross with her right hand then continued, saying, "Bless mi Father, it's three week since mi last confession".

There was slight movement behind the screen as the priest adjusted his position on the chair.

"Why do you seek God's absolution?"

It was a voice she recognised, soft and calming which gave her the courage to continue.

"Father, I've done somert s' terrible". There was slight trembling to her voice.

"Remember my child why you are here. You have come to ask Our Lord Jesus Christ for forgiveness and he is waiting to absolve you of all your sins".

"But Father, I've brought great shame upon me an' mi family". She said in-between snuffles.

If the priest was intrigued or believed he had heard it all before, he remained pious and neutral, giving nothing away.

"My child, The Almighty is all forgiving. Repent and allow God's blessing to cleanse your soul and wash away the stain of sin".

"Father, I've bin wi' a man".

She could not see him furrow his brow and look directly at the screen.

"Explain yourself, my child". His tone was chiding.

"Fornication Father, out o' wedlock. I succumbed t' mi desires an' now 'e wants nowt t' do wi mi". The sobbing resumed.

"Tell me exactly what happened".

She paused before replying, "Wi' respect Father, can yer not just gi' mi some penance an' I'll swear t'

Almighty God that I'll never stray off t' path o' righteousness again".

"If it was only that simple. You are here to receive The Blessed Sacrament of Penance and must show sorrow in offending God and truthfully repent. Before I pronounce absolution I must be satisfied that you are truly repentant. Through the power of Jesus Christ Our Lord I am able to forgive your transgressions in His name, but are your sins venial or mortal? I must know the very nature of your offending to God".

"Oh Father, it's a mortal sin, there's n' doubtin' that".

His patience was evaporating.

"I shall decide the gravity of your sins and the sincerity of your contrition. Before I can pronounce absolution and impose a suitable penance I must have detailed knowledge of your confession. Avoiding the truth is not the path a sinner should take. Only by the admission of one's guilt can you win back God's love".

"I understand Father, but where do I begin?"

"Start with the fornication". He answered quickly.

Her head remained bowed more out of shame than contrition.

"A few week back a gentleman's tailor came a callin', t' size up t' master o' the' 'ouse. Called abaht 'alf-a-dozen times in all an' 'e allus came t' kitchen fer a brew. As I'm senior domestic after Mrs. Tomkins, t' 'ousekeeper, it wer mi place t' attend t' 'im like. It wer no 'ardship neither as 'e wer a good lookin' fella. 'E med no secret of 'is intentions an' 'is charm an' gabble fair impressed me, that's no secret either Father. An' one thing led t' tother, if yer know what I mean".

"I am a servant of Christ and do not surrender myself to the weakness of the flesh, hence my child I am un-shockable and do not take a salacious interest in matters of sexual impropriety. Continue with your confession and I shall inform you when you have recounted sufficient detail to enable absolution".

The priest slowly reclined himself on the chair and closed his eyes.

"It wer a few weeks back, 'e delivered t' suits fer Mr. White then came down t' kitchen. As soon as I saw that wicked look in 'is eyes I knew what 'e wanted. We wer alone an' wi'out sayin' a word 'e took mi in 'is arms an' kissed mi like I've never bin kissed afore. T' truth was Father I wanted 'im as well".

The priest recognised the name as one of his parishioners, Lieutenant General Sir George White and could now put a face to the servant beyond the screen. He had seen the pretty blonde attend Sunday mass with the rest of the household on many occasions, and yes, she was a bonnie lass, he thought to himself.

"Continue my child. A kiss does not constitute fornication".

"We began t' fumble wi each others clothes, when I 'eard t' front door bang shut, so I dragged Tom, er that's 'is name Thomas, int' t' laundry room an' locked t' door. 'E pushed mi ont' t' sacks of washin' an' began touchin' mi".

The priest interrupted. "Where did this Thomas touch you child?"

She was too lost in her own thoughts to register the slight breathlessness of the priest. He had pulled his cassock above his waist and was rubbing his groin fervently.

"Well places a woman doesn't like talkin' abaht".

"This is no time to be bashful. You have violated God's trust with a grave act of lewdness and your soul must be cleansed. That is why you are here. Now where did Thomas put his hands?" His tone was almost dream-like.

"Erm, between my legs".

"What happened then?"

"Well what d' yer think 'appened?" She was beginning to regret her quest for salvation.

"Young lady, do not presume my mind to be as sordid as yours. I am a Roman Catholic Priest and therefore a stranger to matters of the flesh, but I am no stranger to listening to sinful, lustful and unchaste confessions. So far you have told me nothing that could be regarded as a mortal sin. Do you want God's forgiveness or not?"

"Of course I do Father".

"So where did he put his hands?"

"Inside mi underwear an' inside mi blouse".

"Are you saying he touched your bare breasts and womanhood?"

"Yes Father".

"And did you touch his manhood?"

36

"Yes Father".

"And did you want to receive his manhood?"

She hesitated.

"Well did you?"

"Yes I wanted him". She answered quickly.

The priest had now exposed his own erection and was caressing himself in a well-practised manner. "And you lifted up your skirt to expose your pubic area, did you?"

"I'm so ashamed Father".

"Did you show him your pubes and groin?"

"I showed 'im mi quim, is that t' same thing?"

"And you took hold of his erect member, pleasuring him before covering it with your quim, did you?"

"Somert like that". Her voice reflected her self-loathing at that moment.

"And then you fornicated like the devil on sacks of laundry. Did you enjoy this carnal act?" Father Fairfax uttered between gasps.

"Can I ever bi forgiven Father?"

There was movement from within the priest's side of the confessional. He opened the door and peered around it before stepping into the aisle. He quickly scanned the church and saw it was deserted and then opened the cubicle door facing him.

The servant looked up surprised, ready to chastise a hasty and inpatient confessor and became confused on seeing the parish priest standing over her.

"Father Fairfax! What are yer doin'?"

He hitched his ankle length cassock to his waist, showing her his erection that was ready to burst, as if offering an explanation to her question. The priest entered the small confessional pushing the kneeling servant against the wooden side panel, his engorged phallus inches from her face. He gripped her head with both hands and pulled her face towards him. Squirming, she tried to push the sixty-year old man away, but his bulk and strength were overpowering, so in desperation she screamed for help.

"No, no. I don't want to harm you, please just satisfy me like you did the tailor". His eyes pleaded with her, still hoping that consenting gratification would happen.

The servant, a good thirty five years younger than the priest, huddled in the corner, her screams quite deafening in the confines of the confessional.

The priest was overwhelmed by sexual excitement which ran through him like electricity. His lust became a trembling foul rage.

"Silence girl! You are nothing more than a harlot. Satisfy my needs whore and be grateful for it".

He shouted above the din, lashing out with his hand, slapping her hard across her face.

Shocked by his fury she cowered beneath him. "Please Father, please, don't 'urt mi, I'm beggin' yer. I never told yer but I'm with…". She did not finish the sentence.

"Take me in your mouth whore and pleasure me". The priest was shaking uncontrollably as if convulsing.

She screamed with all the power of her lungs.

His arms shot forward and large hairy hands gripped her throat and squeezed, instantly stifling the screams. Blindly she thrashed out with her hands as he crushed her larynx, the throttling cutting off the air supply to her brain and for a few seconds the choking was terror beyond comprehension.

His insane eyes stared at the lifeless face, the open mouth no longer rasping and it was only the smell of her emptying bladder, an aroma he savoured, that withdrew him from his paroxysm of violence.

He removed his hands from her neck and in-between his panting gasps, breathed in the sour stink of urine that filled the cubicle.

7

The full moon was hidden behind jostling grey clouds which seemed to be in no hurry to move on, despite the breeze wafting in the salty smell of the Irish Sea less than two miles away.

Even though it had gone midnight, Auntie Vena was on the terrace stirring the gloopy liquid in a large iron cauldron, which sat on a metal stand straddling an impressive wood fire.

The one-eyed cat rubbed itself against her ankles, purring in anticipation.

Auntie Vena did not feel the change in temperature, she was always cold, even so welcomed the bleakness and darkness of winter. She remained uncomfortably chilled throughout the seasons. Her coagulated blood, putrid from centuries of corruption, bore no symbiosis to her withered heart, lodged inside her like an unpicked fruit, rendering the miracle of oxygenation to the pages of medical journals (or was her own existence an even greater miracle?).

The witch did like to dress for the cold months accordingly, which is why this mid-autumn night she wore a long black woollen overcoat, perfectly tailored and of course her polished brogues.

She was careful not to let the spluttering, glutinous dark green liquid splatter her coat as she stood close to the pot, stirring with a long wooden pole, feeling the end catch the iron base. As the pole was extracted to resume the stirring cycle, a strange red creature with mottled scales, no discernible eyes and no bigger than a newt, was clinging to the wood with its six legs as if attempting to climb to safety. Auntie Vena firmly knocked the pole against the rim, dislodging the animal and as it hit the surface, floundering, Auntie Vena using the wooden pole, pushed it to the bottom of the cauldron where it was hottest.

She found this amusing and cackled out loud.

The burning logs had reduced to glowing embers and the brew was a rolling simmer, the surface occasionally burping like a small volcanic vent of lava. Fortunately the smell from the pot was carried away on the sea breeze. Had the night air been still, alarmed neighbours would have been forced to investigate the source of the gagging stench.

What made the witch think of her Bavarian friend, Walpurga Hausmannin, she would have found difficult to say. It was possibly that the last occasion she had made such a brew, such a powerful potion, was at Walpurga's farmhouse.

It had been the year 1850 and rumours were whispered in and around the village of Dilligen that Walpurga was a witch and vampire and already under investigation for child abduction.

Auntie Vena knew the truth and understood why the local villagers were fearful of Walpurga. She was not a vampire of course, they are something completely different, but certainly a witch, a witch of great power and a child stealer: name a witch

41

that's not. Auntie Vena had convinced Walpurga, who even then was being called the Bayern Witch, of the need to leave Dillingen. She could feel the tension in the town and knew only too well how quickly gossip and finger pointing turned into mob violence, so together they travelled to Ingolstadt around fifty miles away, abandoning the farmhouse and the children chained together in the old cowshed.

Walpurga was not a witch like Auntie Vena, a Demdike, a necromancer. She was mortal and had passed fifty years on the earth plane. She needed sustenance as anyone would need food and drink and she did enjoy the pleasure of food consumption. Walpurga was fat, so fat she had difficulty walking, her creaking leg joints protesting forlornly against her increasing weight.

They stayed with Walpurga's old friend, Victor Von Frankenstein who was studying chemistry at the town's university and rented a large house away from the campus. He was aloof, arrogant, but a brilliant scientist, completely obsessed with his work: to discover the hidden laws of nature.

Frankenstein had little contact with his two house guests, leaving them to fend for themselves while he worked in his laboratory at the top of the house. They had been there for two weeks and had not seen or spoken to Frankenstein for several days when one evening, as they listened to a thunder storm outside, he suddenly appeared in the reading room excited, thrilled as if charged by the static electricity from the lighting flashes outside. He insisted they accompany him to his laboratory.

Auntie Vena cared little for the scientist, but at Walpurga's insistence she followed them up several flights of stairs, Walpurga breathless as Frankenstein held the door open and the two witches entered the laboratory.

It was a large room, the ceiling made up of massive glass panes with connecting pulleys and ropes, allowing the lightning storm to illuminate the laboratory in flashes.

Electric arcs crackled overhead, huge glass vats of luminous green liquid bubbled continuously. Numerous control panels flashed erratically and an enormous generator hummed and emitted a phosphorous blue light as flywheels whirred and large glowing bulbs pulsated all around.

In the middle of all this was a long table bearing something colossal and covered in a white shroud. The gaunt looking scientist told the two visitors that after years of experiments he was now ready to fulfil his dreams and reanimate a corpse. A corpse made up of limbs and organs from selected human specimens.

The witches exchanged nervous looks. Auntie Vena was a necromancer and could raise the dead through black magic, and had done this many times, but what was being proposed now was wrong. She tried to tell Frankenstein life cannot be created this way, but he would not listen, pushing her aside as he pulled a lever, setting ropes and pulleys into motion, instigating the rise of the central table towards a myriad of cables and terminals high above them. Two large panes of glass slowly opened inwards, allowing the torrential rain and wind to blast into the laboratory as the table stopped a few feet from the opening, swaying, and the shroud moving eerily in the storm. Frankenstein pulled another lever which slowly sent a large lighting conductor rising through the opening into the night sky, wires trailed down to apparatus below and ultimately to whatever lay under the shroud.

Within minutes a lightening bolt struck the copper conductor, sending sparks and flames in all directions, the generator vibrated worryingly and the hum of circuits and bubbling chemicals seemed close to exploding. The shroud caught fire from the arcing electric charges dancing above the suspended platform, but the flames were soon extinguished by the driving rain.

Frankenstein, looking wild and mad, became even more excited as he pushed a lever forwards and watched the table descend as smoothly as it had risen. It came to a gentle stop on reaching the supporting frame and through the commotion of decelerating flywheels and diminishing hums, the scientist remained still and stared at the smoking partly covered figure laying on the table.

Auntie Vena and Walpurga were also transfixed, not daring to believe what they may witness. As if to answer their secret thoughts, the charred shroud fell to the floorboards, as huge legs with feet encased in rough hewn leather boots twitched and kicked as the two spectators watched a life force surge through the creature, and within seconds, arms displaying raw stitched hands reached out as if trying to grab life itself.

"It's alive, it's alive!" Frankenstein screamed with joy. Then the thing sat upright, legs swinging awkwardly onto the floor and with what seemed a great effort, it stood upright, swaying, tendrils of smoke wafting from its bulk.

The witches gawped at the monster. It was at least seven feet tall and not in proportion. The large head displayed neat stitching around the forehead and neck, just below electrical sockets either side. The skin was yellow in contrast to the black, patchy lustrous hair and the top of the head was abnormally flat. The eyes were black and watery and the lipless mouth resembled a slash below the bulbous nose, which had also been stitched in place.

Frankenstein rushed forwards to greet his creation and the monster, dressed in a tattered black suit, turned to meet him. It was more alive than it looked and silently wrapped its large hands around Frankenstein's neck, squeezing hard, indicating murder would be the monster's first action.

Auntie Vena brought both hands together and pointing them forward sent a visible pulse of energy, which could never be created in any laboratory, hitting both man and monster, sending them sprawling backwards. Walpurga rushed towards her friend, who was sprawled on the floor semi-conscious and as she helped him to his feet, the same rough hands and arms wrapped around the witch, once again squeezing with unnatural strength. The monster groaned, seemingly pleased with itself and effortlessly lifted Walpurga off her feet, the very life being squeezed from her, as a constrictor would kill its prey.

Once again Auntie Vena, with hands pressed together as if in prayer, pointed fingers towards the monster, releasing a deadly blast of shimmering energy. The creature turned in a split second, letting Walpurga take the direct hit, bowling her and the monster across the laboratory, knocking into trestles, upturning apparatus and crashing into a large glass tank of glistening sulphuric acid.

The glass encasing the sloshing liquid cracked like a macabre cobweb, the pressure within shattering the fractured container, releasing gallons of the deadly corrosive acid like a wave onto the floundering Walpurga. Her blood curdling scream froze Auntie Vena with horror as she saw her friend's hands dissolving and the flesh continue to burn and disappear along her arms and feet, exposing the skeleton beneath.

Flames erupted as chemicals mixed and reacted and the acid combusting as rain water made contact. The monster, for all its size, was stunned by the attack and struggled to get to its feet. Walpurga rushed towards it, screaming, her head and body ablaze, running on skeletal feet that snapped free at the ankle. She continued on the stubs of her exposed tibia, colliding with the huge creature. Her size and momentum carried both of them towards a large window, the flames relishing the monster's clothing as witch and monster hit the glass, smashing through it instantly, allowing them to topple together into the driving rain. As they struck the ground the monster rolled away, smothering the flames, and looked across to see the witch burn and bubble as fire and acid consumed her completely.

The laboratory was already an inferno. Auntie Vena had reached the shattered window and could see Walpurga still burning fifty feet below.
There was no sign of the monster.

Frankenstein had escaped the laboratory and was already rushing through the house collecting his treasured research, thick choking smoke chasing him.

Auntie Vena casually stepped through the broken window and slowly descended to the lawn where her friend was nothing more than unidentifiable embers.

She was going to hunt down the monster and its creator, to rip them apart limb by limb, letting the other witness their demise, attesting to the scientist that it is always easier to destroy life than create it, but decided to let the mortals deal with their own creations. Instead, her next journey was to Munich railway station and from there perhaps take the train to Bucharest 800 miles away, and then a further train to Sibiu in the shadows of the Carthpathian Mountains to visit Queen Witch Vanda, an old friend from the last Great Gathering.

While she sat in the Great Hall of the *Munchen Hauptbahnhof* Auntie Vena was unusually reflective. The town of Sibiu, the capital of Transylvania, was the home of the Wallachia from the House of Dracul. She did not know a lot about the Wallachians, only what Vanda Moldovan had told her. Auntie Vena knew the peace agreement between the Romani and the Wallachia was often broken by the vampires, despite the Romani elders providing live victims, usually travellers dragged from their guest house beds, then tied to posts on the outskirts of Sibiu. The bloodthirsty Draculs could not be trusted, they always wanted more.

Auntie Vena had only encountered vampires on one occasion, in central London, not many years ago. But a vampire is no match for a Demdike. These bloodsucking parasites are hampered by their arrogance and constant hunger, they act without thinking and the Demdike had sensed the nosferatu clinging to the archway roof as trains trundled overhead into Kings Cross Station. As it plunged towards her, she took off its head before it had got within ten feet. The others were hanging from the damp brickwork like stalactites, wide eyed, hissing and unsure, their need for blood urging them to drop and feast, even though this blood smelt different, somehow sour like curdled milk. The vampires did not respond to the witch's flick of the wrist as a fireball suddenly engulfed them. Their screams brought out the whores from adjacent alleyways to investigate, their clients running in the opposite direction.

Her decision had already been made. She would leave a visit to the gypsy witch until another time, and instead travelled first class to Calais. Auntie

Vena had no luggage or money. When the latter was needed, she could conjure any amount of wealth.

She took a sailing ship to Dover, and then a train north, arriving in Manchester several days after leaving Munich.

Auntie Vena had been out of the country for numerous years and thought better of returning to the Forest of Pendle, the locals would talk and the witch finder would soon be on to her. The market town of Preston seemed a logical choice, an acceptable thirty miles from Pendle Hill and twenty miles from the graves. She contacted a land agent and 'Hoarstones' was only the second property she viewed. Auntie Vena could see the potential in the detached house and out buildings, but more importantly as she strolled around the secluded garden, the land agent pointing out the obvious, she saw the one eyed black cat sat on the verandah watching her.

"Hello old friend, I wondered when you would turn up", Auntie Vena said with genuine pleasure.

She emerged from her reverie; *was it really only fifty one years ago? It seemed centuries in the past.*

The potion was still hot, not quite a simmer, when Auntie Vena suddenly rose rapidly into the night in a vertical line, like a bell-ringer caught off guard. She reached out with both hands, then dropped gracefully to the same spot by the cauldron.

The witch opened her right hand to see a small mammal, a pipistrelle bat, looking up at her terrified. She closed her hand tightly, squeezing, feeling blood and fluids run through her fingers then threw the half dead bat to the black cat, who immediately pounced and carried it into the night. Her other hand revealed an identical flittermouse, possibly the mating partner of the first. It too was on its back and tried to fly away. The witch quickly ripped the membrane on both wings, rendering flight impossible and tossed it into the scolding brew. The small mammal, only days from hibernation, shrieked in agony as the gloop sucked it below the surface like a wild pony straying into a moorland swamp.

8

The head, arms and legs of 'Tommy Ten-Pints' were found near to the Serpentine Lake in Moor Park the following afternoon. In fact most of his body was intact, it was the torso and internal organs that had been ravaged and eaten by the hyena.

Sergeant Huggins spoke quietly to the two patrolling officers who had found the remains while Detective Constable Collier set up the tripod and camera and began photographing their dead colleague where he lay face up by the water's edge. Back at the Central Police Station on Lancaster Road, Detective Inspector Meadowbank was in the C.I.D. office reading the post mortem report on Bridie Wilkes, whose body had been discovered in Winckley Square Gardens.

'Cause of death: Strangulation. Forceful constriction of the trachea and neck structures resulting in occlusion of the air passage'.

One sentence he re-read several times, 'the deceased was four weeks pregnant'.

He was rocking back on the rear legs of his wooden chair, the pipe he was holding long extinguished, when the door opened. Superintendent Malone remained by the open door.

"Inspector, I'm surprised to see you here".

Meadowbank gestured to the pile of paperwork on his desk.

"Would your time not be better spent supervising your team on the ground?"

"My team don't need supervision. They do what they are paid t' do an' do a bloody good job as well, sir".

"Rank structure is a curious thing Inspector. Some men find promotion a natural consequence of their ability being recognised, others accept the responsibility with reluctance but try their damnedest to succeed, while others are promoted beyond their ability and are completely out of their depth. Do you understand the point I'm making Inspector?" He had a strong Dublin accent.

"No sir I don't".

Superintendent Malone stepped into the office, limping as he approached the inspectors desk, resting both hands on the back of a chair.

"It's quite simple. Men need leadership just as a flock, herd or swarm of animals, birds or insects do. They look for guidance, in fact more than that they need guidance to survive. Take His Majesty's Armed Forces for instance. Have I ever told you I am a former captain with the Royal Dublin Fusiliers?"

The inspector was still lounging back, balancing the chair on its rear legs.

"Yes sir, I do believe you 'ave mentioned it".

"Well I think it's worth mentioning again so you understand where I am coming from. Let's not be coy. I am a natural leader, that ability was recognised by others a long time ago. My father and grandfather were both Brigadier Generals, so you see I was weened for leadership. Call it destiny. Subordinates appreciate decision making. I lead from the front Meadowbank. That is why I was wounded at Talana Hill. Took a bullet in the charge". He slapped his right thigh twice to emphasise this.

The Detective Inspector had heard this claim before and knew there was no 'charge' at the Battle of Talana Hill. He had made it his business to establish what had happened that day on 20th October 1899 and it was well recorded that the Boers had forced the British to retreat undercover of darkness.

He looked at his Superintendent closely, possibly for the first time, and realised Superintendent Malone's ego towered above his small frame. He was at most 5'9", slight build, his short black hair side parted with brilliantine matching perfectly his neatly trimmed moustache. Meadowbank considered that Mr. Malone would be popular with the ladies as he was quite a dashing fellow and decided he could not be more than thirty five.

"I was medically discharged with honours", the Superintendent continued, "and once back in civilian life I was soon offered a commission with Preston Borough Police. I like a challenge Meadowbank, gets me through the day".

"That's verra interestin' sir, but I must crack on wi' this paperwork. T' Chief is expectin' a briefin' later today".

It seemed the Superintendent could not have been more offended.

"That is my point exactly Inspector. I do balk at your leadership style and your lack of comprehension of rank structure. You brief me, I brief the chief superintendent and he briefs the chief constable. There is no leap frogging the chain of command, that is how it works. I shall bring the Chief Superintendent up to date on events, is that clear? Now where are we up to with the body found in Winckley Square Gardens?"

"As yer wish sir. T' young lass 'as been identified as Bridie Wilkes, nineteen years old. An 'ousemaid for a...". He dropped the chair down with a thud and flicked through a slim binder, "A Mr. White, 10 Winkley Square. George Stuart White t' be exact. Sergeant 'Uggins is on 'is way t' interview 'im as wi speak".

The Superintendent was stroking his moustache. "George Stuart White you say? Not Sir George Stuart White, retired Lieutenant General by any chance?"

Meadowbank ran his tobacco stained finger across a report. "'Appen I do. That's t'very man. D' yer know 'im sir?"

"Sir George was my commanding officer at Ladysmith, of course I know him. When did Huggins leave?"

"Abowt ten minutes ago. 'E set off on foot".

"Right Inspector, arrange for a carriage and driver to meet me at the front immediately. I'll conduct the interview with Sir George. This calls for tact and diplomacy and Sergeant Huggins should be nowhere near".

"What abowt t' briefin' wi' t'chief, sir?" He called out to the superintendent who had done a quick about turn.

"You take it Inspector. I cannot do everything around here". With that Superintendent Malone disappeared.

9

As the night clouds filtered the light from the moon's waning crescent, in an unconsecrated corner of the cemetery, near to Miller Road, a lone figure dressed in black stood by a graveside as if in silent prayer to a dear departed. Auntie Vena's eyes were wide open as she stared at the huge boulder sitting on top of a stone slab, measuring at least five feet square.

The inscription on the slab was simple enough,
'Meg Shelton Buried 29th May 1612'.

This was the first occasion she had visited the grave, but Auntie Vena knew Meg Shelton was buried under all that stone, head first and in a deep hole. These obstacles were intended to stop 'The Preston Witch' from scratching her way to the surface, and up to present seemed to have worked, as Meg Shelton had not been seen for nearly three hundred years.

Auntie Vena stood straight in her dark woollen coat and black bonnet, her gloved hands casually clasped to the front. She was saying something, not speaking to herself, but gently reciting an incantation, a soothing cadence of words repeated over and over while staring at the boulder.

The graveyard was quiet, as would be expected during the early hours of a late October night, so the sudden movement of the two ton boulder seemed especially loud as stone moved on stone. The huge rock of sand stone was slowly inch by inch sliding across the granite grave stone, leaving a trail of crushed rock and obliterating the inscription that had weathered storms since 1612, as the boulder continued its journey. The noise of grinding rock did not seem to bother Auntie Vena who continued with her enchantment and only stopped when the boulder dropped off the granite slab, rolled down a grass slope before smashing into and demolishing a large marble cross.

Auntie Vena stepped onto the gravestone and moved to the centre, putting out her right hand, her open palm facing towards the ground. Once again she began to quietly utter repeated words which flowed to a rhythm, a rise and fall of words that would be meaningless to anyone listening. It did not take long for the stone slab to relent and with a loud crack similar to tectonic plate movement, the thick granite split in two, an inch from Auntie Vena's brogues. She pushed her hand down further as if pressing against an unseen force and stepped back on to the grass as the slab broke into countless pieces. With a gentle flick of the wrist the granite chunks were sent hurtling away into the shadows, like a swarm of insects, revealing bare earth.

It would take two gravediggers several hours to exhume a corpse, using spades and a block and tackle to lift the coffin, especially one buried ten feet deep, but for Auntie Vena it took a matter of minutes. The earth began to churn and erupt as if a giant mole was digging its way to the surface, the coffin poked through the soil and continued to rise. Soon the rough wooden planked oblong casket was standing upright like to a strange totem pole, and then without warning it crashed to the ground like a felled tree, sending loose earth in all directions. The lid, together with countless six inch nails that had held it in place for so long, flew into the air simultaneously, following the direction of the gravestone pieces.

Auntie Vena remained where she was and put her hands behind her back like a headmistress waiting for a delinquent child's explanation.

Grunting and retching came from within the coffin and the rank odour of decay spread like an invisible fog that would have made the most experienced mortician gag and move away.

A pair of dirt-rotten hands with grime caked nails which had stopped scratching at the wooden lid a century ago, gripped either side of the coffin and Meg Shelton slowly heaved herself into a sitting position, cricking her neck as if repairing the damage the hangman's noose had caused.

She had her back to Auntie Vena as she slowly stood up, swaying as if she was standing in a small boat in choppy waters. Her grey hair was long and foul, the sack cloth and sacking breeches she wore were tied around her waist with a heavy cord and they too were soiled and rancid, alive with beetles, weevils and grubs.

Looking up to the moon Meg Shelton breathed in deeply.

"Come on Meg, we haven't got all night. There's work to do".

She turned to face Auntie Vena, only now aware of her presence. Her face was grotesque, fixed with rage, a rage that only being buried alive for 289 years could produce. Her eyes were nothing less than black pits of malignant loathing, her nose was hooked and her chin protruded unnaturally. Ingrained dirt covered her face and suppurating sores pitted her flesh. Her mouth opened hideously, as if attempting to smile, revealing remnants of teeth stained like tar. She made a guttural noise to clear her throat and spat out a glob of black phlegm animated with plump maggots.

"Well, well…", she hesitated, croaking, coughed, spitting out another ball of black mucous and maggots then tried again. Her voice was harsh, rasping like a file against cold metal. "Well, well, well, what have we got 'ere?" If Meg was glad to see her visitor, it did not show.

"I've always wondered why they didn't burn an old hag like you at the stake?"

"The fools showed compassion. They under estimate us Auntie Vena, or should I call you Vena Demdike?"

"Call me what you want, but we must be gone from here".

"What does a Demdike want from a Shelton?" She turned to look again at the crescent moon as it appeared through the clouds.

"As your necromancer I already have your loyalty and it is now time for you and I to work together".

"But first I must to return to Cuckoo Hall. There are things I need". Meg was still distracted by the moon.

Auntie Vena picked up a hooded robe from by her feet and offered it to Meg. She carefully and slowly stepped from the coffin. Her bare feet were the colour of charcoal and with small awkward steps, as if afflicted with a paralysis, she stomped forwards. Auntie Vena put the robe around Meg's shoulders, like a shawl and pulled the hood over her head.

"Meg, there is no Cuckoo Hall anymore. It's gone with everything else". She spoke quietly.

"What do you mean?" demanded Meg as she turned to face Auntie Vena.

"Destroyed by fire. They burnt your house to the ground just after they put you in that hole".

Her black baleful eyes searched Auntie Vena's rose coloured complexion. She was confused and suddenly deflated. "Why?"

"Have you any idea what has happened and how long you have been buried for?"

Meg was searching for memories or recollections, but it was too soon.

"Come on home with me. I have a carriage nearby". She was concerned with Meg's condition and spoke to her like a mother to a child.

The landau, owned by AuntieVena, waited in the shadows by the cemetery entrance on Miller Road. The black carriage and two black Thoroughbred mares were almost invisible against the dark stone wall. The tall driver, wearing a grey flat cap, a dark cape over his black woollen suit, and immaculate hob-nailed boots, stood by the horses, hastily dropped his cigarette, crushing it underfoot, when he saw his mistress returning.

"Mr. Ambrose, help my friend into the carriage. She's not herself at the moment".

"Of course ma'am". He opened the carriage door and picked up Meg Shelton and placed her on the seat as if she was a small kit-bag, ignoring the stench and infestation of larva and crawling creatures with multiple legs.

If Mr. Ambrose was aware who or what this stranger was he remained expressionless. As he took Auntie Vena's hand helping her step into the carriage she said, "Take us home please Mr. Ambrose".

He bowed his head in acknowledgement, deftly flicking maggots and oversize ticks from his sleeves.

10

The senior clerk at Preston Cemetery sat at his desk and a hard boiled egg sandwich sat on a smoothed out newspaper in front of him. A steaming pint mug of tea completed his lunch, but he had lost his appetite.

On the wall above the fireplace hung a portrait of the new king, Queen Victoria's son, Edward V11 who seemed to be enjoying the view from the window of headstones, mausoleums and numerous granite and marble monuments.

The clerk looked up at the two police officers. "You've sin it wi' yer own eyes Inspector, so don't stand there an' tell me I'm over reacting. I've worked 'ere since I were a lad, nearly fifty year ago and I've never sin anything like this. We've 'ad grave robbers in the past, but this is not the work o' grave robbers". He ran a hand through his thinning grey hair to emphasise his perplexity.

"Exactly Bob, wi don't know what were dealin' wi at t' moment an' until wi do, we shouldn't bi jumpin' t' conclusions".

"What are yer on about? There's only one conclusion t' jump to an that's the Preston Witch 'as risen from 'er grave an' the Devil only knows where she is now".

"Whoa Bob, whoa! Wi don't need that sort o'talk. We are tryin' t' keep things in perspective 'ere and until we've done a thorough investigation you'd bi better keepin' those sort o' thoughts t' yersel'". Meadowbank was losing his patience with Bob Acres, the senior clerk.

The clerk pushed his sandwiches to one side and rested his clasped hands on the desk with a sigh, clearly indicating he too had lost patience. He looked towards Sergeant Huggins.

"Sergeant, per'aps yer can 'elp Mr. Meadowbank see what is plain as day? It would tek two shire 'orses or a dozen men t' shift that boulder. It hasn't moved for 'undreds of years an' yet overnight it has been pushed aside an' that three inch thick granite slab is in a thousand pieces. Not even gunpowder could do that. An' what about the coffin? It's as solid as the day it wer buried nearly three 'undred year ago an' that's not right. It should 'ave rotted away t' nothin'. An' where are the remains of Meg Shelton, eh? There should be bones an' dust at the very least. There's no sign that she was ever in that coffin".

"Well perhaps that's your answer. There was no body in t' coffin in t' first place". Sergeant Huggins suggested.

"That doesn't mek sense. Why go to all this trouble of extractin' an empty coffin from a bloody deep 'ole? You'll have to do better than that Sergeant especially now the papers have got hold of the story".

"What?" Meadowbank shouted.

"Cemetery manager informed the Preston Herald and Guardian this morning. They've already bin down an' taken photographs of the coffin an' what 'ave you".

"He should 'ave spoken t' us first. Reet, listen t' me. As far as Preston Borough Police are concerned that grave site is a crime scene, and no one must go near it until I say so. Police officers will b' patrollin' t' cemetery grounds twenty four hours a day, until further notice and you better tell yer boss that as well, an' anyone tryin' t' get near will be arrested". "You can tell 'im yersel', 'e's on 'is way down 'ere with the mayor t' pose for some photographs".

The inspector shook his head, "Christ Almighty! Sam, let's get owt of 'ere before I do somert I'll regret". They followed the footpath to the far end of the cemetery. "Don't be too 'ard on 'im Albert. You've got to admit it is a strange set of events".

"There's a logical explanation to this Sam, somewhere, and we'll find the answer and it won't involve 'unting for T' Preston Witch".

"Not everythin' 'as a logical explanation. Remember The White Lady at Samlesbury Hall a couple o' year back? We went down to investigate a night time prowler an' came face t' face with The White Lady floating down that corridor towards us not ten feet away. That 'orrible face of sorrow starin' at us. Still gives me a shudder thinkin' about it now'.

"We should 'ave bin told that t' hall was supposed t' be 'aunted. It was ridiculous t' let us wander around the place in t' middle of t' neet looking for a flamin' prowler. It shit me up as well and I don't mind admittin' that".

Huggins laughed hearing this. "But would it 'ave made any difference? We couldn't say 'we are not going to Samlesbury 'all cause it's 'aunted'. Anyway, you don't believe in t' supernatural d' yer? So it couldn't 'ave bin a ghost".

"I must admit I didn't until that neet. Who wouldn't think twice abowt t' existence o' ghosts after what we saw? That doesn't alter mi views about this one though. I still say that a local villain will be behind this an' not a local witch whose bin dead nigh on three 'undred year".

The sergeant was going to mention the haunting of Miley Tunnel incident and last year's murder by the possessed Eleanor Knox they had investigated with neither brought to anything like a satisfactory conclusion, but instead said, "I'll tell thee somert for nowt Albert, I've got a bad feelin' about all this".

They had reached the exposed grave and Meg Shelton's coffin still lay where it fell the night before.

"Sam, I want yer t' organise that grave t' be dug owt completely and examined. Get that coffin on a cart an' bring it back t' nick where' wi can 'ave a proper look at it an' it'll be owt t' way o' pryin' eyes as well".

He turned to the constable who was stood near by and said, "Charlie, if t' press turn up, refer 'em t' Superintendent Malone, it's abowt time 'e earned 'is money".

11

The house was called 'Hoarstones'. The letters had been skilfully carved into both of the large stone posts supporting heavy wooden gates. The grey brick driveway led to double bay windows with an old oak door in-between. Ivy covered one side of the house, and was creeping across the upstairs windows. The herbaceous borders looked unkempt, but nothing a capable gardener could not put right in a weekend.

Next to the house, separated by a glass covered passageway which gave access to the rear garden, were the stables where Auntie Vena kept her black mares and carriage.

It would be described as 'a gentleman's residence' with the servants' quarters on the third floor. This is where Mr. Ambrose resided.

Shutters were pulled across the ground floor windows at the front of the house and curtains drawn across the rest. In the rear parlour the perpetually banked glowing fire would have made any blacksmith smile with pleasure, but it made the room stifling.

The two occupants did not appear to be uncomfortable in the oppressive warmth.

Auntie Vena was sitting in her armchair and Meg Shelton was sitting back on the rocker, both held cut glass tumblers of Glen Garioch malt whisky, Auntie

Vena's favourite drink anytime of the day. The one-eyed cat seemed displeased at losing its napping spot and stared at the visitor as if willing her to move.

Meg Shelton was still in her sack cloths. Auntie Vena had considered putting her in more appropriate attire but as the infestation of bugs and creeping grubs had disappeared from her clothing and hair, she decided to leave Meg as she was.

It was mid morning and Meg had been liberated for several hours. She was not responding as expected, or similar to any corpse Auntie Vena had summoned from the grave previously. Admittedly she had not practised her knowledge of necromancy for many, many decades, but Meg was too subdued, as if she was not pleased or even grateful for her resurrection. Meg stared at the flames in the hearth.

"Meg, I know you don't need it, but have a sip of your drink. I think it will do you good". She looked down at the tumbler held on her lap. It contained a decent measure for even the hardened drinker. "What is it?" she asked quietly.

Auntie Vena smiled, a rare occurrence in itself, and held her crystal glass towards the fire, rolling the malted barley around the tumbler, as a sommelier with a fine wine.

"Possibly one of the mortal's greatest creations. Something I've only discovered in the last 100 years". She looked at Meg. "Drink it, you've had a shock, it will make you feel alive inside".

She did as she was told and drained the glass, swallowing awkwardly. Meg opened her mouth and released a loud gasp, filling the room with a fetid stink and polluting the aromatic bouquet of the Western Isles single malt.

Auntie Vena settled back in the chair. "Now Meg, what do you want to do? Go back in the hole or take revenge on the bloodline that put you there? Remember the Witch finder Roger Nowell, the one who trapped you then torched your home, Cuckoo Hall? It appears that the Nowell's of Read Hall are still breeding and just as powerful. A distant grandson of the witch finder, bearing the same name, has been told of your coffin being unearthed and he is asking questions. I want you to stop him".

"What do you want me to do?" Her movement and speech already had more vigour.

It would seem Auntie Vena was right.

"I want you to rip out his beating heart and bring it back to me. I have a particular potion to brew and a witch finder's heart boiled overnight will do nicely. It may also give you pleasure, eh Meg? And you may also decide to turn his lovely home into a bonfire and roast his wife and children".

Meg was enthusiastically pushing herself back and forth in the rocker and Auntie Vena reached over, refilling her cut glass tumbler.

12

The cemetery superintendent, Mr. Cripps; the Lord Mayor Baron Stanley of Preston and Sir Roger Nowell arrived at the cemetery by a hired brougham carriage, not long after the inspector and sergeant had left.

Mr. Cripps directed the driver past the clerk's office, towards the north side of the eighteen hectare park. He knew exactly where Meg Shelton's grave was situated as he knew with most graves here. The cemetery boss led the two dignitaries on foot along a path, passing the impressive vault where the brewer Matthew Brown was buried, to a secluded spot near the boundary wall with Miller Road and froze when he saw the churned heap of soil and open coffin.

Sir Roger examined the disturbed mound of earth surrounding a collapsed hole.

"The coffin has not been dug from the grave, it has been extracted by sheer force".

"What are you saying Roger?" Enquired the mayor. He seemed irritated.

"It is clear no one with a spade has been at work here. It's as if the coffin has been pulled or pushed from the hole".

"Balderdash!". The Lord Mayor Baron Stanley could not think of anything better to say.

The cemetery superintendent had gone quite pale as he took in the scene of devastation. He was quickly coming to the same conclusion as his manager, Bob Acres, that the Preston Witch had risen.

Sir Roger turned his attention to the coffin. It was a pauper's coffin, rough sawn, the un-planed planks nailed neatly together but not the work of a carpenter proud of his trade. He ran his fingers over the deep scratch marks in the rough wood of the coffin lid and had to agree that it was remarkably well preserved.

"What are your thoughts Frederick? Supernatural, superhuman or superstition?"

"I am a disciple of Doubting Thomas and do not subscribe to the fantastical or supernatural. I am fully aware of your antecedents Roger, heir to the witch finder legacy and I am sure you would have me believe that whoever was in that coffin is now wandering the streets of Preston, but we both know that is impossible. The police have launched an investigation and I have every confidence that they will find the person behind this stunt and put them before the magistrates".

" A stunt you think?"

He turned to ask Mr. Cripps his opinion but he had already gone and could be seen hurrying towards the administration building and the safety of Bob Acre's office.

"An elaborate stunt you would agree? I know the circus is in town but this is an illusion their magicians would be proud of", Sir Roger said, shaking his head to decline a cigarette offered by the Mayor.

Baron Stanley wore his usual top hat and black frock-jacket, matching trousers and spats over his black hand stitched shoes. He was six feet tall but his ever present top hat made him look taller. He drew on the cigarette with a slight wheeze and replied through a release of smoke.

"A stunt nonetheless, or the work of the ignorant or criminal. There is no other explanation".

Sir Roger had walked away several yards to study the pile of granite jigsaw pieces and inspect the boulder that had toppled the eight foot cross of solid marble.

He felt a chill wrap around his neck and travel down his spine, he pulled up his overcoat collar and could not rid the feeling he was being watched.

Across the parkland and the rise and fall of white headstones, angels, cherubs and crosses, stood Mr. Ambrose, hidden amongst a coppice of hawthorn trees, observing through binoculars with interest.

The sound of trundling cart wheels on the tarmac road caught the attention of Sir Roger and the Lord Mayor Baron Stanley, who both turned to watch four horses pull an open wagon towards them. There were several uniformed police constables on board and a sergeant sat next to the driver.
Following behind on foot, four grave diggers carried spades and shovels, laughing and chatting amongst themselves.

The police sergeant addressed Baron Stanley and Sir Roger, "Excuse me gentlemen, I'll 'ave t' ask you t' leave this area. It is now a crime scene an' you could interfere with t' investigation".

"What crime has been committed sergeant?" asked Sir Roger.

The sergeant glowered at the question, "Body snatchin' and wilful damage to start with".

The police officer recognised the Lord Mayor, but not his companion so he decided it would prudent to treat them both with due regard, rather than tell them to 'fuck off and mine your own business'.

"Whose body are you alleging has been taken?" Sir Roger enquired.

"May I ask who you are sir an' what your interest is in t' matter?" asked the sergeant as if already bored with this conversation.

"Of course, I am Sir Roger Nowell, Lord-lieutenant of Lancashire and I am conducting a private investigation on behalf of the borough".

On hearing this the Lord Mayor gave Sir Roger a puzzled frown and throaty cough. The sergeant was flummoxed at the introduction. He was now facing the two most senior dignitaries in the county and borough.

"It was Meg Shelton's grave an' we're t' dig out the 'ole properly t' mek certain she still ain't down there". The sergeant answered with as much charm as possible.

"And what of the coffin?" pressed Sir Roger.

The sergeant turned to the Lord Mayor. "Answer Sir Roger please sergeant, then we will get from under your feet".

"The coffin is goin' t' station fer a proper examination sir".

"Carry on sergeant, you and your men have a long day ahead of you" replied the Lord Mayor, walking towards the brougham.

"Come along Sir Roger, there is the matter of your private investigation to discuss". Sir Roger could not help but smile.

* * *

Inspector Meadowbank was enjoying a quiet lunch in The Stanley Arms, away from the C.I.D. office, the non-stop ringing of the telephone, the stream of questions from his detectives and the constant updates for Superintendent Malone. He had chosen one of his favourite dishes; tripe and onions in milk, served in a bowl with plenty of bread and butter.

The inspector was concentrating on his food and did not notice a woman enter the ale-house and approach the bar. He heard his name mentioned and on looking up saw the landlord William Walmsley pointing at him. The woman walked towards his table smiling.

"Mr. Meadowbank, I was told I may find yer in 'ere".

He looked at her with an open mouth, then hastily swallowed a piece of tripe as he recognised her immediately.

"Mary, blow me!" He stood to give her a hug and she quietly sighed as his arms wrapped round her. "Sit down Mary". He pulled a chair out for her.

"Thank you. Am I disturbin' yer lunch?"

"Not at all, I've nearly finished anyhow. Let mi get yer a drink an' do yer fancy owt t' eat? The grub 'ere is excellent", he said eagerly.

"I'm still not drinkin' booze, so I'll 'ave a cuppa please and I've already eaten, thank you".

He cast a glance to his near empty pint and decided against another, at least till later and called across to the landlord to order a pot of tea for Mary. She unbuttoned her woollen charcoal slim fitting coat, revealing a high waisted grey chiffon skirt and lace neck cream blouse.

"Well Mr. Meadowbank, we never did 'ave that drink, did we? Even though mine would 'ave bin a cuppa". She adjusted her wide rimmed purple velvet hat.

Was he being paranoid, or was that a dig at him?

"Mary, that's my fault entirely. It wasn't 'cause I didn't want to, times flies an' I always seem t' 'ave a lot on mi plate". He knew he sounded feeble, but it was true.

"And Mary, please call me Albert. No more Mr. Meadowbank nonsense, you sound like mi bank manager".

She laughed and Meadowbank realised once again how attractive she was and possibly the same age as him, but her blonde hair pulled back into a bun making her appear years younger.

Mary pointed to the files next to his bowl of tripe. "Bringin' office t' ale-house, that's not a good thing Albert".

"This is normal. I actually get a lot done in 'ere. It can bi nice an' quiet".

"Oh! I'm sorry, I never thought. I'll go an' leave yers in peace".

Meadowbank nearly knocked his pint glass flying as he reached across to put his hand on hers. "No, no. I didn't mean that. Stay please, finish yer brew".

"You an' Sergeant 'uggins 'ave become quite famous since yer fettled Jack t' Ripper, an' yer still found time t' sort owt mi widow's pension while all that was goin' on. I'll always bi grateful for what yer did". It was her turn to reach out as she squeezed his hand.

"Speak of t' devil, Sergeant 'uggins is 'ere". He pulled his hand away swiftly.

"Sam, you remember Mary, don't yer? Mary Babbitt".

Huggins doffed his deer-stalker.

"Name rings a bell. Oh, yes, of course. You're t' mother of one o' t' Ripper's victims. I remember now, was it yer daughter t' first t' bi murdered by 'im? Nasty work that. Anyway, 'ow are yer doin' now love?"

Mary went quite pallid and without further preamble she stood, offering her thanks to Meadowbank.

"I'd better be off, but I still 'ave same lodgin's on Fishrgate 'ill. Yer welcome t' call anytime Albert, I 'ope yer know that?"

Meadowbank smiled, "I do know that an' I will visit, very soon".

She nodded to Huggins with a scowl and left.
"Nice one Sam! Thanks fer bloody nowt".
"What? Is it somert I said?"

13

On the death of Old Ted, his son, Young Ted, who was fifty seven but could pass for seventy seven, became sole stablehand at the Central Police Station, looking after the six constabulary horses, stables and yard on Earl Street.

He was preparing two horses for Inspector Meadowbank and Sergeant Huggins. Knowing which they each preferred he had the two Cleveland Bay mares saddled, including leather rifle mounts. "Ted, you're a shining star. Bernadette looks a beauty as usual". Meadowbank ran an appreciative hand along the horse's neck. He did not need to check the saddle and straps, but slipped his Lee-Enfield rifle in to the saddle holster.

"She's a bit feisty today Mr. Meadowbank sir, she ain't bin out fer a while so the lass will be glad of the exercise.
Same fer you Mr. Huggins, Floss ain't as tetchy, but she'll be ready t' stretch her legs, that's fer sure".

Huggins also secured his Lee-Enfield and took the reins, thanking Young Ted, and giving him a friendly slap on the shoulder. Both police officers wore constabulary black woollen riding breeches with black riding boots and both carried a Webley service revolver holstered around their waist.

"Are yers 'oping t' catch this crazy 'ound that's causin' 'avoc?"

"That we are Ted, an' once an' fer all an' put an end to this malarky", said Huggins.

"It ain't any malarky Mr. Huggins. How many 'as the beast attacked now, at least ten?"

The officers did not correct him, it was four as far as they knew. The only fatality being Tommy 'Ten Pints' Molloy, the other three still in hospital with serious chunks of flesh missing from them and of course there was the whelk man who ran a shellfish stall on a Friday outside English Martyrs church. He had not been seen since evening mass last week, his stock of cockles, oysters, scallops, winkles and mussels plundered that very first evening, once word got round that the stall was unattended.

At first the large splodges of blood around the stall were ignored, until a patrolling constable, responding to the commotion arrived.

The strange events whirling around the town like a cyclone, were not just the concern of the local constabulary but the local population as well.

Three children aged between eight and twelve had disappeared over three days. If they had all come from The Shambles, a dilapidated street in the town centre, where the poorest of the poor lived, such as the youngest of the three, Mary Scott, then their disappearance would probably have gone unreported. But two boys never returned home from playing football on Moor Park on consecutive evenings. One was the son of a local physician, Doctor Randall and the second boy was the youngest son of Jacob Swan of Swan and Son, Quality Butchers and Purveyors of Cooked Meats on Friargate. They were demanding action from the police.

The two officers arrived at the junction of North Road and Saint George's Road. Sergeant Huggins dismounted and scrutinised the pavement, the blood stains still visible. He looked around and said to the inspector, "'Ow can a full grown man just disappear? Doesn't mek sense".

"Sam, what abowt that waste land o' yonder. 'As it bin searched?", the inspector pointed to overgrown scrubland next to The Unicorn Hotel.

"I would bloody well 'ope so", replied the sergeant.

"Let's 'ave a look while we're 'ere then". Meadowbank responded.

The sergeant led his horse across St. George's Road, following Meadowbank. He dismounted and gave the reins to Huggins. The land had been bought for house building, but that now seemed to have been forgotten about. It was dark and the street lighting had little effect in illuminating the site. Meadowbank lit the wick of the small 'bulls-eye' lamp he held and moved forward, watching where he placed his feet amongst the rubbish now being dumped there, including toilet waste from someone's ash pit. Even through the stink of faeces and urine, the smell of rotting flesh was unmistakeable.

The glow from the lamp picked out a ghostly hand and arm amongst the human waste and undergrowth. Meadowbank found himself stood over the head and remains of the whelk man, still wearing his white coat, now shredded in parts and blood soaked.

"Sam, I've found t'poor bugger. We need t' protect this area, 'till mornin', so we can 'ave a proper look in t'daylight", the inspector said with no jubilation.

He lit his pipe as he walked backed to his colleague.

"At least we knew what we're lookin' for. An hell'ound rather than a maniac like Jack t' Ripper", offered Huggins.

Meadowbank looked back towards the congealed mess of flesh and bones and thought there was not much difference in the end result.

Sergeant Huggins stayed at the scene while Meadowbank headed back to the police station on Earl Street. The inspector arranged for Doctor Archie Byers, their most reliable police surgeon, to make an examination of the body before it was moved to the mortuary. He also organised for a uniformed constable to relieve Sergeant Huggins on St. George's Road.

While at the station he nipped to his room on the first floor and produced a black leather bound hip flask from the bedside cabinet drawer. He knew it was full with a decent brandy and pocketed that, together with another pouch of tobacco.

As he was leaving he stuck his head into the canteen kitchen and found Phoebe Tanner, the resident charwoman at the station, busy rolling out pastry, even though it was well past eight in the evening.

"Phoebe, the light o' mi life. What culinary marvels are yer creatin'?"

"Now listen 'ere Inspector Meadowbank. I don't want no flannel from you. I 'aven't time, these pies are fer tomorrow". It could be argued that Phoebe Tanner single handedly kept the station oiled and running smoothly with her constant supply of hot tea throughout the day, every day, but more importantly she made the most delicious pies.

Phoebe mixed the flour and dripping to make the pastry, lined the mould then filled and hand crimped around thirty savoury pies, different for each day.

There was a seven day calendar pinned to the canteen wall, listing what pie, which day, all in beautiful calligraphy, produced by one of the uniform sergeants:

Monday - Pigeon pie.
Tuesday - Steak and ox kidney pie.
Wednesday - Minced beef and onion pie.
Thursday - Pork pie.
Friday - Butter pie.
Saturday - Cow heel and ox tail pie.
Sunday - Beef suet pudding.

Meadowbank pushed his luck a bit further.

"Phoebe mi sweetheart, me an' Sam are workin' late. 'Ave yer owt we can scoff t' keep us goin'?"

The cook turned round and said, "Mr Meadowbank, I am not t' personal cook t' yer plain clothes department…".

The inspector interrupted, "I bet yer wish yer were though. We'd look after yers".

"I'm looked after verra well, as you know. But as it 'appens, there are three sausage rolls int' larder yer can 'ave. They were fer t' superintendent's supper. I'll do 'im a bacon barm instead. 'E'll bi none t' wiser".

Phoebe was fifty three and quite tall at 5' 10" and remarkably slim for someone who spends most of her time pie making. With greying black hair in a pony tail, she had one or two secret admirers in the station. She just wished one of them would get on with it and ask her out for tea, particularly Station Sergeant Thackeray. As the inspector headed towards the stables he bumped into Superintendent Malone, and slowly moved the newspaper bundle behind his back.

"Ah, Inspector, just the man. I'll be having drinks with the Chief Constable later. Are there any updates I can pass on to him?"

"We've just found t' body of Joshua Pope, you can tell 'im that sir".

"Joshua Pope?"

"T' missin' whelk man".

"Excellent news. And what are your thoughts on his death inspector. Is foul play suspected?"

"Until t' doctor 'as a look, I'd say 'e was eaten alive and there ain't much left of 'im".

Meadowbank noticed the superintendent wince.

"Hmm, interesting. Possibly the hyena was responsible?"

"That is a strong possibility sir".

"Well carry on inspector and keep me posted". Superintendent Malone was wearing a dinner suit, black bow tie and cummerbund and the inspector could not resist commenting on his attire.

"Yer lookin' very dapper sir, if I may say so?"

"A lodge meeting Meadowbank, something you should consider. It certainly would not do your career prospects any harm".

"Thanks for t' recommendation sir. I've not considered becomin' a Freemason afore".

"I am not recommending you Meadowbank. It would be inappropriate for an officer of my rank to introduce a junior rank". He pulled on the white gloves he had been holding.

"Canapes at seven, better not keep the chief waiting, eh! Inspector?".

Meadowbank walked away shaking his head and within minutes he was back on his horse, again thanking Young Ted, no longer distracted by adverse thoughts of Superintendent Malone.

Sergeant Huggins was chatting to a constable when the inspector arrived back at St. George's Road. He gave them both one of Phoebe's sausage rolls then passed the brandy flask round.

Ten minutes later, Huggins and Meadowbank had re-mounted and resumed their patrol, leaving the constable to wait for Doctor Bayers and protect the scene until daylight hours. They continued along Garstang Road in the direction of Fulwood, keeping the horses at a steady walk and turned right into Moor Park Avenue, with the expanse of Moor Park to their left, overlooked by large baroque houses.

Huggins pointed in front, saying, "Up yonder is where poor 'Tommy Ten Pints' met 'is end".

Meadowbank nodded, only too aware of what happened along this stretch of road. Both horses suddenly reared, whinnying and snorting, their forelegs thrashing the air. As the officers fought to control the horses a large animal appeared from the darkness of the park and with its head down looked on at the commotion. The black striped male hyena was snarling, exposing bone crushing teeth, its front legs longer than the rear ones, giving it an unusual stance and it slowly moved nearer to the terrified horses, Meadowbank and Huggins too occupied to be aware of its presence. As the hyena stalked nearer, the horses jumped from side to side, rearing on their hind legs, bucking, spinning and kicking out as they sought to evade the predator. Meadowbank and Huggins tried in vain to steady their mounts, but Meadowbank was thrown backwards from the saddle and hit the cobblestones hard, his back taking the impact. He lay winded, but conscious and saw Bernadette bolt along the avenue towards Deepdale Road.

Huggins was fighting to stay in the saddle when Meadowbank caught sight of the wolf-like hyena, looking directly at him, not fifteen feet away and sniffing the air with relish. He reached for his sidearm, unclipped the holster, pulled out the Webley and fired a shot towards the hyena.

The gun-fire spooked Floss even more and she galloped into the parkland with Huggins clinging to the reins and the startled hyena loping along Moor

Park Avenue in the same direction as Bernadette. Meadowbank sat up for his next shot and holding the revolver with both hands, fired two more rounds at the fleeing animal.

Within seconds all was quiet. Meadowbank was alone, bruised but intact. He painfully got to his feet and scanned the area, but there was no sign of the hyena, Bernadette, Sergeant Huggins or Floss. He started walking towards Deepdale Road, stretching his back and shoulders, the revolver still in his right hand, when he spotted blood on the cobblestones. It was fresh, the drops glistening in the street lighting as they disappeared into the distance. He now knew he had hit the hyena and it may be nearby wounded or better still dead.

He followed the spots of blood for a hundred yards when the trail stopped in the middle of the road. Holding the revolver with an outstretched arm Meadowbank slowly turned full circle, when he heard a horse galloping towards him. Seconds later Huggins rode into view and he too had drawn his revolver.

Still mounted he said, "Albert, are you alright? What were you shootin' at?"

"I'm fine Sam. Glad t'see you".

"What t' 'ell 'appened?"

"We were attacked by t' hyena. I managed t' get a few shots at it an' it looks like I hit t' bloody thing as well. 'And us yer lamp, will yer?"

Huggins dismounted, lit the wick before handing over the bull-lamp. Both detectives scoured the area, but there was no further evidence of the blood trail.

Sergeant Huggins rode off to find Bernadette, before the rifle and ammunition harnessed to the saddle, fell into the wrong hands.

"T' hyena can't just disappear into thin air". Meadowbank said to himself.

He looked at the large houses facing him and walked towards the nearest one. It had a five foot high brick wall, topped with a three foot high railings and the name inscribed onto the gateposts was, 'Hoarstones'. Looking between the railings he could see the house was in darkness and then movement at one of the first floor windows grabbed his attention. He shone the bull-lamp at the house front, to little effect, but Auntie Vena who was watching the police inspector with interest, stepped back into the shadows.

14

It was the early hours of the morning and Meadowbank was laid in bed, his aching back keeping him awake, allowing him to mull over the events earlier in the evening.

Sergeant Huggins had retrieved Bernadette from a good spirited member of the public, not far away on Deepdale Road, who had caught the runaway horse and was then wondering what to do with it when Huggins arrived, much to the relief of them both. He met up with his inspector back on Moor Park Avenue and together they returned to the station and finished the night off in The Stanley Arms.

Meadowbank was certain someone had been watching him from the house called 'Hoarstones'. There was nothing too suspicious in that, he acknowledged to himself, but nonetheless he had an uneasy feeling about the place. It was puzzling how the blood trail stopped a few yards from that large house. Could the hyena have taken refuge in the grounds or nearby and could it get over eight foot walls and railings? He had clearly injured the animal, which made that feat less likely.

His encounter with the hellhound, as the local papers were calling it, made three confirmed sightings on or around Moor Park Avenue. Was that coincidence or was there a connection?

Remembering what his old sergeant used to say to him, "'Ey lad! There's no such thing as coincidence", Meadowbank was swaying towards the law of probability. And what else did his old sergeant say? "Always follow your gut instinct, it'll rarely let you down". He had decided that house to house enquiries would commence along Moor Park Avenue as soon as possible, starting with the house called 'Hoarstones'.

Even though catching or killing the hyena was not his number one priority, it certainly was for the local residents and once this latest encounter hit the news stands there would be pandemonium. He could already picture the headlines in the Herald and Guardian, 'Hellhound Attacks Police". That would help to calm everyone down, he thought with a slight smile.

His room was quite small, but longer than wide. A single bed filled one corner, next to the window, which overlooked the courtyard and gaol. A washstand and bowl stood in the opposite corner. A pine desk and a Windsor style chair was against the wall, beneath a row of wall mounted shelves, displaying a few law books, with a small chest of drawers facing the bed end.

The room had everything he needed and it was rent free accommodation, allocated to him as the Borough's senior detective and in lieu of the married man's housing allowance. Meadowbank had often thought of renting rooms, comprising of a drawing/breakfast room and separate bedroom, just like Sam Huggins did on The Colonnade off

Avenham Lane. The rent there was not too bad, and Huggins had a lot more privacy than he had. The inspector had given up counting how many times he had been woken in the middle of the night, always off duty, to visit the scene of a bloody crime or a fallen drunk with a head injury. It was too easy for the station sergeant to knock him up at all hours, rather than contact Superintendent Malone, who would invariably refer the station sergeant back to Meadowbank anyway.

The two rooms which Huggins rented, overlooked Avenham Park and were in a very desirable area, just off Avenham Lane. It had been the matrimonial home for Huggins and his former wife for a good three years, before she ran off with the landlord several years ago. The owner of the building, who liked having a resident police officer as a tenant, offered Huggins the position of unofficial landlord/ rent collector together with a favourable weekly rent, which Huggins accepted at once.

Meadowbank heard a yell from deep within the police station, possibly from someone larking about on nightshift or a prisoner in custody protesting their innocence. He always slept with the curtains open and this night the quarter moon offered little light into his room as he restlessly changed position to a part of his body that did not ache. Meadowbank became aware of the room getting darker and colder or was he imagining this? Still laid on his side he strained to see into the gloom and was sure something moved in the corner where shadows met, he was certain the darkness shifted like curtains caught in a draught. And then he saw the old woman, barely discernible, stood in the pervading dark. She faced him, watching from the invading blackness, her eyes glowing like embers, lank hair to her shoulders. He froze, silently calling to a God he no longer believed existed and as the figure slowly emerged from the darkness he watched the dark shape grow in size, her open mouth releasing a low cackle, a sound that would not have been out of place within the wards of a lunatic asylum, as the ever growing hag slowly floated towards him, arms outstretched, as if inviting an embrace. Petrified, he scrambled back from under the bedding, pressing himself against the wall, and fumbled for the matches, eventually lighting the bedside candle. The woman had gone, but a fetid stink occupied his room.

His heart was still racing when he heard a scratching sound and in the glow of the candle light he saw a black cat sat on the chest of drawers, watching him as the old woman had done, seconds ago. Except the cat only had one eye. Meadowbank was almost relieved on seeing the cat and spoke to it as any pet owner would do.

"What are you doin' in 'ere an' 'ow did you get in Puss?"

The cat remained passive, as if mulling over what had just been said, its green eye fixed on Meadowbank who was stood in his long johns and vest. Still unnerved, he looked around his room once more, pulling his nose at the rank smell he could almost taste, then opened the door, checking the corridor.

"Come on Puss, out yer go".

The cat was not in a hurry to leave, so the inspector moved towards it. The cat jumped to the floor and left with its tail held high in the air. As he shut the door and locked it, he did not see the cat saunter along the corridor and enter the C.I.D. office, looking like it belonged there. It jumped on to the inspector's desk and began scratching at the neat pile of files, as if searching for one in particular.

At half past six that morning, Meadowbank was up, shaved and dressed and on his way to the kitchen. It was still dark and the burning gaslights gave the kitchen a welcoming feel, together with the aroma of bacon frying. Phoebe Tanner was always in the kitchen for 6am, apart from Christmas Day. She had a room next to Meadowbank and he was keen to hear what she knew about the black cat.

"Phoebe love, any chance of a brew t' tek t' mi office?"

"Inspector Meadowbank, yer up early, 'ave yer wet yer bed?" she quipped.

"Ey! It's too early fer cheek off you. Anyway, 'ow long 'ave we 'ad a black station cat?'

"We 'aven't. Napoleon is t' station cat and 'e's a ginger tom. I've just let 'im out".

"Well last night a one eyed black cat was sat in mi room, as large as life".

"I think yer spendin' too much time in t' Stanley wi' Sergeant 'Uggins, Inspector. Anyway, a black cat is considered lucky".

This was not what he wanted to hear and he certainly did not feel good luck was coming his way.

15

St. Wilfrid's presbytery was at the corner of Chapel Lane and Friargate, next to the church. The front door displayed a cast iron 'praying hands' knocker which the plump middle aged lady rapped twice. She was wearing her usual cream bonnet and matching woollen shawl over a dark blue dress. The housekeeper immediately recognised the visitor and could see she was agitated.

"Good afternoon Mrs. Fields."

"Hello Miss McEvedy. I need to speak to Father Fairfax on an urgent personal matter, if he's available please?"

"Of course. Father Fairfax is in his study. I'm sure he will be able to see you".

Mrs. Fields took a seat in the black and white floor tiled hallway.

A few minutes later the hefty priest entered the hallway from his study. His thick greying hair needed cutting but his pockmarked face was clean shaven. He wore a clerical collar and black cassock, the thirty three buttons, each representing a year of Christ's life on earth, were buttoned from his neck to his feet.

"Emily dear, Miss McEvedy tells me you seem upset. It's not about organising the tombola is it?" he asked with genuine concern.

"No father, I'm more than happy with that. It's about young Bridie".

The priest dragged a chair across the tiles and sat close to Mrs. Fields.

"Who is Bridie?"

"Bridie Wilkes. Sir George's maid who was murdered". She put a handkerchief to her mouth to catch her gasps. "I think I know who killed her". Father Fairfax stared at the governess as if listening to a deranged confession. His blue eyes wide open, his chin dropped and his hands became clammy.

"You know who killed her? Are you certain?" he said, clearing his voice.

"Well, I know she was with child and the father is the tailor's young assistant, Tom Morgan".

The priest put a hand to his forehead as if not believing what he was being told.

"With child, how do you know that?".

"Bridie told me only two days ago and that Tom Morgan wants nothing to do with her now and denies he is the father. She was beside herself, I can tell you".

Father Fairfax was not being deliberately dim-witted, rather feeling his way in a confused fug when he asked, "I don't understand. Who do you think killed Bridie?"

He had a deep mellow voice which suited his build and well spoken tones from Lytham St Annes but his throat had become quite dry and his vocals hoarse.

Mrs. Fields was feeling more composed by the minute, and at last she was able to share her theory based on the slightest of evidence.

"Tom Morgan of course. Who else? Anyway, Bridie told me she was coming to see you the day she disappeared. I think she wanted to confess or something. I'm just wondering if she said anything to you father?"

The parish priest was thinking fast, trying to stay several questions ahead of Mrs. Fields.

"Who else knows about all this Emily?"

"Me, you now and that scoundrel, Tom Morgan". "You haven't mentioned any of this to the police yet or your husband?"

"The police are coming to the house tomorrow morning to interview the staff. I wanted to speak to you first. As for Harold, he told me not to get involved".

"Emily, why don't we go into my study, have a nice cup of tea and some of Miss McEvedy's scrumptious scones while we decide what you should do?" He patted her lap to reassure her everything would be alright.

Father Fairfax opened the study door, allowing Mrs. Fields to enter the inner sanctum of the presbytery. The room was quite dark with just a single window overlooking the small courtyard and a floor to ceiling bookcase, crammed with serious looking dark tomes lined one wall. Mrs. Fields sat in one of the two leather Chesterfield armchairs placed either side of the hearth and stared at an impressive crucifix and graphic crucifixion of

Christ, on the wall above the fireplace. The priest left her alone while he went to the kitchen.

Miss McEvedy was quietly singing to herself as she wiped the pine table top, when Father Fairfax entered the kitchen.

"Ah! Miss McEvedy, I'm going to have a chat with Emily in the study. You take the rest of the day off. I won't be going anywhere now and I'll see you in the morning".

"Come on now Father, I won't be doing that", she said in her melodic Galway lilt.

"No, I insist. You deserve some time to yourself. Here take this and treat you and your mother to something special from Booths on Fishergate". He proffered a one pound note from his wallet.

The housekeeper stared at the bank of England note in silence. That was more than a weeks wages.

"And do me a favour, if you see any fresh ground coffee get me a small pack, will you?"

Miss McEvedy was very quickly persuaded to take the money and left the presbytery less than five minutes later.

The parish priest was no stranger to the layout of the kitchen and what was behind each cupboard door. The kettle soon boiled on the range and he even used the best china tea service. The tray carried the usual tea accoutrements, pot, jug, cups and saucers and four freshly buttered scones. He poured the milk into the the two cups and from his cassock pocket, produced a small phial sealed with a rubber stopper. Into one of the cups, indicated with a teaspoon on the saucer, Father Fairfax poured the contents of the phial. The opaque tincture had no obvious smell to it. The priest had made the solution of alcohol extract and heroin many times and knew it would work perfectly.

Emily Fields was still in the armchair when Father Fairfax returned. He placed the tea tray on his desk and while the tea brewed, sat on the edge of the desk and asked, "Now Emily, what exactly did Bridie tell you?'

The governess confirmed she knew about the young couple's goings on and had even heard their moans of pleasure on one occasion weeks ago, coming from the laundry room. The priest shook his head as a member of a jury might on hearing morally outrageous allegations.

"And what did poor Bridie say about visiting the church that tragic day?"

He turned to stir the pot and poured the tea into the two cups, handing Mrs.Fields the cup and saucer with a teaspoon. A matching plate was placed on a side table with a tempting scone within reach.

"Not a lot Father, to be honest. It may be that you were the last person to speak to her or see her alive. Tom Morgan could have followed her to the church, waited outside and struck as she returned to the house".

She was warming to her theory.

"Did you tell Harold you were coming to see me today?" he asked casually.

"I did tell him, but he wasn't listening. He's just not interested Father, all he thinks about is the smooth running of the household and tugging his forelock to Sir George and Lady Edith".

"How's the tea and scone Emily?"

She had separated the two halves and nearly eaten one in between sipping the tea.

"Lovely, thank you Father. Miss McEvedy knows how to look after you".

The parish priest smiled.

A few minutes later, the governess put a hand to her mouth and made a deep yawn, immediately apologising to the priest. The narcotic solution soon took effect, as the priest expected. He took the empty tea cup and saucer from her drooping hand and gently pushed her drowsy head back against the chair. Mrs. Fields mumbled more apologies before falling silent and unable to speak.

The opioid concoction rendered Emily Fields conscious and aware of sounds and sensations, but devoid of movement in any way. Her open eyes looked like the eyes of a dead rabbit hanging from a butcher's hook, but unlike the dead animal waiting to be cleaved, she could see and hear very well. The priest looked into her eyes, his face close to hers. He had done this on so many occasions and it always fascinated him.

"I know you can hear me Emily", he whispered, his halitosis warm against her face.

"You should have listened to Harold, instead of sticking your nose into matters that do not concern you". The anger was rising inside him.

He unfastened and gently removed her bonnet, plumping up her grey hair that was brushed back into a bun.

"What shall I do with you Emily? Decisions, decisions".

The priest had already decided what he was going to do with Emily Fields. He bent down and started unbuttoning his cassock. To unfasten that many buttons was time consuming, but he was not in any hurry. Leaning forward he kissed her lips, tentatively at first, but as his fervour rose his mouth enveloped hers with passion. The cassock was unbuttoned to his waist, revealing black trousers recently pressed by Miss McEvedy. The belt was removed and carelessly dropped to the floor, then he unfastened his trousers, hastily pulling them down to his knees.

His hands wandered to the shawl still around Emily's shoulders and once drawn back allowed him to see her ample chest and he lusted to expose what was behind the fabric. He gasped, his desire to kill her increased his ardour. He had produced a switchblade knife from a trouser pocket. Pressing a button allowed the blade to spring out with a loud click and he began cutting away the buttons of her dress, starting at the collar.

Three loud raps of the door knocker seemed to blast through the house. Father Fairfax froze, similar to Mrs. Fields' condition and he held his breath at the intrusion.

He listened and believing the visitor had gone, relaxed, continuing his appraisal of Mrs. Fields.

Three more strikes from the iron knocker forced him to step back from his prisoner and with an impatient sigh, he pulled his trousers up and made himself presentable.

As he opened the front door, the man standing on the doorstep was holding out some sort of identification for the priest to see. "Excuse me sir, are you Father Fairfax?'

"Yes I am". He tried to sound unconcerned, but knew where this man was from.

"I am Detective Constable Huxley from Preston C.I.D. I am making enquiries into the deceased recently found in Winckley Square not far from here and need to establish whether you knew the deceased".

"I doubt it, but do you have a name for the young lady, officer?"

DC Huxley looked at the priest, "I did not say the deceased was female. Why would you think that sir?"

He silently cursed his carelessness.

"Officer, forgive my lack of manners. Rather than discuss it on the doorstep, come inside will you please?"

The detective entered the hallway with Father Fairfax behind him, who was still holding the exposed switchblade in his pocket. The study door was slightly open and Emily Fields could hear everything being said. She tried to shout, tried to move a limb to make a noise, any noise to attract the police officer's attention, but she was completely immobile. DC Huxley sat on the very chair Mrs. Fields had sat on less than an hour ago and the priest sat next to him. He pointed out that his housekeeper was not available to provide refreshments and apologised. The parish priest explained it was a local rumour that the body was that of a young woman, but he could not remember who had actually told him. When asked, he told the officer he did not know a Bridie Wilkes and did not know that was the name of the deceased, but she could have been one of his many parishioners. On the Thursday in question he confirmed he was busy with clerical duties in the church, such as taking confession and preparing his vestments for a Christening the following day. The detective made notes as the priest spoke and he asked if the police were close to naming a suspect.

"It's early days yet sir. Is there anyone else in the house at the moment, I could speak with?"

"I live in the presbytery alone. A housekeeper visits each day. Miss McEvedy, she'll be back in from seven in the morning if you need to speak with her".

The detective thanked the priest as he was walked to the front door.

Mrs. Fields heard the officer leave and the door shut with a thud. The priest's footsteps echoed on the tiled floor as he returned to the study. This time he closed the door and locked it.

He was already unfastening his trousers. "Now Emily, where were we before the interruption?"

16

The road to Clitheroe was tarmacadam for most of the way, it was only the Old Roman Road near Sabden that was dirt track. Mr. Ambrose, driving the polished landau, had no idea how to get to Read Hall, but the two Thoroughbred mares knew the route exactly and were eager to complete the journey.

It was that time of the year when the night crept into the afternoon and the carriage was already displaying illuminated paraffin lamps to the front, even though it was only four o'clock in the afternoon. Street lighting would end at Farringdon Park and then it would be total darkness for the remaining sixteen miles, apart from the inns at the hamlets of Samlesbury, Balderstone and Osbaldeston.

The Preston Witch was the only passenger in the landau. She was in her usual sombre state, which still worried Auntie Vena. Meg had been out of the ground for over a week, and Auntie Vena thought she should be displaying some of her old fiery, if not downright unpleasant traits by now. Auntie Vena just hoped she was up to tonight's task. Meg was still in her sack cloths, but wrapped in an ankle length black robe, the one given to her by Auntie Vena at the cemetery. As usual the hood was pulled far across her head, hiding her bloodshot eyes, which seemed to be ripening like plums prior to harvesting.

Mr. Ambrose did not check on his passenger, if he had he would have seen Meg's hands twitching incessantly as they approached Pendle Hill, similar to someone suffering from convulsions.

She knew that they were in the shadow of the hill.

Meg looked up to her right and smiled, as she if could see the rising mass of over eighteen hundred feet, but the seeping fog and the blackness of the night kept Pendle Hill hidden. She inhaled deeply, gorging on the pervading mystical air, her black wizened lungs expanding with each breath, her shrunken shape began to fill the loose robe, as if hydraulics were in action, her fingers cracked as her decrepit nails slowly became talons, her features even more aquiline. She cackled and smiled, her remaining teeth still like slithers of coal, but her body shuddered and trembled as an energy long forgotten by the Preston Witch, surged through her and like alcohol corrupting an alcoholic, the pleasure was immense.

If only Auntie Vena was present to witness the transformation of pupa to a perverted butterfly.

Mr. Ambrose stopped the carriage near to the main gatekeeper's lodge then turned to look at his passenger. He was startled to see Meg Shelton sat upright, staring at him with dark purple eyes and smiling, her mouth twisting as if it was a difficult endeavour. He continued to look at Meg, realising she had increased in size, she was much larger than he remembered and more alert. He imagined she could leap from the carriage and run to Read Hall if she chose.

"We're here Meg. You know what to do".

"Don't worry, I won't let Auntie Vena down". Even her voice had changed. Gone was the rasping whisper, replaced with a gruff, even pleasant quality to her tone.

Mr. Ambrose climbed down to assist Meg from the carriage, but she was already moving towards the gates to the estate. As he watched the Preston Witch, he had to look twice before realising she was not walking, but floating about a foot off the ground as she continued towards the closed gates.

The high double wrought iron gates, each bearing the Nowell family crest, had been locked on instructions from Sir Roger. The gatekeeper, a sprightly seventy year old was enjoying a mug of steaming tea in the gate house when he heard loud banging from outside.

He grabbed his shotgun and on leaving the grand looking lodge, saw an old woman stood at the gates which were rocking on their huge iron hinges, as if being subjected to a localised earth tremor.

This alone should have alerted the gate-keeper that this was an unnatural phenomena.

"What the 'ell are yer playing at? This is private property, move away".

Meg ignored him and swept a hand forward, in a manner similar to dismissing a truculent beggar. There was a crack of metal fracturing, immediately followed by both heavy gates opening with terrific force; the right hand gate colliding with the gate-keeper, sending him sprawling to the ground.

Meg entered the grounds to the manor, dust and dirt swirling in eddies beneath her.

The gatekeeper was back on his feet. As a former infantry man and now a house servant for over thirty years, he was used to taking orders, in fact he needed them to perform his duties, so it was surprising that he decided to aim the single barrelled shotgun at Meg and pull the trigger.

The blast of the gun discharging even startled Mr. Ambrose, who was tending to the horses out of sight. He then rushed towards the gates.

The lead slug had passed through Meg's chest and out of her back, ripping an unrepairable hole in Auntie Vena's robe. The Preston Witch, unconcerned about the wound and unaware of the damage to the fabric, flicked her right wrist, as if giving someone directions. A lightening bolt, a flash of visible energy flew from her fingertips and hit the gatekeeper like an exploding fire-ball, within seconds reducing him and his shotgun to a bubbling molten liquid.

Mr. Ambrose had sprinted towards the shotgun fire and watched incredulously as he reached the huge York stone gate pillars. He had been with Auntie Vena for many years and had witnessed her carry out many breath-taking killings, but had never seen anything like this.

He watched Meg waft through the black smoke coming from the cooling gatekeepers remains and veer off the drive cutting across the parkland. Just like the two Thoroughbred mares, she knew her destination.

Read Hall, an ancient manor house with extensive landscaped and ornamental grounds, was a fitting home for a wealthy ancestral witch finder. This evening it was well lit with gas lamps on the terraces and the front of the house, illuminating the armed members of staff on patrol.

Sir Roger, stood at the drawing room window, cupping a large glass of brandy in both hands, saw a flash of flames through the sunset and thickening fog coming from the direction of the gatehouse.

He put the glass on the table and turned to a large man sat by the log fire. He too was enjoying one of Sir Roger's fine cognacs.

"She's here", Sir Roger said quietly.

The man nodded then drained the brandy goblet, savouring the liquid with an appreciative sigh.

"How long have we got?", he asked.

"Not long enough for another of those, if that is what you're thinking". Sir Roger resumed his post at the window.

The large man got up to join Sir Roger. John Paslew, The Abbot of Whalley, was 6'5" and towered over the Lord Lieutenant. He wore a white ankle length tunic and the tonsure, a requirement of all Cistercian monks, made him look older than his forty nine years. A black scapula went over the tunic, but it was the holster, ammunition belt and side arm fastened around his waist that looked out of place, even exaggerating his spreading girth. Sir Roger was already cradling his double barrelled sawn off shotgun, loaded with two solid silver bullets he had made himself.

"Arnold!". He called for his butler.

He appeared at the drawing room almost instantly. "Yes sir?"

"Arnold, tell the men danger is upon us and it's time to shoot at anything that moves. Are there anymore staff on the premises?.

"No sir, the domestic staff left the estate in the convoy of coaches this morning. Apart from the few who volunteered to stay and Walter at the gate house of course".

"I fear it may be too late for poor old Walter. We'll check on him as soon as possible. It's time you left as well Arnold. It is probably safer now to take refuge in the cellar than attempt to leave the house".

"With all due respect sir, I've served this house for over fifty years and have no intention of running scared the first time danger presents itself".

Sir Roger touched his shoulder fondly, "In that case, after you've relayed my message to the men, select a weapon of your choice from the gun cabinet and have plenty of ammunition with you. I suggest you guard the kitchen, in the event the house is attacked from the rear. And thank you Arnold".

"Just one question sir, who exactly are we expecting?'

"Supernatural forces. Meg Shelton, The Preston Witch to be exact. My ancestors didn't finish off this witch as they should have, and now she's back from the grave to destroy me, this house and everyone in it". He looked at the abbot and his butler to reinforce the gravity of what he had said. "How can you be certain of that Roger? This notion you have of a witch rising from the grave to take revenge on your family is hard to comprehend, and your insistence that I arm myself for my own protection does stretch our long friendship, I'll be honest. I do regret you talking me into this foolish enterprise. I am a man of God, not a hired gunslinger". The abbott was clearly annoyed.

"John, Meg Shelton has risen, believe that. Not through her own black magic, but through that of an ancient and unholy power of a necromancer, an evil entity who does the work of Satan. The Nowell's were cursed by Elizabeth Demdike on the scaffold at Lancaster. This is her retribution for my distant grandfather, my namesake, persecuting, prosecuting and condemning by fair means or foul, every Lancashire witch he could could track down, including Meg Shelton. If we survive the night, an even greater force from hell will bare down on us in days to come. Of that I am certain".

"Very good sir". Arnold replied, as if taking instructions for afternoon tea.

As the butler left the drawing room, John Paslew withdrew the handgun and with shaking hands checked it was loaded. It was a howdah pistol, a high calibre gun with two barrels. The abbot acquired the handgun on missionary duties in the Congo as a keepsake. It was ideal for killing big cats at close range and could even stop an elephant with a good head shot, but the abbot had never fired a gun in his life.

"What have you got me into Roger?".

"I told you we would be facing a demon from hell, and witches are the right hand of the devil, and must be destroyed. That is why I asked you to arm yourself with firepower as well as your faith. You are not here to perform an exorcism, to save a soul from Satan, just the opposite in fact. We are here to kill not save".

A scream from outside pierced the early evening. Both men turned to the window, but only swirling fog pressed against the glass.

"What hell have you brought me to?", asked The Abbot of Whalley nervously.

Meg Shelton approached the lake where the fog seemed impenetrable and came to a stop. Still hovering above the wet grass she cried out "REVENGE!". The loud call amplified and echoed through the thick mist. Movement could be heard where the woodland meets the meadows and cut grass. Hundreds of wild boar, kept for hunting and eating, appeared, staring through the fog towards the Preston Witch.

"REVENGE IS MINE AND YOURS", she cried out even louder.

The gamekeepers, beaters and hired help from the village, all positioned around the house, froze as those words tumbled at them through the watery mist. The boars set off as one, all maintaining a steady trot, but soon the charge began. The sounder stampeded towards the house, led by huge male swine, bellowing for other boar, females and even piglets to follow.

Meg approached the lake and continued across the water as if it was the Sea of Galilee, the surface rippling as she passed. The boars were not far behind and split left and right at the lake, minutes later re-converging, countless cloven feet churning the manicured grass, their screams and grunts of rage and excitement driving each other faster. By the time the witch had crossed the lake, hundreds of wild boar had overtaken her and disappeared into the fog. She smiled in anticipation.

Some of the beaters and mercenaries, on hearing the sounds of hell getting closer and louder, fired blindly into the eddying vapour. Those with oil lanterns held them forward, hoping to catch sight of the monster they could only hear. The more experienced gamekeepers waited patiently for a target, their weapons already pointing at the cacophony of grunting getting nearer.

A grand old boar, bulky and solid with razor sharp tusks was the first to reach the Yorkshire stone terrace beyond the tar macadam driveway. It was met with a barrage of gun fire. The rest were not far behind. The huge boar was hit many times but did not miss a stride and attacked the first man it saw. With a flick of its powerful neck a tusk gored the gamekeeper's groin, ripping away his genitals in an instant.

A fellow gamekeeper on the estate, who stalked many a wild boar, attempted to reload his shotgun, instead of taking flight. He should have known better. He was hit by a large sow at full charge and hurled backwards, his head splitting open as he collided with the stonework. The sow stepped back, those piggy intelligent eyes watching for movement and when satisfied the gamekeeper was dead, hurled herself forward, smashing through a stained glass window into the dining hall. Immediately other pigs followed through the breach and many more charged against the ground floor windows.

Dozens of boar lay dead, but most were gathered at the front of the hall, goring, trampling, charging and snapping at the few surviving gunmen, vying to scramble into the great hall.

It was even more horrific inside the house. The swines were running amok, destroying furniture and carpets, and sniffing the air for humans.

The servants who had volunteered to stay behind, including Arnold, locked themselves in the basement kitchen. They were soon sniffed out, the bolted wooden door pulverised in minutes as strong bristle covered shoulders heaved against it. The boars rushed in, their high pitched squeals and cries drowning out the screams of the men as they attempted to escape. Very soon the chomping, slurping and crunching started, and as boars will eat anything, so they began to feast.

Sir Roger and John Paslew had remained in the drawing room and could only watch the carnage unfold outside and listen to the ensuing horror within the house.

Remarkably the boars had not attempted to enter the drawing room, the stained glass mullioned windows remaining intact and the door leading to the hallway unscathed.

The drawing room was well lit by gas lights, the heavy drapes were open, but the wild pigs paid no attention to the two occupants even though more than a hundred marauded through the house. The beasts trampled upstairs destroying beds and furniture and reached the servants' quarters on the top floor. Not a single door, locked or otherwise remained intact, carpets and varnished wood floors were soon covered in excrement and urine. Mirrors were smashed as raging boars charged at the interloper reflected back, but still the drawing room remained a sanctuary.

"We cannot just stay here and do nothing. Men, your men are being slaughtered, we must help". John Paslew was pointing his pistol at the door as he walked towards it.

"John, if you open that door we will be dead within minutes. This is all a sideshow, a horrific sideshow, but we must wait for the main event. The witch will appear soon, of that I am certain. We must hold our resolve".

The Preston Witch had reached the front steps to Read Hall. She glided gently up the stone steps towards the solid oak door that had kept the Nowells secure for centuries. It had been shattered, chunks of wood attached to the hinges hung precariously. A piglet with a dismembered arm in its mouth ran squealing from the house passing Meg Shelton as it disappeared into the fog.

She stood outside the drawing room double doors, which without warning opened suddenly as if blasted by a hurricane. The witch floated into the large drawing room with its Adams fireplace, Persian rugs, Chippendale furniture and crystal chandelier. She pulled the robe hood down, turning towards Sir Roger, revealing her face to a witch finder once again.

John Paslew, still brandishing the howdah handgun, reached into his tunic and produced a crucifix. Holding it in his left hand he thrust it at the witch, calling out,

"In nomine Patris et Filii et Spiritus Sancti. I command you unclean one to depart to whence you came…".

She interrupted the abbot, her harsh voice still nurturing. "You priests never learn. It is you who should depart".

The monk was lifted off his feet and pitched backwards, as if an invisible battering ram had hit him. He was hurled thirty feet across the room, smashing through a floor to ceiling stained glass window, landing in a heap on the terrace. His presence immediately attracting the attention of the wild pigs snuffling amongst the carcasses. The abbot attempted to use the pistol he was still holding, but the nearest boar was far quicker and lunged forward, swiping a tusk through the abbot's neck and into his throat. The boar shook its huge head violently, the explosive force decapitating the prostrate monk.

Sir Roger looked on in disbelief. He had asked his friend, The Abbot of Whalley, to help him battle Meg Shelton, but he had underestimated her power and now his friend was dead. He heard the witch laugh. It was not a jocular or even gloating sound, more like a vixen being strangled by a huntsman. Sir Roger looked at the Preston Witch for the first time. Her grey hair was to her shoulders, lank and foul. Her skin was the colour of sour milk, suppurating sores weeped rank puss, and her bulging purple eyes were devoid of pupils. The nose was hooked and hairy with flaring nostrils secreting black snot. Her mouth was gruesome, lips resembling charred fish skin, and a large hard bristled wart protruded from her jutting bony chin. And still she hovered, motionless, returning Sir Roger's stare. He realised he was in the presence of pure evil, a creature that had somehow crawled from hell and invaded his home. The malevolence wafted over him like a breeze from an abattoir, gagging and eye watering. Sir Roger knew he had to act fast.

In a single movement he swept the sawn off shotgun towards the witch and squeezed one of the two triggers. A silver bullet hit the witch in the shoulder. She dropped with a thud to the floor and staggered backwards, looking at Sir Roger confused. "What have you done?" she rasped.

For the next shot, he put the gun to his shoulder and took aim. The second silver bullet travelled the twenty feet separating them in a fraction of a second and hit the witch's forehead, dead centre. She was propelled over a small table, falling against a bookcase, lifeless. Sir Roger cautiously approached the witch, prodding her with his shotgun barrel.

He let out a sigh and left the drawing room. The wild boars were leaving the house as quickly as they had entered, leaping out of windows, sprinting along corridors towards open doors, as if the mating season was calling them from the woodland.

Very soon the house was quiet.

Sir Roger stepped outside, passing through the opening where his front door used to be. The fog had lifted and the sounder of boars were heading nonchalantly back to the woods. The slaughter was everywhere. Bodies lay limbless and eviscerated, pigs littered the terrace and driveway, many shot to pieces.

Mr. Ambrose was waiting by the gatehouse and could only guess at the carnage inflicted by Meg Shelton. He decided to see for himself and followed the driveway towards the house. It helped now the fog had gone, at last he could see where he was going.

A handful of survivors assembled at the front of the house as Sir Roger checked for signs of life amongst the fallen. He returned a short time later and spoke to his head gamekeeper.

"We have to finish this now. James, get a rope from the workshop and bring some paraffin. I need someone to help me bring the witch's body out here".

Two beaters entered the house with Sir Roger and they dragged Meg Shelton outside by her feet. There was an ancient oak tree a short distance from the house. It had stood there longer than Read Hall. Sir Roger took the rope and threw one end over a low branch then wrapped the other around the witch's corpse. The watching men understood what was about to happen and two of them took hold of the slack rope and heaved until Meg Shelton was upright. And there she stood, her feet still on the ground but swaying like a common drunk, supported by the rope.

Sir Roger carried large pieces of the oak front door and placed them around the witch's feet. James then doused the body and wood in paraffin and Sir Roger tossed an oil-lamp at the impromptu pyre. They watched in silence as the witch burnt.

As if waking from a nightmare, Meg Shelton's eyes opened with sudden terror. Already the robe was alight at her feet and the blue flames were rapidly consuming the flammable substance. Her scream was ear-shattering, forcing the observers to press their palms against their ears. It was a single, continuous scream of unimaginable panic, a scream no human could make. Her mouth wide open, her face contorted with fear and not once pausing for breath allowed the scream to endure. Even the wild boars already dozing with bellies full, lifted their heads nervously and nocturnal creatures scurried away.

The flames had joined forces and the Preston Witch disappeared in the inferno. The rope holding the witch burnt away and she toppled to the grass, no longer writhing, the screaming stopped. Sir Roger and his men maintained a silent vigil around the immolation of Meg Shelton.

Mr. Ambrose kept low and to the shadows as he approached the house. He froze on seeing Meg dragged across the churned lawn, strung up and set alight. His mind was racing. The scream was distracting, this was not supposed to happen. What will Auntie Vena say?

Once Sir Roger was satisfied with the finality of the smouldering corpse, he tentatively recovered the two silver bullets, still hot, first crushing the charred rib cage and then the skull with his boot heel. He sent four men to check on Walter at the gatehouse. They were armed and carried lanterns, still fearful of further boar attacks. As the men advanced towards Mr. Ambrose's position, he dashed across the lawns, now avoiding the driveway. He had to get back and still had a twenty mile journey ahead of him.

17

Auntie Vena sat by the fire, it was banked high as usual but there was no coal scuttle nearby, in fact no coal had ever been delivered to the house and Mr. Ambrose had never needed to clean the grate or remove the ash-pan. This had often puzzled him, but he knew better than to ask questions of Auntie Vena.

She tightly held the half filled tumbler of whisky and looked away from the dancing flames to the man who had been stood by the open door for several minutes.

"Mr. Ambrose, close the door and sit down. Help yourself to one of these, you know where the glasses and bottles are kept".

The tall man did as he was told and sat down in the rocking chair with a controlled sigh, tensing, as if bracing himself for a sudden eruption of sorts. He glanced nervously at the one eyed cat, squatting on the hearth rug, staring back at him intently, as if the cat was about to start interrogating him.

But it was Auntie Vena who spoke, not the cat. "I was never convinced Meg was ready to take on the witch finder, but I had to act. She was a disappointment and I can only think she had been buried in that hole too long. Nearly three centuries buried alive had taken its toll I fear. I hope the others fair better".

"With respect ma'am, the witch that left here last night was not the witch that arrived at Read Hall. Meg had literally grown into something frightening. She actually floated down the driveway and set fire to the gatekeeper with a lighting bolt". He was quietly spoken and his accent was clearly from the city of Newcastle-upon-Tyne.

Auntie Vena was not particularly impressed with what she was being told. "That is basic black magic. If she could do that then she could have used her energy to obliterate Read Hall and everyone in it and bring me the witch finder's heart as she was supposed to". Auntie Vena smoothed her dark green tartan dress several times, which seemed to placate her rising anger.

"Instead Meg has left behind a messy situation for me to sort out. The witch finder will now come looking for Meg's necromancer, me. So we must be vigilant Mr. Ambrose. I think a more basic approach to the witch finder's destruction is called for. There are several ways to skin a cat", she paused and smiled gently at the cat now looking back at her with his one eye wide open. "I could never skin you, dear. I never wear cat fur". She cooed at the animal.

Mr. Ambrose could not decide whether the Demdike was serious or not.

"Yes, the witch finder must die very soon and you Mr. Ambrose will kill him and bring me his heart". The faithful servant relaxed and gently rocked the chair, taking a large glug of the single malt as if already considering his method of execution.

"How long have you been with me Mr. Ambrose?" She knew exactly to the day how long. "Over thirty years ma'am".

She thought back to how they met thirty two years, two hundred and twenty four days ago. Auntie Vena was visiting Black Chantel of York, staying in her town house on Little Blake Street, in the shadow of the great Minster.

Black Chantel was from Haiti, a 'Creole dark sorcerer', a 'bokor' who introduced Auntie Vena to the secrets of a voodoo queen. Mr. Ambrose had been found hiding in the stables at the rear of Black Chantel's house. He had been beaten and handcuffed, having broke free from the two constables who had arrested him for an attempt robbery on nearby Stonegate. He had been discovered by Malcolm, Auntie Vena's coach driver, while he tended the two Thoroughbred mares.

Malcolm's presence no longer pleased Auntie Vena. She approved of him in the early days, when she found him sleeping on the streets. Then he was young and eager to please. But her only member of staff drank too much by then, even by her standards and his rowdy behaviour when intoxicated was infuriating to say the least. But a good coachman is hard to come by, so she had mistakenly turned a blind eye on more than one occasion to his inebriated singing, as he entered the house by the rear door and noisily climbed the stairs to his room on the top floor.

That was until one evening.

Auntie Vena was dozing by the fire and did not hear the drunk servant open the door to the warm sitting room. He quietly approached Auntie Vena, watching her chest gently rise and fall with each breath. She was leant back in her armchair, the whisky tumbler empty on the tiled hearth, her slender legs in silk stockings and polished brogues slightly parted. The lavender perfume she always wore by *Floris of London* gently fragranced the room. His own breathing quickened and he wet his lips. Malcolm ignored the hissing black cat stood on the sideboard and moved furtively towards the sleeping witch. Spurred on by a gallon of bitter inside him, he had already formed the unhinged notion of being intimate with Auntie Vena, and had convinced himself the old woman would be receptive, even grateful for his advances.

Auntie Vena awoke confused. She was being smothered and her Merino wool cardigan unbuttoned. Opening her eyes she saw Malcolm's closed eyes inches from hers and his open mouth roughly pressed against hers.

She could not have moved quicker and as she stood up, her right hand slapped his face hard, then her left hand and again her right hand struck his face. He staggered backwards, "Ma'am, I'm sorry...", before he could finish his pleading the one-eyed black cat launched himself from the sideboard, landing perfectly on Malcolm's head, sinking numerous claws into his face and skull. The servant fell to the floor screaming, blood streaming from puncture wounds with the cat seemingly content to stay embedded to his head.

As Auntie Vena approached her stricken servant, the cat released itself and jumped back on the sideboard. With her polished right shoe, Auntie Vena kicked Malcolm hard in the stomach again and again, and again, forcing several pints of bitter to spew from his mouth onto the varnished floorboards. "I'll pretend this never happened, are you listening Malcolm? And you had better clean that mess up before the morning".

The servant remained huddled on the floor moaning apologies, arms folded across his stomach.

Auntie Vena and the cat left the room, making a rare visit to her large bedroom upstairs.

This had occurred a week before the visit to York.

Mr. Ambrose had been presented to Black Chantel and Auntie Vena who listened with admiration to his plight and flight from the law. Auntie Vena could see possibilities with the young fugitive and the York Witch had no real use for him, other than draining and bottling all the blood from his body. That amount of fresh blood was difficult to obtain at the best of times.

Malcolm was stood nearby, the cuts to his face still evident. even in the candlelight. He was ready to step forward and redeem some grace from his employer, should the escaped prisoner do something foolhardy, especially as the handcuffs had suddenly dropped from his wrists onto the matting with a thud, as if an invisible hand and key had unlocked them.

The next morning Malcolm's body was found washed up on the shoreline under the nearby bridge that crossed the Ouse River. His throat had been cut and every drop of blood had been drained from his corpse. Later that day, the young and grateful Mr. Ambrose drove Auntie Vena home across the Pennines back to Preston.

18

It had just gone eight in the morning and Meadowbank had lit the fire in the CID office an hour earlier. He was at his desk and sat round him were Sergeant Huggins and three detective constables. The CID office was on the first floor overlooking the covered market on Earl Street and Lancaster Road. It was a grey, late October day and again the rain hammered down on the pavements and people below, many believing St Swithin's Day was either three months late or nine months early.

Even though the office door was fully open, Station Sergeant Thackeray knocked as he entered. "Sorry t' interrupt Inspector. There's someone to see yers at t' enquiry desk".

"Blimey Ernest, they're keen at this time. Who is it?"

"Says 'e's Sir Roger Nowell, Lord Lieutenant of Lancashire, and 'as some important information for yers". Meadowbank raised his eyebrows at Sergeant Huggins.

"Thanks Ernest, I'll come an' speak t' him".

They shook hands at the enquiry desk and Meadowbank asked what could he do for Sir Roger, who in turn replied that he had information of the utmost importance regarding an ongoing police investigation. The inspector took Sir Roger to one side and asked what information it was, he was intrigued.

"It is to do with the disappearance of Meg Shelton's body".

"Sir Roger, with all due respect but t' cemetery incident is at t' very bottom of my enquiry list. I'm not convinced that a crime 'as even bin committed. As far as I am concerned t' borough police 'ave already spent too much time on what did or did not 'appen t' Meg Shelton".

"Inspector, if you would hear me out. I appreciate you are busy but I must bring to your attention a recent event which involved the murder of a good friend and the deaths of fifteen of my staff". Sir Roger was immaculately dressed in a charcoal grey three piece woollen suit, matching raincoat and a black Derby hat. He wore a white shirt favouring a modern collar with a black and red striped tie. As far as Meadowbank was concerned Sir Roger could have been on his way for an audience with His Majesty the King. But he did get the inspector's attention.

"Why hasn't this bin reported before?"

"I contacted the police yesterday. There is a major investigation at Read Hall as we speak. Inspector Rutherford is in charge".

"I know Joe Rutherford. He's a good man and a damned good copper".

"I do not doubt that Mr. Meadowbank, but I want you to lead the investigation".

125

The inspector shook his head. "It's not that simple Sir Roger, there are procedures such as protocol an' jurisdiction to follow and…".

Sir Roger interrupted, "Forgive me inspector, but I have already taken the liberty of contacting Major Little and he is ready to re-assign you and your team to the investigation at Read Hall. It needs someone with your tenacity and after putting paid to Jack the Ripper, you are the right man to confront an evil menace beyond belief".

First of all, the inspector was surprised that the Chief Constable of Preston would agree to this and said as much and secondly, was Sir Roger exaggerating the danger?

"I agree that my request is unorthodox, but being the Lord-lieutenant of Lancashire has a few advantages and I say this with no arrogance. You may not yet be aware of the evil permeating the town, but believe me, you will very soon".

Meadowbank looked at Sir Roger for a few moments before saying, "I'm 'aving a briefin' at t' moment wi' mi team. I think we should all 'ear what you 'ave t' say".

The detectives were still sat around the desk each with an enamel mug full of steaming tea and in the middle of the desk was a plate piled with buttered tea-cakes, thanks to Phoebe Tanner.

The inspector made the introductions and Sir Roger gratefully accepted a mug of tea, poured by Huggins.

"I will start with events which took place at my home, Read Hall yesterday evening. Since the grave of Meg Shelton was disturbed and found empty a few weeks ago, I've had my staff on high alert". He held up a hand to gracefully silence D.C. Collier who was about to ask a question. "You will probably share your inspector's doubts about a woman rising from the grave after nearly three hundred years, and who could blame you? But Meg Shelton did exactly that, and how do I know that? Well last night I burnt her alive and crushed her bones underfoot once and for all".

"Are you being serious?" exclaimed Meadowbank. He nearly spat a mouthful of tea across the desk.

"Gentlemen, do you honestly think I would come to you with such a fantastical story, a story you would dismiss as coming from the wards of Whittingham Lunatic Asylum if it were not true? Come to Read Hall and see for yourself. I will show you the death and destruction there after Meg Shelton and hundreds of wild boar invaded my house. Fifteen of my staff and local villagers, including a dear friend, the Abbot of Whalley, John Paslew were slaughtered defending my life and my property".

He placed two pointed cylindrical objects on the desk. "I came face to face with the Preston Witch not twenty hours ago and shot her with these solid silver bullets. They did not kill her of course, but they temporarily stopped her wanton annihilation. It is worth remembering there are only two ways to kill a witch, decapitation and incineration.

My ancestors made that mistake with Meg Shelton, you cannot hang a witch to death".

The five detectives had gone quiet as they looked from the silver bullets back to Sir Roger and for once the warm buttered tea-cakes were going cold. "What about t' Pendle Witches?" Meadowbank asked.

"What about them, Inspector?"

"Well they were 'anged, so what are yer sayin'?"

"You are right of course. Nine were hanged in 1612 at Gallows Hill at Lancaster Castle. After that, there is no record as to what happened to the bodies".

"You don't know where the nine witches are buried?" Huggins asked with disbelief.

"If I knew, believe me I would have dug them up long ago and reduced them to ashes, but I don't, so they lie dormant in the soil somewhere, like seeds waiting to flourish, and all it would take is the black sorcery of a necromancer for them to rise again, like Meg Shelton".

"Sir Roger, what do you want from us exactly?" Meadowbank was becoming irritated at this deluge of foreboding, especially as the files regarding the Winckley Square murder, three missing children and a man-eating hyena were demanding action.

"Apart from what I have respectfully asked or that you at least liaise with Inspector Rutherford, there is nothing more you can do at the moment. It is now a waiting game for the necromancer to be exposed, trapped or reveal themselves. I have much to do going through the records from my ancestors and see if there is a clue amongst the archives to help identify this witch who can bring the dead to life". He took a long drink of tea before continuing,

"With the demise of Meg Shelton, the danger to you and I and the townsfolk of Preston has not gone away. If anything I fear it will become greater. There is an evil presence out there, far more powerful than Meg Shelton. It must be a priority to find this monster".

Sergeant Huggins was the first to speak. "I heard rumours last night of a fire at Read Hall and not what you have described".

"That was a cover story for the press. A decision made by myself, Major Little and Inspector Rutherford. Can you imagine if the true events were released to the papers? That the Preston Witch had somehow gone from her grave to my home in Read resulting in countless deaths. If the public got wind of this there would be panic on the streets, vigilantes, the press breathing down your necks making your job and mine very difficult".

"And what of your family? Are they unharmed?" Huggins asked.

"They are quite safe, thank you for asking Mr. Huggins. My wife's parents reside at Lytham Hall, her father is the Squire of Lytham. She has been there with our daughter, son-in-law and grandchildren for over a week, protected with my own security personnel and they shall remain there until the necromancer is identified and put to death".

"Sir Roger, I'm 'avin' difficulty tekin' all this in to be honest", said D.C. Grimes.

" I have said enough gentleman for today, but will finish on a quote from the good book, Exodus 22 - 18: Though shalt not suffer a witch to live".

He looked at his audience for effect.

"Christ Almighty, that's all I need to 'ear". Meadowbank sighed.

19

Auntie Vena moved quietly through the house carrying the oil-lamp, but Mr. Ambrose had heard her. It was past 3am and he rarely slept. She left by the side door and entered the stables, the two Thoroughbreds with their heads poking over the closed bottom door, relaxed when they recognised the visitor. Auntie Vena patted each one in turn, then passed the third stall which was empty and stopped at the fourth and last stable door with both halves fully closed. She unlatched the two doors, swinging them open, and holding the lamp in front of her, she entered the stall, illuminating the hyena laid on the straw. It had a bandage wrapped around it's chest, just behind it's forelegs and it's breathing seemed laboured. Apart from opening its eyes briefly, the animal paid no attention to Auntie Vena. The main stable door opened with a loud click as the latch was lifted and someone else entered with a lamp, their footsteps loud and heavy.

Mr. Ambrose approached, carrying a tray with a lead crystal tumbler of her favourite single malt whisky.

"I thought you may like a nightcap while you are checking on our guest, ma'am".

Auntie Vena nodded her thanks, took the glass and said, "I must say Mr. Ambrose, you have done an excellent job dressing his wound".

"Thank you ma'am, fortunately the bullet only grazed his stomach. It needed a few stitches, but he should be right as rain in a couple days".

"You also did sterling work recovering the injured animal".

"I was cleaning the stalls when I heard the gunshots. I saw the poor beast collapse, and you know what I'm like with animals ma'am, I couldn't leave it there to be finished off, so I carried it in here".

A purring sound made Mr. Ambrose look up to his left and there was the black cat splayed across the wooden partition, just above head height. He shuddered slightly. For someone who claims to like animals, he did not like that cat. If he had been asked why, he would have mentioned its age to start with. From what Auntie Vena has told him the cat must be at least fifty years old, if not a damn sight older and it never eats. In the thirty years he had been in Vena Demdike's employment he had never once seen that cat eat anything, never seen it fed and it followed Auntie Vena like a shadow, as if it had the ability to appear from nowhere. He had never seen Auntie Vena eat for that matter, but that did not bother him, as he believed he knew what she was. But she was much more than just a witch. He could not possibly know she was The Necromancer; Queen of All Cunning Folk, Sorceress of the Unknown Realms of Darkness and Last of the Lancashire Witches, the most powerful coven these islands had ever seen.

"There is a police inspector, the one who shot our friend here, he may be paying too much attention to our activities. His name is Meadowbank, the cat found that much out for me". He forced himself not to look at the black cat, which he knew was listening.

"I want you to follow him, discreetly, find out if he is in cahoots with the witch finder. The cat has seen them together. We do not need any mishaps so close to All Hallows' Eve. I have already paid him a brief visit, but I fear this may have increased his curiosity rather than curb his enthusiasm, so a more subtle approach is needed".

"Of course ma'am. Do you want me to have a chat with this Inspector?"

"By 'having a chat with him' I presume you mean, should you subject him to gratuitous violence and the answer is 'no', certainly not yet. I will let you know when you can beat him to a pulp, but for now, just follow him please and keep him out of trouble until we know whether he is a threat or not".

"Of course ma'am. And what of the children?"
"What of the children, Mr. Ambrose? Is there cause for concern?"

"No ma'am, not as far as I know, they are eating fine, couple are a bit blubbery, wailing for their parents, but we only have three and you need five".
"I am aware of that. That is my next priority to get the five then I'll have one brat for each point of the pentagram. Let me know when our friend here is back on his feet, he could prove a useful distraction".

20

The Stanley Arms on a Monday evening is usually quiet and tonight was no different. Meadowbank and Huggins were each scoffing a bowl of mutton, onions and carrots, topped with sliced potatoes which some ale-houses were calling Lancashire hot-pot. They agreed that Mrs. Walmsley's mutton stew was delicious and she was a marvellous cook and that William Walmsley was a lucky man.

"Runnin' an ale-'ouse wi'a good lookin' woman who can cook. That's a dream come true". How many times had Sergeant Huggins said this to his inspector?

Both men had recently returned from an afternoon at Read Hall with Superintendent Malone, where they had met Inspector Joe Rutherford. The trip to Read Hall in the borough police brougham was a quiet one. The superintendent was not one for idle chat or even pleasantries, choosing to read The Times for most of the trip, leaving the inspector and sergeant to their own thoughts and providing the first opportunity for the detectives to see Pendle Hill for themselves. Meadowbank paid little attention to the huge monolith of rock, but Huggins was drawn to the barren isolated hill dominating the view from the carriage window to the north. The hill was as Sir Roger had described to him: bleak, majestic and brooding, but an evil lifeblood for black magic?

That he could not understand. Evil comes from the heart and soul, nurtured, unresisted, not from Mother Nature's breathtaking creation such as this. He stared at the sloping plateau and wondered what witchcraft did take place up there all those years ago.

The sergeant had heard of the Pendle Witches, but could not recount a single fact about them, other than a few were hanged for their trouble. But now the Lord Lieutenant of Lancashire was claiming a witch, who was hanged over two hundred years ago, had left her grave and destroyed his home. He was not surprised his inspector described the story as 'baloney'. Why were the three of them even making this journey (apart from the fact they had been instructed to by their chief constable)?

The carriage turned off the Clitheroe Road travelling west towards Read and Padiham, arriving at the hall just after lunchtime. The sun had come out for a change, which allowed the devastation to be laid out for them as the coach made its way along the driveway to the house. The once manicured lawns sweeping from the surrounding woodland looked like a lunatic with a plough had been at work, as the churned grass swept either side of the formal pond straight up to the house. As they got nearer, the carcasses of numerous boar lay where they fell, the ones outside the house had all received fatal shotgun, pistol or rifle fire. A team of slaughter men from local abattoirs were due to arrive that afternoon and remove the carcasses. They would struggle to recover the three dead boar from the downstairs kitchen, especially the huge male with an axe still lodged in its head. It is not known which brave volunteer or hired help was responsible for that. It was too soon to recognise individual acts of bravery. The fifteen dead, twelve from the front of the house and three from the kitchen had already been taken away for a post mortem. The bodies had all been photographed in situ and now lay in a makeshift mortuary in Whalley village hall. Identifying some of the deceased already presented a problem. For some reason the boars tended to eat the face first, leaving many unrecognisable. These would have to be identified by jewellery, clothing, scars, tattoos or an unusual feature. The Abbot of Whalley had his head stitched back into place by one of the mortuary assistants. It was not a particularly good effort as the the head was skewed to one side, leaving the Abbot looking like one of Doctor Frankenstein's creations, but it was acceptable and a fellow Cistercian monk was able to say for certain that the body, or at least the head, was that of John Paslew.

Superintendent Malone had disappeared very quickly after arriving. Looking quite pale he had taken the brougham to Clitheroe police station to meet Chief Superintendent Joe Wolfe, a no nonsense copper who was soon to retire. The meeting between him and Superintendent Malone would be a quick one.

Inspectors Meadowbank and Rutherford were acquaintances from a murder investigation when they were both sergeants. They had a mutual respect and Joe Rutherford was more than happy to let Meadowbank and Huggins know what he had found out, which was not that much really. It amounted to what Sir Roger Nowell had already told them.

Meadowbank was skeptical to put it mildly, about Meg Shelton rising from the grave let alone being responsible for such mayhem and death. Rutherford was more convinced. He had interviewed some of the survivors who had seen the Preston Witch and described her as 'from hell' and there were many witnesses to her being set alight by Sir Roger and the horrific minutes that ensued.

Inspector Rutherford took the two Preston detectives to the large oak tree at the front of the house, away from the driveway, and pointed out the charred grass where Meg Shelton had died. He explained the ashes had been collected in an earthenware pot by the monk who identified the Abbott's body, and the pot was now buried in an unmarked grave within the hallowed grounds of Whalley Abbey.

Meadowbank stared at the burnt spot below the scorched sturdy bough, struggling to believe that Meg Shelton died here few a days ago. He would have to write a report on the missing corpse at some point and had anticipated charging a couple of local idiots with 'disinterring, disturbing or interfering with a corpse', an offence with a maximum of two years imprisonment, and that would have been the end of the matter. Standing in the grounds of Read Hall, he had a bad feeling where this was heading. He could hear Sam and Joe Rutherford talking between themselves, but he was not listening to what they were saying. The sergeant then laughed and Meadowbank could not help but think, 'what's so bloody amusin' about all this?'. He then remembered something else his old station sergeant used to say, 'if you haven't got a sense of humour you should not have joined up'. With a shrug, he took out his pipe, rubbed the tobacco briskly between his palms, filled the bowl, lit the tobacco with a match and flicked it air bound, watching the flaming match land on the blackened grass and instantly snuffed.

Meadowbank decided they had spent enough time at Read Hall and as the phone lines were still working, he was able to ring Clitheroe Police Station, enquiring what time Superintendent Malone would be picking them up on his return to Preston. Why was he not surprised to learn that the superintendent had already left for Preston nearly an hour ago with his driver? He had left a message for Meadowbank and Huggins to sort out their own return transport.

Inspector Rutherford had arrived in a hansom cab, on temporary hire to Lancashire County Police along with a driver and he offered this to the two detectives to get them back to urban life.

It was 7pm when they finally returned to the town and as neither man was in any mood to engage with Superintendent Malone, they went straight to The Stanley Arms.

As usual Huggins finished his meal first. With a belch he appreciatively sat back in the chair, savouring Mrs.Walmsley's mutton stew and showing off a portly stomach, underneath a dark brown tweed waistcoat. He drained the pint glass and left for an early night. Today's 6am start had caught up with him.

Meadowbank ordered another pint of bitter as he thumbed through his notebook and after half an hour he too decided to call it a day. He considered visiting Mary Babbitt. He had made a note of her address and the folded paper was still in his pocket, but then thought better of it as it was getting late and apart from that, it was a mile walk at least. Lancaster Road was quiet, even for a Monday. Meadowbank briefly looked at the progress of the new session house being built opposite, then noticed the black carriage also on the opposite side of the road, but not seeing Mr. Ambrose inside, watching the inspector from the shadows of the landau.

As Meadowbank walked passed Crooked Lane, a dark alley next to the ale-house, he was roughly grabbed from behind. His arms were viscously yanked back and a wire looped around his neck, dragging him backwards into the unlit thoroughfare. It happened so fast. He struggled to keep his balance, his feet unable to gain purchase on the cobbles as the wire dug deeper into his throat and windpipe. Meadowbank clutched at his neck, his body weight suspended by the wire and forcing him against his attacker. He knew he was choking and did not have much time left.

He was close to losing consciousness when the restraint fell from his neck and he was no longer being pulled back. Meadowbank toppled against the ale-house wall, rubbing his neck, gagging and retching, unaware of the commotion around him.

It took the inspector a few minutes to regain his senses and then saw three men laying unconscious on the floor. There was a short wire, the ends wrapped around peg like pieces of wood at his feet. He kicked it away. Someone was stood next to him, motionless. Meadowbank swiftly moved to one side, craning his head to see who it was, then saw the knife handle protruding from their chest. The long blade had been plunged with such force, the blade was pinning the man to the wooden gate of the ale-house yard.

Confused, Meadowbank examined the three men sprawled in front of him. Two were face down, one on his back. They were alive, but had been beaten brutally. He recognised them, they were the stevedores from the other day. Meadowbank looked around then went to the corner with Lancaster Road. He noticed the black carriage had gone.

21

The attempted murder of a police officer was a serious enough offence for Superintendent Malone to attend the police station outside his working day and he in turn thought it prudent to contact his superior officer, Chief Superintendent Montague-Fox. Both senior officers were now listening to Inspector Meadowbank's re-telling of the incident he had scant knowledge of.

Meadowbank was feeling uncomfortable with the number of questions asked of him, none of which he could answer.

Three stevedores were in custody and one in the mortuary. Doctor Archie Bayers was also in attendance. He examined Meadowbank's bruised and swollen throat first, before tending to the half-conscious stevedores. The inspector was grateful for the distraction, as the doctor commented that he had been very lucky that the wire had not permanently damaged his windpipe and he would certainly been close to death by strangulation. Still struggling to speak, Meadowbank rubbed his neck and nodded, only too aware of his brush with death.

They were in the Charge Office as Meadowbank explained once again that he had no idea who intervened and saved his life and, in doing so, was responsible for the murder of one man and inflicting grievous bodily harm on three others.

The superintendent and chief superintendent exchanged glances that Meadowbank spotted, but could not interpret. He did not have to wait long. "Inspector, you say you left The Stanley Arms public house just after 8.30pm, having arrived at the premises at 7pm. During that time, how much alcohol did you consume?" asked the chief superintendent.

"What's that got t' do with owt?"

"Inspector, please address senior officers as 'sir'". Superintendent Malone interjected.

"What's that got t'do with owt, … sir?"

"You haven't forgotten Inspector that drinking alcohol on duty breaches the discipline code?" the chief superintendent continued.

"You must 'ave forgotten sir, that me and Sergeant 'Uggins went off duty at 7pm as recorded on t' duty sheets. But fer t' record I drank two pints o' bitter, which I paid for an' unless I'm mistaken, attempted murder contrary t' Common Law and an offence punishable by 'anging ranks a bit 'igher than any officer allegedly drinkin' on duty".

He turned angrily to the superintendent. "Sir, you seem pre-occupied with accusin' me of consumin' alcohol on duty".

"Inspector Meadow, do you have a drink problem? It seems to me you do". Said Superintendent Malone.

"Is that a serious question…sir?"

"You do spend a lot of your time, on and off duty, in licensed premises. Do you not?".

142

Still looking directly at Superintendent Malone he replied. "I go into licensed premises fer a bit o' peace an' quiet, t' speak t' informants an' t' enjoy a pint. I do 'ave a problem though wi' senior officers not 'avin' a backbone".

"Inspector, it is doing you no good getting your dander fired up at questions that need to be asked and frankly, your tone already amounts to gross insubordination and you would do well to think before you speak. The last thing we want is a discipline hearing, but if we do not ask these questions, the Chief Constable and others, such as the press and the Mayor certainly will and I only want to prevent or nip in the bud any suggestion of impropriety on your part. Your answers satisfy me at the moment to that end. And I am well aware of the statutory legislation and the schedule of offences listed under Common Law. I do not need you to remind me of the law of the land". Chief Superintendent Montague-Fox said slowly. He was well into his seventies, wore the uniform of his rank, spoke the Queen's English as a retired brigadier would do, and had been with the police force ten years, entering as a superintendent like Declan Malone.

Meadowbank looking over the shoulders of the two senior officers saw the station sergeant behind the Charge Desk, pretending to read a report. Ernest Thackeray looked up and gave a friendly wink, which Meadowbank gratefully returned. The inspector had another ally in the room.

It was Doctor Bayers who interrupted. "Gentlemen, Mr. Meadowbank has done enough talking for tonight, he needs rest and a good few sips of warm tea. I must insist he be allowed to recuperate overnight from what was a savage, traumatic and near fatal attack".

"Very well doctor, but Inspector be at your desk for 9am please. There are still questions that need answering. In the mean time I will brief the Chief Constable". Chief Superintendent Montague-Fox said in a more conciliatory tone.

As the two senior officers left the office, Superintendent Malone said. "Fancy a snifter sir, my office, before you go?"

"Damned fine suggestion Declan. You do keep a good cognac to hand, I'll grant you that".

Their chortling diminished as the charge room door closed behind them.

Meadowbank was at his desk by seven the following morning, an hour earlier than usual. The welt around the front of his neck was raw looking and so tender he was unable to shave. The inspector was at the office early so he could speak to Sergeant Huggins, before the circus and ringmaster were due at nine o'clock.

Huggins arrived within half an hour, took one look at the inspector and exclaimed,

"Good God! What th' 'ell 'as 'appened t' you?"

Meadowbank was now wishing he had worn a cravat. It had taken at least ten minutes assuring Phoebe Tanner that he was still fighting fit. He told his sergeant what had happened after he had left

144

The Stanley Arms to walk the two hundred yards back to the station.

"Bloody 'ell Albert, I leave you alone fer 'alf an hour!"

"An' it was yer round", Meadowbank joked, "but seriously t' only clue t' all o' this is t' black landau, waiting outside t' Stanley when I left. There was no driver present. It caught my eye, cause it wer immaculate, yer know? Gleamin'. Belongs t' someone wi' a few bob, that's fer sure. How many landaus d' yer think are 'ere in Preston?"

"That's if it's from Preston, could be from out o' town. T' answer yer question though, I reckon not that many. At a guess, fifty at t' most. Not like hackneys', there are 'undred's o' those".

"From today, we need to check every landau we see, whether it's on t' road or in a driveway. Whoever was in that carriage is either a witness to t' attack on me or responsible for savin' my life an' until we get their version o' events, they are now a murder suspect themselves".

"Look Albert, I don't want t' be t' one t' piss on yer fish an' chips, but you've said yersel' there was no one with the landau, it could 'ave bin empty, the driver could 'ave bin in T' Stanley for example. We need t' ask William Walmsley if 'e saw anythin'".

Meadowbank nodded his agreement.

"But my thinkin' is the timin' of its leavin', the landau passed within feet of Crooked Lane, where all bloody 'ell was taking place. Mi gut feelin' is that carriage was in t' wrong place at t' wrong time and is involved somehow".

"Albert, you're t' boss, so it's your decision, but t' four of us are workin' flat out as it is. What yer suggestin' is a mammoth task, personally I wouldn't mention it unless Malone or Montague-Fox do".

Ignoring his sergeant's concern he continued. "We'd 'ave t' involve t' uniform lads, an' all t' night-watchmen who pass information to us. In fact I'll offer a fiver t' anyone who locates the landau, that will 'elp. T' other thing Sam we 'aven't mentioned is, who th' 'ell can lay out four thugs armed wi' cudgels an' knives like that? Three were dropped unconscious an' t' fourth stabbed through t' 'eart. In fact Archie Bayers couldn't pull t' knife out o' t' body, it had gone int' th' wood a couple o' inches. I mean who do we know who could do that, apart from a Samurai swordsman?"

Sam picked up a spare mug of tea left by Phoebe and sat opposite his inspector. He did not reply, as he did not know anyone who was capable of doing what Meadowbank had described. The inspector had not finished. "I know a few bare-knuckle fighters an' they couldn't stop four stevedores like this. These weren't four tossers lookin' for a bit o' trouble, they all 'ave records fer violent offences, they are 'ardened merchant seamen, armed an' bloody dangerous an' quite prepared t' murder a police officer, simply 'cause o' that fracas t' other day". He painfully stretched his neck without thinking, at the very suggestion at what had happened less than twelve hours ago. Huggins grimaced, seeing the extent of the injury. "That's somert else Sam, who would want t' save

146

my life? I mean there's these four wanted t' end it a couple o' days ago, fer Christ's sake".

"That is strange I admit. Yer right, you are hated amongst t' underworld".

Meadowbank looked at his sergeant pulling a frown.

"Come on Albert, you know that's true, you're either lockin' 'em up or givin' 'em a good hidin'. That's 'ow it works an' they understand that, but they don't like you fer it, an' it's t' same animosity toward me an' every copper in town. It's them an' us. So whoever stepped in an' sorted these four out, wasn't yer usual villain an' they must 'ave 'ad a damn good reason for doin' it as well".

Before Meadowbank could reply, an unsmiling Superintend Malone entered the office, his peaked cap under his left arm.

"Inspector, you're early for the meeting". He ignored Sergeant Huggins.

"Yes sir, it occurs sometimes when being punctual". Meadowbank gave Huggins a slight smile.

22

Lytham Hall, an 18th century Georgian mansion set in 8,000 acres of parkland has been the family home of the Cliftons for nearly three hundred years and where Lady Vivian was born and raised, before her marriage to Sir Roger Nowell, when she moved to Read Hall.

Lady Vivian was not too upset when they made the temporary move back to her family home, while the extensive repair work took place at Read Hall. In fact she was rather pleased with her suggestion. It was Sir Roger's idea that they hold an informal dinner party for a few friends and local personages to help them get their feet back under the table, so to speak. Lady Vivian agreed immediately, she relished the planning and inviting.

Three of the invitations were hand delivered to the Police Station on Lancaster Road. Meadowbank and Huggins opened the ones addressed to them, left on their desks by the station sergeant.

A carriage would collect them at the Central Police Station 6pm prompt that evening, to arrive at 7pm for cocktails.

"Bloody 'ell Sam. If this is informal, what would formal b' like?" Meadowbank was holding the printed invitation they had each received.

"Are yer goin' Albert?"

"Of course I am an' so are you. We're not missin' a free piss up like this an' there's a carriage provided. What is there t' think abowt?"

"What are cocktails an' what d' we wear fer a start? I think I'll 'ave t' buy a new dinner suit".

"Sam, are you a complete peasant? Cocktails are, erm...", his voice trailed off as he thought about this.

"Yeh! What are cocktails? Blowed if I know. Anyway the invite says 'informal' so we go in what we've got on now. Anyhow, you've got more suits than a tailor's shop, you don't need any more".

They took a leisurely walk to The Stanley Arms: it was four o'clock in the afternoon and as they had both been on duty since 5am decided to book off early in preparation for Sir Roger's invitation.

Huggins ordered two pints of bitter and said to the landlord, "Oy, William. Me and Albert 'ave bin invited to an informal dinner at Sir Roger Nowell's place in Lytham. D' yer think we'll do like this?" He stood back, opening his arms so William Walmsley could fully appreciate his attire.

"Yer a couple o' bobby dazzlers. You two always look like yer off t' yer daughter's wedding. When is it yer goin'?"

"Thank you William for yer considered opinion. It's toneet. A carriage is pickin' us up in two hours". Meadowbank replied giving a thumbs up gesture.

"In that case gents, 'ave these two on me t' get yer in t' mood".

A couple of hours later as Meadowbank and Huggins were walking back to the station, they saw a hansom cab waiting outside the front door.

"Is that hansom for us?" asked Huggins.

"It's only ten to six, so it's flamin' early if it is. I'm busting for a leak as well". Meadowbank said checking his pocket watch.

Huggins approached the driver.

"Ey mate! Are yer 'ere t' collect Inspector Meadowbank and Sergeant 'Uggins?"

The young driver was immaculately liveried in Sir Roger's own design of black knee length double breasted tunic with silver buttons, black knee high stockings and a top hat. He looked at the small rotund man addressing him, and hoped he was not one of his passengers.

"Who am I speaking with sir?'

"Samuel "Uggins. Detective Sergeant Samuel 'Uggins to b' exact. So are yer 'ere fer us or what?"

"Compliments of Sir Roger, I am here to transport you and Mr. Meadowbank to Lytham Hall". He was almost chap-fallen.

"Reet yer are. Albert, er, I mean Mr. Meadowbank has just nipped int' t' nick fer a piss an' I think I'll 'ave one as well, t' be ont' save side. Just give us a minute will yer young man?"

"Certainly sir, but I would like to leave at six o'clock prompt".

"Keep yer 'air on, I'll be two shakes, literally". He walked away chuckling at his innuendo.

A few minutes later the two police officers emerged from the station, both laughing raucously at a joke Station Sergeant Thackeray had just regaled.

"Go on Albert, tell t' driver that one. 'E may even crack a smile".

The driver had got down from the rear seat, opening the folding wooden doors that protected the passenger's legs.

"Listen t' this my friend. What's t' difference between a magician's wand an' a policeman's truncheon?"

The question was met with momentarily silence before he said, "I've no idea sir".

This was the inspectors big music hall moment. "One is used for cunning stunts…".

Meadow and Huggins, still feeling the effects of their afternoon drinking session threw an arm around each other in a noisy cheer of the unsaid punchline. The driver answered without the flicker of a smile,

"Most amusing sir. May we continue?"

Meadowbank gave him a slap on the shoulder, "Don't worry lad, it may never 'appen".

By the time the cab had reached Blackpool Road at Ashton, the two detectives were asleep, and even stopping at the Lea Gate turnpike did not disturb their snoring, eventually opening their eyes on arrival at the entrance of Lytham Hall an hour later. The tarmacadam drive, nearly a mile long, led to the front of the Georgian mansion where a footman, wearing a similar uniform to the cab driver, was waiting. He took the invites from Meadowbank and Huggins, showing them into the main hall, where more footmen in the Clifton liveried uniform handed champagne flutes to the guests as they arrived and other servants proffered silver platters of canapés with caviar and other dainty morsels.

"Are these cocktails?" Huggins quietly asked as he examined a small piece of toast piled with salted sturgeon roe.

"Could be Sam. They taste a bit funny though", he replied after swallowing his first bite.

Superintendent Malone, who was with his wife, saw his senior detectives before they spotted him. He promptly walked across the large hallway, his limp appearing more pronounced in his mess uniform.

"Inspector, sergeant, what is the meaning of this? What are you two doing here and drinking champagne on duty?".

"Superintendent Malone, what a pleasant surprise seeing you 'ere". Meadowbank said and acknowledging the fluted glass the superintendent was holding, "cheers sir"

"This is a private function by the Lord Lieutenant of Lancashire, so you better have a damn good explanation".

Before the superintendent got a reply, Sir Roger joined them, putting an arm around the shoulders of Meadowbank and Huggins saying, "Why am I not surprised to find you three huddled together talking shop, but there is someone I want the Inspector and Sergeant to meet. Come with me gentlemen and refill your glasses. Excuse us Mr. Malone".

Huggins kept his head down, but Meadowbank with a beaming smile said, "Yes sir, please excuse Sergeant 'Uggins an' misel'".

Superintendent Malone was left seething and red faced as he watched Sir Roger escort his two senior detectives into the room opposite.

The drawing room was brightly lit by a huge Waterford crystal chandelier, reflecting on the lime green hand painted wallpaper panels. The log fire blazed and crackled behind the etched glass fire screen, drawing the parties towards it.

Nearest to the fireplace were a handful of guests stood listening to a small woman in her mid-forties. Sir Roger interrupted them. "Miss Cook, allow me to introduce to you Detective Inspector Meadowbank and Detective Sergeant Huggins. Their names may be familiar as they were instrumental in tracking down Jack the Ripper".

The small lady with shoulder length black hair pinned back looked at the officers confidently and offered a hand. Sir Roger continued. "Gentleman, this is Florence Cook, a good friend and the country's foremost spiritualist clairvoyant".

Meadowbank took her hand feeling her firm grip. She said, "Yes I am familiar with the case of course".

Her grip became firmer, uncomfortably so for the inspector. Looking at her bemused, he saw her eyes roll up briefly revealing white orbs. Suddenly, after what seemed an awkward pause, her voice broke the silence.

"I see darkness all around you, a malevolent darkness that means you harm".

"I get that every day at work, love". He tried to make light of what this strange woman clutching his hand was saying, as he watched her brown eyes return to a normal position.

"Do not scoff Inspector. There is a supernatural power moving very close to you".

She dropped his hand and put hers to her chest, as if catching her breath.

"I have never come across this entity before, I can only see a shape, it is towering over you and means you harm. You need to be on your guard Inspector".

"What does all that actually mean?" he asked whimsically, ignoring the shocked faces looking on.

She did not answer, instead pointed at Sir Roger, "You are also in danger Sir Roger, from this thing, this Monster and it is a Monster and it wants your soul as well".

Sir Roger, standing in-between the two police officers, appeared mortified, as if he understood the prophesy.

Miss Cook, wearing an ankle length black dress, moved away and sat down. She looked like she was about to faint.

Sir Roger approached her, "Florence, would you like some water?"

Without waiting for a reply he sent a waiter to fetch a glass of water then quickly changed that to a large brandy. "Florence dear, how do you feel?"

"I'm fine thank you. I need to freshen up before we sit in circle, if I may Sir Roger?" She touched his arm. "I bring you both a warning, there is a real horror, something evil and not of this world stalking you and the Inspector. I wish I could tell you how to prepare yourselves, but there will be a confrontation soon".

Sir Roger was visibly shaken and called for Lady Vivian to escort Miss Cook to the bathroom. The clairvoyant was unsteady on her feet and Lady Vivian put an arm around her as they left the drawing room. There was a washroom on the ground floor and Florence Cook insisted she would be fine on her own. Lady Vivian held the door open and did not see a black cat follow the clairvoyant into the washroom.

Ten minutes had passed when Lady Vivian gently knocked on the door, "Miss Cook, are you alright?"

There was no answer.

She knocked harder and tried the door handle which was unlocked. The door would not open fully, something was stopping it from opening.

Lady Vivian manoeuvred her head through the gap and saw Miss Cook sprawled on the floor.

Trying to keep calm she shouted for help. Within seconds Sir Roger, Meadowbank, Huggins, servants and other guests rushed to her aide. Sergeant Huggins shoved the door further open, enough for Joseph Lister, a Scottish surgeon and friend of Sir Roger's, to squeeze through. After a few minutes, Joseph Lister opened the door fully allowing everyone to see Florence Cook laid on her back, staring lifeless at the ceiling, her mouth gaping.

"I'm afraid Miss Cook is dead. It would appear she has suffered a massive heart attack".

The bathroom window was open slightly and no one noticed the black cat jump from the windowsill.

The dinner was cancelled and Meadowbank arranged for Miss Cook's body to be transported to the hospital mortuary. Joseph Lister, 1st Baronet, confirmed life extinct, but could not provide a death certificate until a post mortem had established cause of death.

Sir Roger arranged carriages for the guests, then took Meadowbank to one side before he climbed into the hansom cab with Huggins.

"Inspector, you and I need to have a chat about this. It is not something we can ignore".

"It's somert I can ignore Sir Roger, even if you can't. I don't 'old any importance t' what astrologers, sooth-sayers an' table-rappers 'ave t' say. An' another thing, I would not 'ave accepted yer invitation if I'd 'ave known yer were plannin' t' 'old a seance. That wasn't mentioned on t' invite". His anger was real.

"Florence Cook was not a charlatan if that is what you are saying…".

Meadowbank interrupted. "She said she could speak t' dead. Of course she wer a charlatan".

"She was a gifted clairvoyant who had done private sittings with Queen Victoria, for God's sake! What is the matter with you, Inspector? She had a message for us both and it would be foolish of you

156

indeed not to pay heed to what she said". It was Sir Roger who was now rattled.

"I'm more concerned about t' living than t' dead".

"But who are you more afraid of Inspector, the living or the dead? After your visit to Read Hall, I wanted you to meet Florence Cook, I thought she may have opened your mind to the supernatural, to the unexplained, but the evening to begin with her tragic death cannot be coincidence. The events of the last few weeks are connected, I can see that even if you cannot".

It was that single word 'coincidence' which seemed to slap the inspector across the face.
Lady Vivian appeared at the top of the stone steps and called to her husband.

"I must go gentlemen, goodnight". He had much on his mind.

Superintendent Malone and his wife were next to leave, and he saw Meadowbank and Huggins get into the cab, gesturing for them to wait. The inspector rapped on the roof, signalling to the driver to move on.

It was barely 9pm, as they headed back to Preston. They had not eaten a thing, consuming only a few sips of champagne and were present when the country's most respected clairvoyant collapse and died inexplicably. Huggins had to say something.

"Albert, don't you think you should listen t' Sir Roger? What 'e said may sound mumbo-jumbo t' you, but it don't t' me. You cannot deny weird things are 'appening at t' moment".

Meadowbank had not mentioned to anyone about the old hag he had seen in his room a few days ago and how she floated towards him. It was a terrifying sight he would never forget. He knew it had not been a dream, so logically he reasoned it must have happened. Something plainly evil was in his room, something not of this world appeared to him. Was this the life threatening darkness Florence Cook had warned him about?

"I don't know what t' think Sam. Perhaps you an' Sir Roger are right. It's just that t' believe somert supernatural, a ghost or whatever you want t' call it, is out t' get me an' Sir Roger, doesn't mek sense. Why? How? I lock criminals up, like you do, that's all, so what 'as this got t' do with me?"

"I can't answer that, but maybe you are gettin' t' close t' somert or someone with an investigation an' you need to be stopped".

He turned to his sergeant and could just make out his features in the glow of the bull lamps.

"Such as? T' missing children file is goin' nowhere fast. We 'aven't 'ad a single lead on that. The Winckley Square murder is still early days an' we 'aven't finished t' 'ouse t' 'ouse enquiries yet or even got a suspect. As fer t' maraudin' hyena, that could b' anywhere and there's no criminality involved there, it's just a case of an escaped circus animal".

"What about the attempt on yer life last week?"

"We know who they are, they're still locked up. Nothing supernatural about those idiots. And one 'as admitted it was purely a revenge attack on me". Huggins said, "I think we need t' be armed all t' time now, even off duty, if you'd agree t' that? We don't know what we are dealin' with an' I've a bad feelin' abowt this fer a long time".

Meadowbank nodded. "Fair enough Sam, that 'ad better go for t' rest of t' team as well".

Sir Roger Nowell sat at the heavy oak desk in the first floor study, facing a window looking onto the large courtyard. His father-in-law, John Talbot Clifton, and mother-in-law, Violet Beauclerk, the owners of Lytham Hall were on an extensive tour of the Americas and away for several months.

It was nearly midnight, the oil-lamp on the desk illuminating the pile of documents, files and ledgers Sir Roger had transferred from Read Hall.

All the guests had left, Florence Cook's body had been removed to the mortuary and Lady Vivian had retired to her apartment. He pondered over what the clairvoyant had said to him and the inspector, convinced even more that many lives were in danger, his in particular and Inspector Meadowbank's.

He was sure the identity of the necromancer lay in the records he had stacked in parish and year order, going back to the trial of the Pendle Witches.

There was a knock on the door and the Squire of Lytham's butler, Didier Pascal, entered carrying a tray with a glass of hot milk, a plate of homemade biscuits and a tumbler of brandy.

159

"Your night cap, sir". His Parisian accent gentle and soothing. Add the impressive black handlebar moustache, flecked with grey and it was easy to understand why many of Lady Vivian's visitors, male and female, could not take their eyes of her Father's lithe and graceful butler.

"Thank you Didier. You may retire also. If I need anything further I'll see to it myself". Since the death of his own butler, Arnold, at Read Hall, Sir Roger had come to trust and depend more on the French servant.

"Very well sir. Just one thing, the black cat that is roaming the house, has your family brought it here? It does not belong to the Cliftons".

Sir Roger did not appreciate the importance of the question.

"I am not aware of a black or any other cat being brought here. If you see it again Didier, put it out please".

"Of course sir. It is very distinctive, totally black with only one eye. It does appear domesticated".

Sir Roger nodded, already pre-occupied, and bid the butler a good night.

He resumed his search, methodically tracing the descendants of each of the Lancashire Witches, comparing copies of parish birth and death records of Chattox; Redfearn; Device; Nutter and Hewitt, eliminating those he could with certainty.

How long he had been absorbed in his work he could not say, but as he stretched and reached for the last few mouthfuls of the warm milk he saw a black cat, sat on the windowsill outside, looking at him intently with its one eye.

Startled, Sir Roger hushed an expletive, then moved closer to look at the cat, which remained impassive. Fearing the cat was in danger of falling twenty feet from the window ledge, he moved towards the casement window to open it. Sir Roger then realised the cat was no longer there. Concerned, he lifted the window open and looked out. There was no sign of the it at all and the animal was not laying injured on the ground below.

Being a little perplexed with the plight of the black cat, he went downstairs to the kitchen, unlocked the back door onto the courtyard. He had not brought a lamp with him, and vainly searched the cobblestones below the study, darkened even more by the shadow of the house.

A noise grabbed his attention, he could hear someone walking towards him. He stepped into the shadows, cursing for not having a firearm with him. "Is that you Sir Roger?" A deep vice asked from behind a glaring oil-lamp.

"James, you gave me a start". Sir Roger was relieved to see his head gamekeeper.

"Is everything alright sir?" The gamekeeper pointed the double-barrelled shotgun to the ground. "Working late, but I fear a cat may have fallen from the study windowsill, I was making sure it was okay". They both looked up to the lit window.

"Ain't no cat round here now sir. I have seen one though, a few times this evening. A black one with a missing eye. A bit of a character it is, following me on my rounds".

"That's the one. Very strange that this cat seems to be everywhere around the estate. Anyway James, it is reassuring to see you are alert and doing a good job. Well done".

"I heard about the incident in the hall this evening sir. A tragedy, just before dinner as well and and all that food going to waste".

"What could be salvaged is in the kitchen, help yourself. It is to be distributed amongst the staff tomorrow anyway".

"Thank you sir. Very kind of you and Lady Vivian". He had difficulty hiding his delight. Sir Roger retraced his steps to the study, locking doors behind him.

The appearance of the black cat was niggling him, as if a forgotten memory was slowly crawling back. He rummaged through a pile of books on the floor until he found the one he wanted. *The Wonderful Discoverie of Witches In the County of Lancaster*, the account and investigation in 1613 of the Pendle Witches by Thomas Potts.

He looked for the words 'black cat' and eventually found them in the definition for *'familiar'*:

a familiar is a demon in animal form, assigned to serve a witch as a spy/companion. Often appears as a black cat. See grimalkin.

Sir Roger's skin began to crawl and his hands trembled slightly as he searched for *'grimalkin'*.

He soon found the definition: *grimalkin: an aged and mysterious cat, usually female with supernatural powers, associated with a sorceress.* He rested his head in both hands as the realisation swept over him. The necromancer has followed him to Lytham Hall. How long before the grimalkin returns with the witch? His family are in mortal danger. He must find the identity of the witch as a matter of urgency, and in the mean time move his family somewhere else.

23

She knew Mr. Ambrose was exercising the horses and would be gone for several hours. He still had to clean out the stables and feed the hyena which was now up and about, keen to prowl the night again. So Auntie Vena had the afternoon on her own.

She was in her bedroom, naked admiring herself in the full-length mirror, the only mirror in the house. There was no bed, she did not need one, instead two upholstered chairs were placed either side of the cast iron hearth, surrounding a glowing coal fire, and the one-eyed cat sat on one of the chairs as if watching with interest.

Auntie Vena liked what she saw, but she did not see what was reflected. She saw a voluptuous figure, a slim waist, curvaceous breasts, firm arms and thighs and desirable to any man she should choose. The witch did not have these thoughts very often. Being a two hundred and ninety eight year old virgin had eclipsed any desires she once nurtured, but occasionally her feminine wants surfaced, despite her hatred of all mortal men, even Mr. Ambrose. She gently swayed, smiling at her mirror image as she watched her hands move over her incredibly smooth body, stroking her delectable breasts any man would want and caressing the neat triangle of hair covering her mons Venus, fingers tantalising as she fantasised which lucky mortal should she allow to take her chastity. Auntie Vena did not recognise the wrinkled and loose leathery skin that hung from her upper arms, stomach and thighs or her sparse wiry pubic hair which looked back at her from the mirror.

She did see the reflected cat watching her, impassive as always.

"What are you looking at? I saved your sight, if not for me you would have lost both eyes, so do not judge me. I am a woman after all". She pouted, pulling her shoulders back and running fingers through her vile hair, seeing blonde ringlets drape her shoulders.

The cat was now sat upright and moving its mouth as if silently speaking.

"I know I am a Demdike, how can I forget that?" she said angrily to the cat's reflection.

Auntie Vena moved away from the mirror, padding across bare floorboards, her toenails clicking on the wood as she paraded her nudity in front of the cat as if taunting it, and picked up a bathrobe draped over an armchair. Now covered she sat opposite the cat, crossing her legs, allowing the robe to fall away revealing skin like tree bark. The witch was still feeling provocative and picking up the full glass of malt whisky she stared at her companion on the chair opposite. The cat looked away.

"How can I ever forget I am Demdike? I have been the last of the Demdikes for nearly three centuries", she said more gently.

"I have not taken part in carnal acts like my grandmother and mother did, to produce an heir to carry on the legacy. Perhaps that is my mistake, but to see the only two people I have ever loved sacrifice their freedom for me, so I can make the past right, as it will be and to take revenge on mankind has dulled my need for the mortal man. A species I loathe beyond the Realms of Darkness". She took a drink of the scotch, sucking in her cheeks slightly as she savoured the sensation.

"Only you know what my plans are and soon, very soon, we shall be three generations of Demdike's once again and this time no mob shall hunt us, we will be the hunters. My mother, grandmother and I will be the last of the Demdikes, the last of the Lancashire Witches".

The one-eyed cat was listening intently, as if a mouse was hiding somewhere in the room.

She caressingly picked up a pair of ivory silk stockings from the arm of the chair and drew them against her hoary cheeks, not acknowledging that the delicate fabric was pulling and tearing on the scabbed pustules and bristles sprouting from the many warts covering her face.

With a genteel sigh, similar to a sound of pleasure any woman would express when immersing into a hot bath, Auntie Vena stroked her right thigh and leg with one of the stockings as she bent forward to slip the expensive knitted hose over her foot. Her long yellowing toe nails, not dissimilar to hen's claws, ripped the silk fabric immediately, as she unrolled the stocking along her bony leg, with skin the colour of servants' tea.

The cat inclined its head when the witch began humming a music hall favourite, *The Boy I Love is up in the Gallery*, as she crossed the room and standing in front of the mirror Auntie Vena sang the chorus:

The boy I love is up in the gallery,
The boy I love is looking now at me,
There he is, can't you see, waving his handkerchief,
As merry as a robin that sings on a tree.

The grimalkin was not to know she was completely out of tune, sounding like a puppeteer providing voices for a Punch and Judy show. As she sang and twirled, admiring the torn baggy stockings covering her spindly legs, she pulled the bath robe aside to appreciate her different poses, some risqué, some blatantly seductive, some coyish and was very pleased with what she saw.

Oh yes! Mortal man's days are numbered with his pathetic phallus and libido. Let us see how they manage to subjugate and survive in the Dark Side, let us see if they desire to fornicate with harlots born in hell and let us see if they can drive women and children from their homes when pitched into the abode of misery and pain.

This thought made her smile. Her immaculate white teeth were now shades of black, like stumps of charcoal with the carbonaceous residue smothering her tongue. Her eyes were a deeper green than the cat's one and the fallowed hands that clasped the whisky glass as she shimmied, pirouetted and swirled like a debutante, were gnarled, knuckles swollen with long finger nails, stained and gross, but razor sharp, as if fashioned by a smithy. Scrunching her shoulders enticingly she turned to the cat, giggling, her thatch of shoulder length hair the colour of lime mortar and as coarse and dead as dried sedge-grass moved as one.

A familiar sound distracted Auntie Vena from her reverie. The gates had opened for Mr. Ambrose and the coach trundled over the neat cobbles towards the stables.

"Where has the time gone?" she said gaily to the cat, then turned her back to the mirror and in an instant the warts and bristles disappeared, her skin, moments ago having the texture of a dead bovine, became smooth and toned, hands and nails transformed to ladylike proportions, her eyes blinked away the mucus green, once again revealing alluring blue irises. As she strode towards the door, still holding the glass tumbler, her soft white hair was pulled back into a neat bun and she was wearing a white blouse underneath a black cashmere cardigan, complimented with a pearl necklace and her favourite woollen knee length Isle of Skye tartan skirt and of course her essential black brogues, which would bring a smile to any sergeant-major.

She left the bedroom door open to allow the cat to follow, the fragrance of *Floris of London* mixing with the stench of putrefaction. After refilling her glass she went to the stables to tell Mr. Ambrose the good news. She had found another brat and he was already caged in the cellar. Everything was almost ready.

24

Walton Summit was a ramshackle collection of caravans, covered wagons, grazing ponies and small wood and canvas constructions being used as dwellings by the current occupiers of the hill, overlooking the Lancaster Canal basin. Originally it was the nomadic 'land navigators', who decades earlier had dug out the canals, the railway embankments, and then the road to Carlisle, who settled on this local view point. Now their descendants, a truculent gang of Irish labourers with strict customs and codes, remained inhabitants of Walton Summit, not far from the town of Preston.

The black landau and two horses slowly climbed the dirt track to the enclave, where numerous camp fires sent smoke tendrils into the darkening afternoon sky. The Thoroughbred mares meandered between the vans and covered wagons and naturally knew their destination. Filthy barefoot children followed, jumping up and down, shouting, trying to see who was inside the carriage. Mr. Ambrose ignored them, looking ahead but keeping hold of the whip in the event things got out of hand. The horses stopped next to a bowtop caravan with its curving roof. It was painted a plain light green and blended in with the woodland beyond and the cream cartwheels looked recently repainted. The rear door was open and a man in his mid thirties was sat on the top step, smoking a hand rolled cigarette. He was about 5'10", solid looking, with a mop of black curly hair and a straggly beard. He seemed disinterested as he watched Mr. Ambrose climb down and open the carriage door. As Auntie Vena stepped from the carriage, wearing a long black overcoat, black gloves, black polished brogues and a black woollen Pillbox hat with a netted veil covering half her face, *Floris of London* wafting around her, the man jumped from the step and said, "Madame Demdike. What an unexpected pleasure".

She did not offer her hand in way of greeting, nonetheless he bowed graciously before shooing the children away who were congregating too near the carriage.

"Evergreen, it is always good to see a friend. This is not a social visit though. We need to discuss the final arrangements".

"Of course, it's getting near". His dialect was working class Dublin. He nodded at Mr. Ambrose, who barely returned the acknowledgement.

"Would you care for a glass or two of my poteen Madame Demdike?" he asked, gesturing for her to enter his caravan, both grimy hands displaying chunky gold rings on every finger and each thumb, some of the rings solid gold sovereigns, which he had stolen from a jeweller's shop years ago.

As an aficionado of the single malt highland whisky, she was no fan of the potato moonshine, which had been outlawed since 1661, and Evergreen's own still produced a particularly potent liquor.

"Evergreen, that goes without saying. Your poteen is the main reason I call. I'll have a large one please", she said, nimbly climbing the wooden steps.

Mr. Ambrose, in his tailored black suit, gleaming black hob-nailed boots and wearing a dark grey flat-cap, remained by the carriage, taking in the sights, sounds and smells around him. He was fascinated by the way of life of the Traveller, seemingly carefree, completely lawless and he admired their tradition of violence that kept them in a state of open warfare with the authorities and locals and quite often themselves. Take Evergreen for example. Evergreen Bartlett was a bare knuckle champion, just like his father and he looked it as well. A cocky charmer with a nose broken many times, scars covering his swollen face and hands.

Over the years Mr. Ambrose had visited this camp many times, always on business for Auntie Vena and his stay would often last for hours and quite often overnight, drinking poteen in the company of the elders and usually involved a provocatively dressed woman or two for his pleasure, at a fair price.

Around twenty years ago on an errand for Auntie Vena, he over indulged their hospitality and after a couple bottles of poteen, was goaded into a prize fight by a buxom widow named Cara, who had promoted her inviting décolletage to Mr. Ambrose as the ultimate prize.

His opponent was Duke Bartlett, Evergreen's father and reigning Irish bare-knuckle champion.

Like Mr. Ambrose he was a big man, but his head was shaved and battle scarred and he had a couple of gold teeth he liked flashing.

On paper it looked an even fight. Both men were in their late thirties, similar to Evergreen's age now, but Duke Bartlett was a bloodthirsty ruffian who would fight as fair as a desert scorpion.

From the opening round his style was to attack fast, inflicting as much injury as possible early in the fight, his huge fists delivering catastrophic head punches, which had killed several opponents. Mr. Ambrose had never backed down to any man in his life and he was not going to start with Duke Bartlett, especially as the mysterious Cara had seductively pushed her perfumed handkerchief deep into one of his trouser pockets as a good luck charm.

As word spread that the big Geordie was to fight The Duke, a large crowd gathered in the middle of the camp. Betting was frantic, some wishing that the arrogant Duke would be beaten, but none believed that outcome was possible, so the betting reflected the odds, and Mr. Ambrose was given no chance to defeat the champion. The Duke was already in place dressed in his knee breeches, stripped to the waist showing off bulging forearms and chest as he shadow sparred, fists jabbing and hooking an imaginary opponent.

Mr. Ambrose, feeling slightly jaded after two bottles of poteen and suffering from severe indigestion, kept his shirt on but loosened his tie and neatly rolled up his shirt sleeves, revealing heavily tattooed arms, the designs clearly Satanic, depicting grinning demons and fallen angels. He chose to keep his immaculately creased suit trousers on, rather than make a spectacle fighting in his long johns with Cara watching. He was told to remove his boots by an unidentified spectator, as The Duke was barefoot and Mr. Ambrose considered that to be a reasonable request and pulled his socks off as well.

This fight was not to the rules of The Marquis of Queensbury, but to the rules of the Travellers and there was only one rule; last man standing wins.

A hand-bell rang from the crowd and both men approached each other. The Duke was eager to punish his opponent and show the spectators what a big mistake this interloper had made by accepting the challenge and was buoyed by the partisan crowd shouting his name over and over.

Mr. Ambrose, who had seen Duke Bartlett in action at a previous fight, adopted a casual stance with fists dropped near to his waist, while the champion had his fists and arms high to protect his head, in a true pugilist's stance. There was no referee to greet the two fighters as they came up to the scratch line, roughly marking the centre of the square, formed by the crowd. Their eyes locked and Duke threw the first punch without any preamble, a sweeping cross to the head, which Mr. Ambrose side stepped and unleashed an astonishing semi-circular counter-hook with his right hand, hitting the left side of Duke's temple with a sickening crunch, sending him face down to the grass like a felled tree. And that was it, in less than ten seconds Mr. Ambrose had floored the current Irish bare-knuckle champion and the stunned crowd fell silent, reflecting their disbelief, and none more than Evergreen Bartlett.

This fight became legend and part of the Travellers folklore. Mr. Ambrose took the purse of over two hundred pounds and spent the night in Cara's wagon.

Two days later Duke Bartlett, humiliated, left for Dublin, returning to his parents home and never to set foot out of that city again. Since the fight there had always been an uneasy peace between Mr. Ambrose and Evergreen, but he knew he would never challenge Mr. Ambrose, as he was one of only two men he had ever feared, the other being his father. This did not stop him from scheming and plotting revenge for his father's and family honour, no matter how long it would take.

The paraffin lamp hanging from the roof did little to dispel the gloom inside the caravan, even with the door open. Auntie Vena, nursing her cup of poteen, ignored the stink of body sweat and damp dogs as she sat next to a pile of foul clothing and bed sheets, which would not even pass for jumble. Evergreen had agreed to provide five covered wagons and twelve of his men for the 31st October, in a few days time, and confirmed work clearing the graves was nearly complete. Auntie Vena called for Mr. Ambrose and within seconds his bulk was filling the door opening.

"The case please, Mr. Ambrose".

He leant in and passed her a black leather attache case. Auntie Vena rested it on her lap, flicked the lock and opened the case so the contents were facing Evergreen.

"One thousand pounds as we agreed, and I have included a further one thousand as a gesture of good will. I always appreciate efficiency, so please do not let me down Evergreen".

The gypsy stared at the neat rows of five and ten pound Bank of England notes which filled the case. He had never seen so much cash.

"What have we got here Evergreen?" The deep voice suited the huge woman stood on the steps. "You must have forgot to tell me that the Demdike was visiting today".

She ignored Auntie Vena, her gaze flitting from her husband to the money.

'Carroty Jane' wore a red vest, which was more or less the same colour as her short hair and showed off the extensive tattoos covering her arms, shoulders, neck and disappearing down her chest. She was old enough to be Evergreen's mother but could have easily been mistaken for his father. She was a virago who terrified most men in the camp.

Auntie Vena handed the case to Evergreen saying, "You will remember to send one of the wagons to my house so we can transfer certain goods and we will meet you at the arranged place that evening?"

"Of course, don't worry about that". He held the case to his wife. "Look at this Carroty, two thousand pounds".

"Have you counted it?" asked 'Carroty Jane', still not acknowledging Auntie Vena.

"That is our business concluded Evergreen. Thank you for the drink and if there is a discrepancy with the money it certainly will not have anything to do with me". She smiled at 'Carroty Jane'.

As she stood to leave, Jane slowly moved aside, emitting a pungent smell of sweat similar to the acrid stink which filled the caravan. Mr. Ambrose appeared and offered his hand as Auntie Vena negotiated the wooden steps.

"Good evening Jane. It is always a pleasure to meet you".

"Everyone round here else calls me Carroty, even Evergreen". She glared at Auntie Vena.

"How interesting". As she reached the grass, Auntie Vena seemed to grow in height, looming over Carroty. She held out her right index finger, the finger nail increased in length by several inches to a tapered point as she pushed the tip under Carroty's flabby chin, forcing her head back, blood trickling down her inked neck.

"Call yourself what you will, but do not dare cross me or I will rip out your heart and boil it in a broth for the dogs". Auntie Vena said gruffly, slowly turning towards her carriage, gliding across the dirt path as if on a hydraulic platform to where Mr. Ambrose was holding open the door.

Carroty froze, fighting to stop her bladder from emptying and looked around making sure no one else had heard the threat from Auntie Vena. Only Evergreen had heard and he looked away.

As the carriage approached 'Hoarstones' the high, solid wooden gates silently opened on cue with the smoothness of a Swiss time-piece and once the landau had stopped, Auntie Vena waited for the door to be opened. She took the hand offered by Mr. Ambrose and as she stepped down, turned to him at the same time as the front door unlocked with a 'click', swinging ajar as if waiting for further instructions.

"Mr. Ambrose, I have been thinking. This whore our policeman friend is showing an interest in, why not pay her a visit and bring her along to our celebration on All Hallows' Eve. I am sure we can find a role for her or perhaps you may have your own thoughts on how to keep the whore entertained?" He bowed his head in acknowledgement, unable to stop grinning, his discoloured teeth set together.

25

The newly opened Turkish Baths in Miller Arcade were proving very popular and Meadowbank tried to get there when the baths opened at 7am at least once a week or certainly every two weeks, as there was no bath in the station. He sat in one of the heated rooms, as he always did, eyes closed, before taking to the cold plunge pool followed by a warm bath. He heard someone else come into the room, their bare feet smacking the warm tiled floor.

A few minutes later the inspector wiped sweat from his face, opening his eyes briefly and immediately aware of a man sat opposite looking at him intently. He returned the stare for a few seconds and after once again wiping his eyes clear of sweat and condensation asked, "Can I 'elp yer?" His tone was neutral.

The man, a big man with dark hair and beard, elaborate tattoos covering his arms, shoulders and chest continued to stare.

"Is there a problem?" Meadowbank asked slowly.

"No, there is no problem, Inspector", Mr. Ambrose replied.

"Do I know yer?"

"That's a nasty wound you have to your neck Inspector. You should be more careful". The Geordie accent was unmistakable.

"Reet, you've 'ad yer fun mister. Now tell mi what yer want or fuck off". He stood up, fastening the towel around his waist.

Mr. Ambrose remained seated. "I have a message from an acquaintance of yours. My employer in fact. I believe you met her the other night. Do not get involved with the witch finder. He's already out of his depth, you do not need to sink with him. Just ignore the crazy accusations by Sir Roger Nowell like everyone else does".

"And if I don't?"

"There may not be anyone around to prevent the next attempt on your life".

"Threatenin' t' life of a police officer is a serious offence, whatever your name is".

"You have been warned Inspector Meadowbank. Oh! while I remember, please pass on my regards to your lady friend Mary, she seems a lovely woman". Meadowbank stepped forward, fists clenched.

"Mary Babbitt. She has lodgings at 140 Fishergate Hill if I remember correctly? I did call there the other day, but she was not home. Pity. Perhaps I'll have better luck next time", he said smiling.

Meadowbank charged at the big man, ramming Mr. Ambrose against the green tiled wall, throwing two hard punches to his stomach. It was as if Mr. Ambrose had erupted. He stood up with ease even though Meadowbank was on top of him, pushing the inspector away, followed with a punch to the side of the head, finishing with a solid palm strike to his chin, sending the stunned inspector backwards and slumping onto the tiled bench he had got up from moments earlier.

Meadowbank felt nauseous, his head was thumping and once the room stopped spinning and was able to focus, he realised he was alone.

He quickly dressed and knew he would not be able to run the mile or so to Fishergate Hill, so jumped into a hansom cab he found waiting on Church Street.

It had just gone half past seven and getting light when he arrived at Mary's lodgings. She had the front ground floor room, which was in darkness. This was the first time he had visited the address and finding the front door locked, rapped on the window several times. Within a minute or two the curtains parted and a sleepy Mary Babbitt looked at Meadowbank puzzled.

He then realised he had not thought his actions through. He could not tell Mary her life was in danger because of one of his enquiries and cause her unknown amount of worry, so he was desperately thinking of a plausible reason for getting her out of bed at half past seven in the morning. The locks unbolted and the door opened a few inches. He had run out of time as Mary's face peeped through the gap.

"Is everything alright Albert?"

"Hello Mary. I was just passin' an' thought I'll call an' see 'ow you are an' 'ave that brew you've bin promising".

She did not know what to say so opened the door fully. Mary was in a cream nightdress and bed-socks, her hair was squashed on one side, but her blue eyes were as striking as ever.

"You'd better come in then, afore t' neighbours see yers. This is a bit of a rum do t' bi 'onest Albert. We're not even courtin' an' 'ere I am openin' t' door t' yer in mi nightdress".

"You look lovely in it as well Mary".

"That's not t' point an' you know it". She was pleased he said it though. "Are yer comin' in or what?"

She held the door open as he passed, "It's first door ont' right".

The room smelled pleasant, not stale like his own. There was a single bed in one corner, a table near the window displayed an oil lamp now on a low flame and two chairs sat either side, a pine dresser with a double gas stove and built in wash stand stood against the opposite wall. Two large green rugs covered most of the floorboards and a mirror hung above the fireplace. Meadowbank caught sight of himself and nearly swore. The right side of his face was red, turning blue and his lips swollen.

Mary increased the flame on the lamp, illuminating the room, then saw his injuries.

"Good God! What's 'appened t' yers Albert?"

"You know what my job's like, there's always someone wantin' t' 'ave a go at yer".

She pulled a chair across the floor and sat him down. Bending over him, her soft fingers gently examined the cuts and bruising, squeezing his jaw as he tried not to wince. She then gave her diagnosis.

"There's now't broken, but your face will bi tender, I can see that from t' bruisin'. It'll hurt shavin' if you decide t' get rid of yer beard. And that's apart from t' swellin' t' yer neck. You'll live though. I 'ave somert that'll 'elp".

Since the earlier attack, he found the solution to a painful shave every morning was to grow a beard, which also went some way to covering the scar around his neck.

From a cupboard in the dresser she took a bottle of ointment, pouring cream onto one of her handkerchiefs, gently rubbing it onto the bruising.

"What's that?" It smelled quite pleasant.

"Arnica cream. It'll 'elp sooth an' reduce t' bruisin'. That's as much as anyone can do I think. I'll mek a pot o' tea for us. That allus 'elps". She softly pecked his cheek as she moved to the stove. He remained seated, unsure what to do.

"As much as it's nice t' see yers, d' yer allus d' yer visitin' at this time of the mornin'?"

"There's bin a lot o' robberies an' break-in's round 'ere, an' I just wanted t' mek sure you were okay, as I was in t' area".

"Ahh. That's sweet an' thoughtful of yers Albert. I 'ave mi own police protection now".

"You must keep yer room locked at all times. Do not answer the door t' anyone until you've checked 'em through t' window first, and if yer don't know 'em, tell 'em t' bugger off. D' yer 'ave a telephone 'ere?"

She raised her eyebrows in reply.

"I'll get t' uniform lads on t' beat t' check on yer when they're passin'. We're lookin' for a big bloke wi' black 'air an' a beard. If yer see 'im, definitely lock yer door".

"Don't worry, I'm not in t' 'abit of invitin' strange men in t' mi room. Well, just one".

They both laughed. Meadowbank finished his brew and Mary walked him to the front door. He felt awkward as he turned to face her, so Mary put her arms around his neck and standing on her tiptoes gave him a fervent kiss.

Meadowbank was like a young man on his first date. For the first time in years he had the feeling of excitement that takes over when meeting that special someone who took his breath away. As he walked towards the town centre he felt good inside, despite the swelling to his face and decided to treat himself to a butter pie for breakfast, hot from the oven at Elsie's Pantry.

If the inspector had turned round before reaching Stanley Place, where the road bends to the right thereby obscuring his view of the road behind him, he would have seen a black landau drawn by two black horses pull up and stop outside number 140, Fishergate Hill.

26

Lady Vivian Hortensia Nowell strode into the morning room, still wearing her riding jacket, breeches and boots.

"Roger! What the hell is going on?"

Sir Roger was placing books into a box. He turned to face his wife.

"What are you talking about?"

"I have just found Iris packing my clothes into suitcases, apparently on your instructions, but she did not know why. So I ask again, what is going on?"

Sir Roger could see she was furious.

"I was going tell you this morning over breakfast, but you did not come down to eat".

"Do you ever listen to a bloody word I say, Roger? I told you yesterday I was going for an early morning ride on the dunes with Kitty, then having breakfast with her and Barnabas. Now for the third time, what is going on and I hope this has nothing to do with poor Florence Cook's tragic death last night?"

She stood a few feet away, glaring at her husband, both hands on her hips, still holding her riding crop. Lady Vivian at forty nine years was twenty two years younger than Sir Roger, and often mistaken for his daughter. Her tousled blonde hair was shoulder length, she was slim and suited perfectly the fitted tweed jacket and at 5'11" was slightly taller than her spouse.

"Vivian darling, there have been developments overnight, since Florence's death". He wanted to choose his words carefully, "Our lives are in danger here. We have to leave, today".

She became flushed and took a deep breath.

"Why are you incapable of answering a simple question instead of offering dramatic platitudes? As usual, I have no idea what you are talking about, but if you think for a single moment that I am leaving this house, my family home for over three hundred years because of something you have imagined, then you are more insane than you sound".

"It is with regret that I did not allow you to see the devastation at Read Hall. I thought it was the right decision at the time, nonetheless the supernatural forces that wanted to destroy our home and our family are still out there and I fear Lytham Hall will be the next target in an effort to kill me. Even Florence warned of that".

"I was informed by you that the incident at Read Hall was nothing more than a freak calamity of stampeding boar, startled in the fog. Now you are saying it was a supernatural event to kill you. Roger, you need to listen to yourself. You are not frightening me, but this kind of nonsense would certainly frighten our daughter and grandchildren. I do not know what has happened to you these past few weeks, but I have had enough and your private army has caused me endless embarrassment. This has to stop. If you want to leave Lytham Hall then get on with it, but I am staying put. Just out of interest Roger, what is this supernatural entity that poor Florence claimed wants to kill you. Does it have a name? No! Let me guess. Beelzebub, Lucifer, Rumplestiltskin or is it Satan himself?"

He looked at his wife, ignoring her sarcasm and said hesitantly, "She did not say, but I suspect it is a witch".

"Good God! It had to be a witch didn't it". She threw her arms in the air and walked towards the window looking onto the driveway. "The Pendle Witches are the Nowell family obsession, so it does not surprise me Roger that you believe a witch is out to get you. It worries me, but doesn't surprise me. What does surprise me is that you have not dug up Witch Wood looking for their graves on a fools errand".

As Lady Vivian moved towards the door she said quietly, "Under the circumstances I think it better you sleep elsewhere tonight. We both need time to think".

"Vivian, what do you mean about Witch Wood and digging up graves?"

She stopped at the doorway and turned, tears running down her face. "It does not matter Roger, I have had enough talk of witchcraft to last a lifetime".

Sir Roger approached her.

"Please darling, what did you mean?"

"Look at you. Our marriage is crumbling and even now all you can think about is bloody sorcery", she shouted.

Before his wife could leave the drawing room, he put his arms around her and embraced her as she sobbed into his shoulder.

After a few minutes Lady Vivian pulled away and said, "I would like you gone before evening dinner".

But Sir Roger had to know, and nodding his head in agreement asked,

"Vivian, I am truly sorry that I have upset and disappointed you, but please just tell me what you meant by digging up graves in Witch Wood".

"The Pendle Witches are buried in Witch Wood, did you not know that?"

"Witch Wood here in the grounds of Lytham Hall?' He could not believe what he was hearing.

"Yes, that is why it has been called Witch Wood for centuries". She turned her back on Sir Roger, but he grabbed an arm to stop her from leaving.

He had so many questions to ask, he did not know where to start.

"Why have you never mentioned this before?" he asked.

"It is something that happened nearly three hundred years ago and no longer a topic high on my conversation list". She glared at his hand holding her forearm.

He let go and said, "Please Vivian, you know how important my ancestor's legacy is to me, and this could be part of it. My great grandfather many times over, prosecuted the Pendle Witches and there is no public record of where they were buried and now you are telling me they are buried within the grounds of your family estate. It does not make sense".

She could see he had been wounded, as if betrayed.

"Roger, I think we could both do with a brandy, even before lunch. Let's sit down and I will tell you what I know about Witch Wood, or at least what I can remember from what is supposedly fact or fiction".

The morning room overlooked the front of the house onto the east lawn and Sir Roger sat in a corner of a large cream settee and his wife chose a matching chair near the marble fireplace and the warmth of the glowing coal fire. He was wearing a light grey three piece suit, white shirt and dark grey tie and as usual his attire was immaculate.

"You must remember Roger, that what I tell you is only hearsay from my father. You say there are no records of where the Pendle Witches are buried, likewise I have seen no documents indicating they are buried in Witch Wood, I am repeating what my father told me many years ago".

Sir Roger sat forward, tense, clasping the brandy goblet with both hands and listened.

"Sir Cuthbert de Clifton, who was a contemporary of Roger Nowell, your namesake and a qualified barrister, was a legal advisor to the prosecution during the witch trials at Lancaster Castle".

Sir Roger interrupted. "This is news to me and I have a copy of the court proceedings. I have never heard of Sir Cuthbert de Clifton...".

"Roger, I am just telling you what I have been told and not what has been written in court records and do not subject me to some barrack room cross examination please". Lady Vivian sat back, with her arms resting on the top of the armchair, her legs crossed she stared at her husband. He nodded an apology.

"Please carry on dear".

"As I was saying, Sir Cuthbert de Clifton is believed to have been involved, either officially or unofficially, in the witch trials. I was not aware for certain that no record of the burials exist, you would know that better than I, but it was decided and clearly with Sir Cuthbert's agreement, that they be secretly buried in woodland on his estate in unmarked graves and to this day, as far as I am aware, that is where they still remain".

"Have you seen the graves?'

"No and I do not know their location, other than in the woods west of the house".

"I was led to believe that the 'Witch' in Witch Wood is a buried race horse of that name".

"I have never told you that, but it is a rumour I know and I believe it has been a convenient distraction as far as the family is concerned. Roger, this news may be of importance to you, but to this family it has become a subject of little consequence, a subject that is never talked about and not for reasons of secrecy. It has been forgotten. It is as simple as that".

"Well Vivian, it certainly has not been forgotten by me. Would your father know the location of the graves?"

"As you are aware, my father and mother have embarked on an extensive tour of the Americas, and could be anywhere north of the Amazon and south of the Hudson river. You could ask him on his return in summer next year".

After nearly thirty years of marriage he had become used to her sarcasm. "That isn't very helpful. I need to find those graves, will you help me or not?"

"When were the witch trials?'

"1612", he replied without hesitation.

"That is two hundred and eighty nine years ago. If they do exist, what do you expect to find? Mother Nature will have reclaimed any clearing or burial site over those years. Witch Wood has never been managed, it is overgrown, dark and broody. I do not think even deer forage in there and I would not know where to begin to look, that is if I was inclined to do so. But there is someone though who may be able to help you. My father's gamekeeper, John Isles, may know something".

"Then let us ask Mr. Isles what he does know, shall we?"

27

Inspector Meadowbank was sitting at his desk enjoying a pair of cold pigs trotters in aspic jelly, compliments of Mrs. Walmsley from the previous evening. Gelid, boiled pig's trotters have a certain aroma about them, especially at eight thirty in the morning.

"Christ Almighty! What's that pong?" Detective Constable Huxley exclaimed as he entered the Criminal Investigation Department office.

"It's probably Sergeant Huggins, yer know what 'e's like after a few pints", the inspector joked.

The sergeant was in earshot.

"Ned, it certainly won't 'ave owt t' do wi' t' boiled trotters t' Inspector is chompin' on".

"What 'ave yer got there Ned?" Meadowbank was pointing a pig's foot to the report D.C. Huxley was holding.

"It's a bit weird sir. Last week, Bridie Wilkes, the retired General's maid was found murdered not far from the General's house and now his governess, Emily Fields, has been reported missing by her husband. Seems a bit coincidental this does".

Ned Huxley came from farming stock and he looked it. Stocky build, ruddy cheeks, about 5'11", big rough hands and he never felt the cold. Even in the depths of winter you would find him somewhere, indoors or outdoors, with his shirtsleeves rolled up. His parents worked Saddle End Farm, near Chipping, at the foot of Wolf Fell. On his days off, Ned would often return to the farm to help with the milking or cleaning out the cow sheds. Ned had a honours degree in law from the University College Liverpool and at twenty six years old, he was the youngest and most academically qualified detective in the borough. Meadowbank took the report in his greasy hands and quickly read it.

"There ain't no such thing as coincidence in this game, Ned, remember that". He was glad to impart this gold nugget of advice. "What yer 'ave 'ere is a sequence of events that will b' some'ow connected. We just need t' find t' connection".

"Well, I think I know the connection sir".

Meadowbank looked at the young detective, waiting.

"What th' 'ell is it then?" he said impatiently.

"Thing is sir, both women worked for Sir General George White…".

"It's Lieutenant General Sir George White an' we already know this, get t' point".

Sergeant Huggins and Detective Constable Button put their nib pens down and sat back to listen and Constable Grimes looked up from his 'Imperial' typewriter.

"Well, the thing is sir, according to Mrs. Fields husband, Harold, who also happens to be the general's butler, his wife had gone to see the priest at Saint Wilfrid's church yesterday morning, the day she disappeared and Mr. Fields states…".

The detective paused while he checked his notebook, "that she told him, Bridie Wilkes had also gone to see the same priest the day she went missing. That was the day before her body was found in Winckley Square gardens, which is only a few hundred yards from the church".

Meadowbank looked across at his sergeant. "Sam, gerra search warrant for t' church an' t' presbytery. Ned, do we 'ave a name fer t' priest?'

"Father Gerald Fairfax".

"Gerra as much information as yer can on t' priest, Ned. I want t' know 'ow long 'e's bin in Preston, where's 'e come from, an' does 'e 'ave a past we should know abowt".

He handed the grease stained report to the detective, "Good work. Find out what yer can, then you an' me an' t' lads will pay Father Fairfax a visit".

"I spoke to him yesterday morning sir. Doing my house to house enquiries in Winckley Square and called at the presbytery. He's a big bloke, in his sixties. He seemed a bit nervous, but people often are speaking to the police. He did stumble a bit when he mentioned the victim was female and that was before I'd revealed that to him".

"What's yer gut feelin' about this man, Ned?" the inspector asked.

"There's something not right about him sir". "That's good enough for me. I'll brief the superintendent t' keep 'im 'appy. And while we are all t'gether, Sergeant 'Uggins 'as gorrus an update".

"Thank you sir. I've interviewed t' three who attacked t' inspector. Two are quite 'appy t' talk an' t' other can't as 'is broken jaw is now wired. T' man who assaulted them is a big bugger, at least 6'6", 'as a black beard, smartly dressed in a black suit and a grey flat cap. They said 'e came from nowhere, never said a word, just laid into t' four of 'em. This is t' same man who assaulted Inspector Meadowbank in the Turkish baths a few days ago. So that's who we're lookin' for an' if you do see someone of that description, do not approach 'im. You follow t' suspect as best yer can, then report back to Mr. Meadowbank or misel'. Then we tek 'im down as a team, 'cause 'e won't come quietly. I'll pass these details onto t' uniform lads as well, so we all know who we're lookin' for".

The inspector remained seated saying, "This man 'as a Geordie accent an' is a street fighter an' strong as an ox. I'm not just saying that 'cause 'e gave mi a good 'idin'. 'E is dangerous an' 'as no fear of t' police. Under no circumstances approach this man on yer tod, as Sam 'as just said he needs to be arrested mob-'anded. A name fer 'im would bi very 'andy as well".

Meadowbank lit his pipe as his detectives got to work and once again picked up the post mortem report on Bridie Wilkes. His priority was not to trace the big Geordie, no matter how satisfying that would be, but to trace the father of Bridie's unborn child. There were only two male occupants at the house, Sir George White and his butler, Harold Fields. Sir George was seventy five years of age

195

and his butler, sixty two, so it was possible that either could be the father. Unlikely though, he considered, having met both men, but still a possibility. He wanted a list of every male visitor to the Winckley Square address over the past three months, no matter how brief their stay.

Meadowbank looked across the office deciding who to allocate this job to and when he saw his sergeant and four detectives engrossed in what they were doing, he made a note on a piece of paper, slipping it into his folder. Compiling the list was the easy part of the enquiry, tracing and eliminating each male visitor would be the ball-ache. He would bob round to see Sir George and Lady Edith later on.

Inspector Meadowbank and Sergeant Huggins were like chalk and cheese in many ways. Huggins at sixty one was twenty years older and at 5'8" a lot shorter than the inspector's 6' 2". He had lost most of his hair, apart from a greying band from ear to ear, unlike his boss's dark brown wavy short back and sides, and the sergeant was on the rotund side whereas the inspector was stocky, but not too overweight. Huggins did pride himself on his selection of the several three piece suits he owned and wore with a certain panache. His inspector tried to take a leaf out of his sergeant's book of sartorial style, but never managed the look with the second hand suits he haggled for at the pawnbrokers.

The two officers did have a few things in common though; they were both damn good coppers with a mutual respect and trust of each other, but more than this, they were good friends,

196

despite Huggins being old enough to be Meadowbank's father.

Huggins had been divorced for five years and Meadowbank going on for eight years and they often discussed, always after a few pints, the advantages and disadvantages of women and relationships. They usually agreed they were better off being single and making do with the occasional visit to Ma Bakers house of ill repute every now and then.

"Paddy, 'Ow are t'enquiries comin' fer t' black carriage and 'ouse t' 'ouse on Moor Park Avenue?" Meadowbank called across the office to DC Button.

"First one slowly sir, and the second one I haven't started yet". Paddy Button had only recently been transferred to Meadowbank's team from the uniform department downstairs and was still finding his feet. He was certainly not used to senior officers addressing him by his Christian name.

"Reet, gi' me t' black carriage folder an' you crack on wi' t' street enquiries. We need t' find that bloody wolf 'ound thing before it teks a chunk owt o' someone else".

The CID office, directly above the parade and reports room, looked onto Lancaster Road and the Black-a-Moors Head Hotel, were police officers were not welcome due to the clientele and a landlord who had a dubious past and a hostile tone to the local constabulary. If you looked the other way to the right, you would see The Stanley Arms further up the road, an oasis of calm for the borough police, amongst the dozens and dozens of ale-houses throughout the town.

There were four desks in the office, the inspector and sergeant had their own and the four constables shared the other two, pushed together. There was a framed picture of Queen Victoria hanging above the fireplace even though she had been dead nine months. The replacement prints of her son and successor, Edward V1 had not yet reached Preston Police Station, but no one had noticed.

28

The old woman walked along Friargate pulling an empty shopping trolley. After a fruitless search, she was leaving the town centre to meet up with her carriage and driver, waiting on Maudland Bank. It was not late, but already dusk was approaching and the gas lamps were flickering on. She did not know she was being followed.

The priest had seen Auntie Vena from the shadows of a doorway near Lune Street and did not really know what drew him to her. She appeared elderly, was on her own, the long black overcoat with the collar up against the evening chill disguised her figure and the black bonnet pinned to her hair hid any features. Could it have been the stockinged ankles and shiny black brogues which attracted his attention? Whatever had caught his eye, Father Fairfax was already aroused with anticipation. It was over twenty four hours since he had defiled Emily Fields in every way imaginable; even her corpse, still warm had not satisfied his longing.

Father Fairfax felt like a gliding raptor, a king condor with wings outstretched, unstoppable in his search for prey to plunder. He was not wearing his clerical dark suit and dog collar, as he normally would when visiting parishioners. Instead he was dressed in a grubby tweed mis-matching jacket and trousers, cloth cap and rubber soled shoes which did not clatter on the pavement like hob-nailed boots or clogs, usually worn by mill workers, one of which he was pretending to be.

He quickened his pace to close the fifty feet or so between them, making sure no early evening revellers where around to interrupt him. The small glass phial together with a chloroform soaked handkerchief were readily accessible in his jacket pocket.

Auntie Vena had reached Old Chapel Yard, the entrance to Saint Mary's church and paid no attention to the chapel that stood behind the shops, as if the church was hiding from its congregation. The priest moved surprisingly fast considering his age and corpulent girth. His arm swept around her neck, the choking pressure against her windpipe was to stifle any scream for help. She let go of the trolley as she was brutally pulled backwards up stone steps towards the chapel main door, a damp handkerchief pressing against her mouth and nose. As Father Fairfax forced the old woman onto the cobblestones, he changed position quickly and was now sat astride her, his bulk pushing down and one hand tightly around her throat, the other returning the chemical soaked handkerchief to his pocket.

Throughout the attack Auntie Vena had not made a sound. The priest began to unbutton his trousers, his mouth was salivating as he pressed his weight down on the woman who offered no resistance. He eyed her shape evident beneath the overcoat and licked his lips, then looked at Auntie Vena's face for the first time as he tugged his trousers below his groin. She gave the priest a gentle smile, but her eyes, like holes in the earth, stared into his.

The priest was puzzled why this old woman was still conscious. To remedy this, he raised a fist above his head, intending to smash his knuckles down onto her face, when she spoke.

"Father, is this behaviour meant to convert me to the Roman Catholic faith?"

The priest froze at the question and the casual manner it was asked and looked for the terror and pleading he relished. There was none.

Without any change to her calm expression she watched Father Fairfax suddenly being propelled backwards through the air with great force, as if swatted by a giant hand and only a brick wall over twenty feet away stopped his flight, the back of his skull splitting open on impact. He fell to the yard floor in a heap, his trousers incongruous around his knees, exposing parchment white hairy thighs.

Auntie Vena stood up and still wearing black leather gloves, removed her overcoat and meticulously patted away the dust and dirt from the back of the garment and gave it a quick shake before putting the coat back on, refastening the buttons. Satisfied with her appearance she walked towards the priest. He was conscious, despite warm blood flowing gently from his shattered skull onto his neckerchief and down his back. Sitting askew like a discarded marionette he looked up at the old woman standing over him.

Auntie Vena removed a long hat pin from her velvet bonnet, stooping down she took hold of the priest's jaw with her left hand forcing his gaping mouth shut and with her right thumb pushed the 6" pin into his right temple all the way to the antique pearl mount. Only his eyes, wide like a beast at an abattoir gave any indication to what was happening.

As she patted herself down one final time, Auntie Vena noticed the counter heels on both brogues were badly scuffed. Her face contorted with rage, revealing teeth too white and perfect for any elderly person as she hissed at the lifeless figure of Father Fairfax and pointing at her brogues. "See what you have done, bastard priest".

She took steps towards the corpse with every intention of grinding the priest into a paste, like a chef would pulp ingredients using a pestle and mortar, but she turned around, retrieved her shopping trolley and continued along Friargate, remembering a more pressing rendezvous with Mr. Ambrose.

29

Sir Roger and Lady Vivian, riding their own horses, cantered along the tarmacadam path towards Witch Wood. Following behind was an open cart pulled by a single horse and driven by John Isles, accompanied by James Black. The two gamekeepers had joined forces and Black was more than happy to let the local woodsman take the lead. Both men carried loaded double barrelled shotguns and wore ammunition bandoliers holding enough cartridges to make any poacher take a discreet retreat. But it was not poachers they were armed against.

The four of them travelled in silence. Sir Roger was still confounded by his wife's revelation, as if it was of no consequence to him. She in turn regretted ever mentioning the family secret of Witch Wood and was glad her father was out of the country and uncertain how he would react on his return, apart from being furious. They took no interest in the surrounding park and pasture land or the herd of grazing fallow deer with their heads up watching the party pass. Witch Wood to the west of the hall loomed ahead, stretching north and south, the deciduous trees already preparing for winter.

The narrow road suddenly turned sharp right, following the edge of the woodland into the distance. It was here that John Isles called out for

Sir Roger to stop. The horses were tethered and the wagon parked off the road.

"With respect sir, I'll take the lead. I know these woods better than anyone". John Isles pointed out. Sir Roger and Lady Vivian both nodded, no one could argue with that statement.

John Isles had already assured Sir Roger he had no knowledge of any graves in the wood, let alone the burial sites of the Pendle Witches. He had heard rumours but dismissed them as just that and as he had patrolled these woods and grounds for over thirty years he had never seen anything remotely resembling a burial place.

They set off in single file, John Isles: Sir Roger, Lady Vivian and James Black at the rear. Much of the undergrowth had died back and they followed an animal trail for a hundred yards when John Isles suddenly stopped. A wider path came into view.

"That path wasn't here last week. I don't know anything about it". He turned to look at Sir Roger, who shook his head. "Nothing to do with me John. What's the significance?"

The path was recent, running left and right, the undergrowth hacked back and trampled down. As the path cut through a bog, several planks of wood had been laid on straw across the quagmire.

"The significance is sir, that someone has gone to a lot of trouble to make this path and I want to know why".

Turning left would take them towards the railway line and right, deeper into the woods. They turned right, following the path.

Witch Wood was silent apart from the distant 'drumming' of a woodpecker and the noise of their own footsteps crunching on the flattened grass and shrubbery and the clunk as they stepped onto several more planks of rough wood crossing wet pieces of ground. They had been walking along the path for ten minutes when they came to a clearing. Numerous trees had been cut down across a fifty foot square area. The felled trees had been placed in pyramid shape piles and undergrowth cleared away, creating an unnatural open space.

The four of them remained at the edge of the woodland opening, staring at the fresh mounds of earth lined in a neat row in the middle of the clearing.

"Oh My God! You've found them". Sir Roger whispered, walking towards the heaps of fresh soil, not hearing his gamekeeper reply, "No, we haven't found them, someone else has".

Sir Roger counted nine graves, all about six feet long and three feet wide. John Isles noticed axes, large wood saws and spades on the ground at the far side of the clearing, as if they had been dropped in a hurry. An uneasy feeling crept over him and he quietly closed his shotgun, turning to look at James Black. He had also seen the discarded tools and was scanning the woodland opposite.

Movement between the trees on the far side grabbed John Isles' attention. There was a sudden flash and explosion as a rifle opened fire. Sir Roger dropped to the ground with a moan. Another shot blasted from the trees and James Black toppled backwards. John Isles fired at the gun flashes then pulled Lady Vivian to the ground, standing over her as he fired the second barrel. She was screaming and reaching out to her husband, who was crawling towards a tree stump, blood covering his left shoulder. John Isles glanced at the Read Hall gamekeeper; it obvious from the ragged hole to his chest he was dead. John reloaded and knew he had to get Lady Vivian to cover. He grabbed her arm dragging the screaming woman backwards and holding the shotgun at his hip, fired two more shots across the clearing. He pulled Lady Vivian behind a pile of tree trunks and called out to Sir Roger.

"Sir, how are you doing?"

"Don't worry about me. How's Vivian?"

"She's okay, sir".

John quietly said to Lady Vivian, "Ma'am, I'm going to get these bastards. Once I've made it across the clearing, I'll give you a signal and you get Sir Roger back to the carriage. I'll meet you at the hall later. Can you do that?"

She was in shock.

The gamekeeper shook her, "Did you hear me ma'am?"

She nodded her head. Without another word John turned, fired both barrels at the lingering gun smoke and sprinted across the open space reaching the tree line within seconds. He stayed behind a wide sycamore, gave a signal to Lady Vivian, then listened to the woodland around him. A noise like a large stag breaking through the undergrowth could be heard going away from him, towards the railway tracks.

John headed off to his left, moving through the woodland like a true woodsman, darting around trees, hurdling over fallen trunks and leaping over tangled bracken in complete defiance of his fifty five years of age. He reached the Blackpool to Preston Coast Line and followed it north, running on the sleepers in the middle of the track. Before reaching the Windsor Road Goods Yard, John crouched behind a pile of railway sleepers and waited.

He did not have to wait for long. Three men emerged from Witch Wood about hundred feet in front of him, laughing, pleased with themselves. They climbed over the fence separating the train line from Lytham Hall estate and moved towards the goods yard. All three carried rifles.

The gamekeeper rested both elbows on the top sleeper and took aim. The first lead slug hit the nearest man in the head, bursting it like a prize marrow and lifting him off his feet sideways. Moving the shotgun to the left slightly he pulled the second trigger. Rather than take cover the two men stood tall, searching the surrounding terrain. The second lump of lead went through a ribcage, exploding the heart in less than a heartbeat of the youngest man.

John Isles reloaded, his gun sight following the third man who was now making a dash for the cover of rolling stock. He squeezed the trigger, as he always did when stalking poachers or culling the deer herd, calmly and with confidence, his shoulder absorbing the kickback of the shotgun. The third man seemed to cartwheel forward as the bullet whacked into his back, sprawling him on the rail track motionless. The gamekeeper approached the three bodies, confident none would rear up and surprise him, then dragged them by their arms to side of the track leaving them in a gruesome line. He collected the rifles, they were all ex-British Army Martini-Henry single shot, in a poor state, but still effective. He slung them over his shoulder, found the two horses where they had been left at the edge of the wood and walked them back to the stables. His mind was in turmoil. Why did James Black just die in Witch Wood? What the hell was going on? One thing John was certain about having looked at the three bodies and gone through their pockets, these men were Irish Tinkers, Travellers, Gypsies. Call them what you will, but they were bad news. By the time John returned to Lytham Hall, Sir Roger was in the basement kitchen, stripped to the waist and holding a wad of cotton towels against his shoulder. Lady Vivian was now more composed and busy offering brandy to Sir Roger, Mrs. Hedges the cook and her assistant Mollie. They all looked far too happy considering the circumstances, as Lady Vivian continued to top up every glass as soon as it approached empty, including her own.

The family doctor attended the hall and decided to remove the bullet there and then as everyone appeared to be inebriated, particularly Sir Roger.

Even though Lytham Cottage Hospital was only two miles away, it would cause quite a stir arriving with the Lord Lieutenant of Lancashire worse for drink and a bullet wound to his left shoulder, especially as his father-in-law, John Talbot Clifton, paid for the hospital to be built. After examining the wound, the doctor decided against a sedative, due to Sir Roger's drunken stupor and produced a set of surgical callipers from his bag, deftly removing the bullet while the patient remained semi-conscious. John Isles was in Sir Roger's study using the telephone to contact the police. He then took the carriage back to Witch Wood and remained with James Black's body, until the police arrived.

30

As rigor mortis was taking over the lonely corpse of Father Fairfax at the other end of town, a group of police officers, consisting of Meadowbank, Huggins, the three detectives, Benny Watts a uniformed sergeant and Constable Jacob Lamb gathered outside the presbytery next to Saint Wilfrid's Church. They were not alone; a small crowd was collecting on the footpath a few yards away keen to see what the police were up to, including a passing press photographer from The Lancashire Evening Post. If anyone was in at the presbytery, they were not answering the door.

"Do yer stuff, Benny". Meadowbank said to the sergeant.

Sergeant Watts was holding a heavy cylindrical piece of solid metal, three foot long, with a grab handle welded in the middle and one at the end. To use this piece of equipment effectively as a battering ram, as it was designed for, would require two officers to take hold and swing it between them for maximum power. But Benny Watts was a former dray-man, who for many years lugged thirty six gallon oak beer-barrels or the larger hogshead casks from wagon to cellar, stepped forward with the 'emergency key', as he liked to call it, handed his helmet to P.C. Lamb, then swung the lump of iron with such power, his colleagues watched in awe as the solid door burst open on impact. All the officers carried the latest dry cell flashlights and once inside the hallway, Meadowbank directed Sergeant Watts to search upstairs. P.C. Lamb had been left outside to keep the crowd back and ensure none of them follow the police into the building, particularly the photographer. The three detectives were given the front of the large building and cellar to search while Meadowbank and Sergeant Huggins would search the rear.

The first door they came to was locked, so Meadowbank stepped back, booting it with his right foot and was quietly chuffed with himself when it flew open at his first attempt. The room had a peculiar smell to it, a whiff of chemicals familiar to Meadowbank and Huggins, but both struggled to identify. There was a further door next to a floor to ceiling bookcase and this too was locked. Huggins searched the desk drawers and found a bunch of keys, one of which unlocked the door. The room was dark and windowless and the smell was even stronger.

"Chloroform", Huggins said, now recognising the sweet smell.

Meadowbank nodded in agreement then lit the wall gas mantle, knowing chloroform was not flammable and hoping there were not other noxious vapours floating around ready to ignite.

The room was fairly small, an annexe to the study with various vestments hanging macabrely from wall hooks. A floor cabinet displayed a selection of clerical collars next to an assortment of blue apothecary bottles and corked flasks containing different liquids. In the middle of the parquet floor was a tarpaulin bundle, tied methodically with a thin rope along its five foot length. The two officers gave each other a knowing look. Huggins produced a small pocket knife, it was exceptionally sharp and soon cut through the cord. Pulling back the loose folds of the sheet Huggins revealed the trussed naked body of Emily Fields. Keeping the flashlight shining on her chalk white face Meadowbank said, "Sam, we need to catch this priest and soon".

There was a commotion in the hallway and D.C. Collier was shouting for assistance.
Meadowbank and Huggins rushed to his aide.

"Sir, we've found a woman in the cellar, tied up". The detective was still startled.

"Is she alive?" Meadowbank asked.

"Yes, she's unconscious, but breathing".

"Reet, call a doctor quick. There's a telephone int' study".

The inspector and sergeant, following their flashlights, descended the stone steps into the cold cellar, now lit with an assortment of candles. Against a damp wall and next to several tea chests and storage boxes was a battered dining chair and sat on it was Miss McEvedy, bound to the chair with identical cord as used in the study. Her head had dropped forward, but the bruising to her face was clearly visible. Constable Collier was right, she was unconscious and breathing, but also reeked of chloroform. One of the detectives was attempting to untie the tightly twisted knot, then moved aside when Huggins attacked the rope with his knife. Meadowbank gently lifted the housekeeper into his arms in one motion and carried her upstairs to the sitting room, laying her on the couch.

"Who is she?" Huggins asked.

"I don't know, but from t' apron she's wearin' possibly t' 'ousekeeper or even a parishioner, and certainly Father Fairfax's next victim".

"Bloody 'ell Albert. This 'ouse of God 'as become an 'ouse of 'orrors. I'll carry on t' search an' 'ave a look around t' church as well".

Miss McEvedy was still fully clothed and Meadowbank had noticed the housekeeper's underwear around her knees. He left them there until the doctor arrived.

31

She suddenly threw the tumbler across the room, glass and whisky exploding against the wall. The black cat, laying on the rocking-chair looked away, not wanting to see her rage.

Auntie Vena glared at Evergreen, silently challenging him to speak further.

"I have paid you a lot of money for you to meet my wishes. I put my faith in your assurance that you could protect the grave site for a few days, now you tell me that three men you left to do exactly that, have been shot dead. Who is protecting the site now?" She suppressed her fury.

"There are police and armed guards all over the place. I've just come from there, we can't get near". Evergreen hoped this explanation would suffice.

Auntie Vena propelled herself forward in a blur, coming to a standstill no more than a foot from Evergreen. Even though they were similar height, she seemed to tower over him, her perfume wafting and swirling, confusing his senses. *Did her eyes blink like a lizard and change from blue to green to blue?*

"Evergreen, I want as many of your tribe as you can assemble to keep the clearing secure until midnight tomorrow. I do not care what it takes or how many police officers have to be killed, just see to it. If you feel the task is beyond you, return the two thousand pounds and Mr. Ambrose will take over from where you have failed and he never disappoints me".

She continued to stare at the gypsy.

"Well, what shall it be?"

"I will have twenty to thirty men down there before nightfall".

"And they must remain there until I say so. You understand?"

At last Evergreen lifted his head and looked directly at Auntie Vena, nodding in acquiescence.

"Off you go then and I shall see you in a little over thirty six hours".

She looked at the cat and sighed. "I should have left you down there. I can always rely on you and Mr. Ambrose".

The cat used a paw to wash itself, as if it had just eaten a sparrow. Auntie Vena opened another bottle of Glen Garioch, her favourite malt scotch, and filled a Waterford crystal tumbler, now one of three remaining from originally four acquired decades ago. She was becoming restless. All Hallows' Eve was getting closer and mistakes should not be happening now.

The witch unbolted the back door in the scullery and stood on the top step overlooking the stone terrace and veranda. Beyond, the unkempt lawn was kept hidden from view of prying neighbours by surrounding mature beech, ash, hawthorne and yew trees. As she sipped the warming amber drink, once again trying to picture her mother's face, movement at the end of the garden caught her attention. It was amongst a row of dense yew trees, hiding a high wall which separated the rear access lane to neighbouring properties. Someone was crouched in the tall grass and overhanging branches, the glint of binoculars unmistakable in the mid-morning sun. Auntie Vena carried on watching her unknown visitor, apparently unconcerned, and after a few more minutes went back inside to find Mr. Ambrose.

Detective Constable Paddy Button had begun his house to house enquiries on Moor Park Avenue, and as instructed by his inspector he started with the house called 'Hoarstones'.

D.C. Button was unable to get beyond the locked front gates, and looking through thee railings he could see no sign of life, apart from a lantern burning on a stable windowsill. He got no response from the houses either side and was scratching his head as what to do next. He did not want to go back to the station and announce that he had failed the one task he had been given; find out who lives at "Hoarstones'. Constable Button had walked from the station, carrying everything he needed in a haversack, including a boiled tongue sandwich and a Dewar flask of hot sweet tea and more importantly a pair of binoculars. He was also carrying a Webley service revolver in a side holster in accordance with his detective inspector's orders: *C.I.D. officers to be armed at all times.*

He found the service road at the back of the houses and eventually identified 'Hoarstones'. Eager to impress his new boss, D.C. Button decided to climb the six foot high brick wall. He was five feet eleven inches tall, thirty years of age and an accomplished footballer, often a substitute for Preston North End's first team languishing in the bottom half of Division One. Paddy Button was physically fit and scaled the wall without any difficulty. The row of mature yew trees provided plenty of cover as the detective crept through the undergrowth. He found a spot between the trees with a clear view of the rear of the house and, lying on his stomach, he removed the flask and binoculars from his haversack, settling down for a few hours of discreet observations.

Not long had passed when he saw an elderly female leave the house and linger under the glass roofed veranda. She was drinking from a glass. D.C. Button could see her features quite clearly through the binoculars, particularly when she looked in his direction, returning inside the house after a few minutes.

A short time later a big man with a dark beard appeared from an outbuilding. He was wearing a black suit and seemed to be looking at the detective, as if he could see him from over two hundred and fifty feet away and amongst chest high grass, bordering the unkempt lawn. He trained the binoculars on the man, who appeared to have a large animal by his side, but it was difficult to identify what it was. This man pointed towards the detective's position and the animal suddenly disappeared from view. To get a better line of sight, Paddy Button raised himself onto his haunches and scanned the rear garden through the binoculars. He spotted something dart across the lawn, coming towards him through the long grass. It had gone from view within seconds.

He put the glasses down and searched the garden. The man was still stood under the veranda and he was looking directly at Constable Button as the old woman had done.

Was he smiling? Paddy Button brought the binoculars back into position and one look at the man immediately confirmed he had been spotted. He was now waving at the detective, as if acknowledging an old friend. It was time to make a hurried withdrawal.

The detective grabbed his haversack, leaving behind the flask as he sprinted towards the wall. Throwing the haversack over the brickwork, he grabbed the top coping stones as the hyena burst through the undergrowth and was on D.C. Button before he was able to haul himself to safety. His left leg was seized in powerful jaws and was instantly dragged backwards. He screamed in pain as his leg below the knee was bitten off and with a flick of its huge head, the hyena sent the dismembered limb flying through the air. D.C. Button rolled onto his back, in an effort to draw his revolver. Hyenas are scavengers in the wild, but this striped hyena, demented after years in captivity, abused and starved, howled like a wolf before lunging at the detective, teeth sinking into his neck, tearing out ligaments and membrane of his larynx with a single bite. Not having the strength to aim the gun, let alone pull the trigger, D.C. Button lay on his back mortally injured, taking last gasps through his ruptured airway as the hyena lapped the blood gurgling from his throat and windpipe.

32

Meadowbank left the presbytery after midnight and walked back to the station alone. His head felt fuggy; he did not know whether it was from the chloroform imbued rooms in which he had spent the last few hours or the sight of poor Emily Fields.

Huggins and Doctor Bayers had gone to the hospital in the ambulance with Miss McEvedy, who had gently been brought to her senses with smelling salts. This may have been a mistake by the police doctor, as she immediately became hysterical and had to be sedated to get her into the ambulance.

Sergeant Watts and two constables were to remain at the presbytery throughout the night to protect the scene until photographed, and wait for the undertakers to arrive, and also in case Father Fairfax returned.

Fishergate was unusually quiet for this time of the night, and the inspector put this down to the rain which seemed to be set in for the next few hours. He turned left onto Cheapside, crossed the Market Square, passing the Harris Museum, on to Birley Street, turning right on to Earl Street and immediately saw someone in the shadows of the covered market, leaning against a stanchion.

He could not make out who it was and without thinking, slipped the brass knuckleduster onto his right fist. As he got nearer to the police station, the person took a few steps forward and called out, "Mr. Meadowbank. I need to have a word with you".

He did not recognise the voice, but recognised the man now standing within the street lighting.

"Evergreen, what brings you 'ere?"

The two detectives had locked the gypsy up a few years back for violent disorder in The Olde Dog. Meadowbank knew he was a handful after a few drinks, so kept the knuckleduster in place.

"You won't need that thing Mr. Meadowbank. I've not come to cause trouble".

Meadowbank crossed the street and they both moved under cover and into the shadows as he put the brass weapon back into his pocket.

"What can I do fer thee, Evergreen?"

"It's what I can do for you".

"How much will that cost?"

"I have information and I want nowt for it. Do you know a bloke called Mr. Ambrose?"

Meadowbank shook his head. "D' yer 'ave a first name?"

"No. I've known him for years, but only ever known him as that. Works for Vena Demdike".

"Am I suppose t' know what yer talkin' abowt, Evergreen?"

"He's the one who gave your attackers a good hiding a few nights back".

That grabbed the inspector's attention.

"Go on, I'm listenin'".

The gypsy smiled, "I thought you would. They are planning something big for tomorrow night. I don't know what, but Vena Demdike has paid me a lot of money to provide armed men to protect some graves at Lytham. Have you heard of that place?"

"Lytham. I was there last night. What's special abowt these graves?"

"I don't know and don't want to know if I'm honest".

"That's somert you've never bin, Evergreen. Where are these graves then?"

"Deep in woodland at a big house called Lytham Hall".

Meadowbank looked at the gypsy without speaking.

"Mr. Meadowbank! What's wrong?"

"That's where I was last night, in Lytham. At Lytham Hall. So what d' yer want t' tell me?"

"That's a coincidence ain't it? Anyway, you do what you want, but me or my men won't be there. I'm supposed to go Demdike's house first and pick some stuff up, but I have a very bad feeling about all this. They're dabbling with the supernatural and that ain't natural. Live near the park they do. Ambrose is Demdike's driver and hard-man, looks after her, but I'm sure she can look after herself, if you know what I mean".

"You don't know what t' job is though? Could they be plannin' t' rob t' big 'ouse at Lytham?"

"You're not listening Mr. Meadowbank. That's not her style, Vena Demdike doesn't need money, she's bloody loaded. It's to do with these nine graves. Took twelve of us days to clear woodland around them, after Ambrose showed us where they where. Carroty thinks it's do with these missing kids. I don't know, but I do know there is something very wrong going on and I won't be here to find out what it is, but it's giving me the creeps. Me and Carroty are leaving for Dublin in a few hours, before Mr. Ambrose comes looking for us and the money and we won't be coming back".

"Where's this 'ouse then, near a park yer say?"

"I've only been once before. It's a big house with high gates".

"What road?"

"You do know I can't read, don't you?'

A house with high gates facing a park. The pieces suddenly fell into place.

"Is the house called 'Hoarstones'?"

"Mr. Meadowbank, look I don't know any more than that. I've got to go, Carroty's waiting for me in Black-a-Moors".

Meadowbank held out his hand, "Good luck Evergreen, I'll tek care o' this".

As he watched Evergreen disappear into the night, he wondered how D.C. Button had got on with his house to house enquiries on Moor Park Avenue.

The inspector now had two names. They did not mean anything to him, but he needed to check the name index in his office.

At 1am that morning he decided to ring Lytham Hall and speak with Sir Roger.

33

Didier Pascall, wearing pristine white pyjamas, had woken Sir Roger in the early hours of the morning, apologising for disturbing his sleep, but informing him there was an urgent telephone call from an Inspector Meadowbank. Sir Roger, in his nightshirt, raced across the landing to his study.

At last he had a name and even though he was not familiar with Vena Demdike, he had certainly heard of the last name. Whoever Vena Demdike was, she must be a direct descendant of Elizabeth and Old Mother Demdike, two of the nine hung at Gallows Hill. Sir Roger checked his files and records, but could find no trace of a Vena Demdike.

This surviving Demdike has got to be the necromancer, there could be no other explanation. This thought kept spinning inside his head. *And the inspector mentioned graves in the woods here at the hall. This Demdike must be planning some grotesque ritual on Halloween now the site has been cleared and nine graves exposed.*

He had to act fast to stop the witches' sabbath he now suspected was taking place in Witch Wood in just over twenty four hours.

The average annual adult male wage in 1901 was £56.00 per year for ten hours a day, six days a week. So when Sir Roger advertised for hired help at £10.00 per day and meals provided he was inundated with applicants. There was one condition, they must own a firearm and know how to use it. By 10am the queue of hopeful employees stretched nearly the length of the driveway to Lytham Hall. John Isles, the gamekeeper, conducted the interviews in the stable block behind the main hall. He sat at a desk brought from the estate office and Didier Pascall brought men forward one at a time. Sir Roger hovered in the background, shaking his head to certain men and nodding to others, much to the gamekeeper's frustration, as he had volunteered to do the interviews, as Sir Roger said he was too busy.

Even those rejected were given a pound note for their trouble and within a few hours enough men had been recruited. John Isles addressed them from the steps at the front of the house. He wanted them back there by 6am the following morning for an early breakfast. They must each have possession of a firearm and ammunition, that was the only stipulation.

At 6am the next day, before the sun had risen, the stable block was illuminated with paraffin lamps. Inside was alive with chatter, and the clattering of tin mugs of hot tea and the welcoming aroma of Mrs. Hedges' bacon sandwiches, as a hundred men sat on rows of wooden benches and bales of hay. Many gathered in the courtyard, filling their pipes or rolling their own cigarettes.

Sir Roger was dressed in a dark brown tweed belted jacket, matching breeches, gaiters with brown boots and a Harris tweed deerstalker.

Noticeably he wore an ammunition bandolier across a shoulder and in his pocket were a dozen solid-silver slugs. Around his waist was holstered John Paslew's large calibre hand-gun, the howdah, but this was not for any sentimental reasons. He knew the gun's capabilities an it was fast to reload. The opposite holster carried a Very pistol, already loaded with a flare. Firing the flare was the signal for Didier Pascall to leave the hall and come to their assistance in Witch Wood. The Frenchman carried an identical Very pistol should help be needed at the hall.

At 7.30am John Isles waited in his four wheel cart watching the men who had travelled on foot clamber into the back. Sir Roger sat next to his gamekeeper and smiled to himself as a hundred of the volunteers assembled on the driveway. Many were ex-infantry from the 47th Lancashire Regiment of Foot, who had returned from the Boer Wars battle hardened and could certainly handle a weapon. They formed an orderly line of men on horseback, some on foot and others crowding into farm wagons, and there was even a Thwaites's Brewery dray wagon with two majestic shire horses lined up with at least ten workers from the Blackburn brewery on board. It was a good humoured gathering, but only John Isles knew what the mission entailed and no one questioned why the end wagon was piled with tied faggots of split branches and large tin cans of paraffin.

The procession headed towards Witch Wood, and Lady Vivian watched anxiously from her bedroom window, again regretting her disclosure to her husband of the legend of the graves. Her heart pounded as she watched the small army, led by her husband, amble blindly towards the unknown.

The rising sun brought welcome daylight to the estate, with a cloudless sky promising sunshine, as the train of men, horses and wagons arrived at the bend in the road with the woodland directly in front of them. John Isles raised an arm signalling they were stopping. Sir Roger, standing in the cart faced the men, all looking eager to to get to work and get paid, called out to the gathering.

"In the woodland in front of you are the graves of nine witches buried here nearly three hundred years ago. Our mission today is to dig each one from their grave and burn the remains".

A discernible murmur of surprise rippled through the assembled men.

"I know this proposal will sound insane to you, but two days ago James Black, a member of my ground staff, was murdered by men paid to protect these graves, and I was shot in the shoulder".

His left arm was still in a sling and he painfully raised this supported arm to emphasise his injury. "Make no mistake, this will be dangerous work. As far as we know the grave site is deserted. John here has been keeping an eye on the area, but these men, paid to protect the devil's children, could return at any time. You will need strong stomachs. To dig up a grave is not a pleasant task, but when the coffin contains hibernating witches, who were hung at Lancaster gallows and now waiting for the moment to be resurrected, you will need all the fortitude you have. I could go on, but this is not the time for talking, but the time for action. Anyone who feels this mission is beyond them, feel free to leave and you will be paid for half a day. The rest of you follow John and I, and we will travel to the graves on foot. My stable boys will look after the horses".

As far as Sir Roger could tell no one turned round and headed back to the hall. Volunteers carried the faggots of tied sticks, tin cans and branches and most men these days had at least one box of safety matches on them, but John Isles had enough with him for a second gunpowder plot. A sombre mood descended on the men as they reflected and discussed their task ahead. Weapons and spades were clutched tightly as cigarettes and pipes were drawn on heavily, hacking coughs accompanying the trample of footfall. Sir Roger had left a further fifty mercenaries guarding the hall, under the command of Didier Pascal, a former French Legionnaire before injury forced his retirement. These men came from villages and towns around Read, the majority being former foot soldiers of the East Lancashire Regiment. Sir Roger was not taking any chances after the ravaging of his ancestral home. He also considered each group could act as reinforcements to each other if events went horribly wrong and each group of men had been told to react quickly if a flare was fired from Witch Wood or Lytham Hall.

Sir Roger had not informed Inspector Meadowbank what he was planning or of the murder of his gamekeeper. Now that he was certain he was dealing with a Demdike as the necromancer, he wanted to avoid any interferences, distractions or delays. He did not want to be digging out the coffins approaching midnight on the eve of The Great Assembly of Witches.

34

The cleaner opened the heavy wooden doors of Saint Mary's church and began to mop the stone steps leading to the small cobbled courtyard. She did not see the body of Father Fairfax until she turned to pour away the water, dropping the bucket with a scream as the galvanised pail bounced noisily on the cobbles. She continued to scream as she hurried through the church to find Father Burne-Jones.

Saint Mary's parish priest did not recognise his neighbouring colleague at first. It was only when he took particular interest in the hat-pin protruding from the dead man's skull, that he realised it was Gerald Fairfax, dressed in odd clothing.

Instead of using a telephone to contact the police, Father Burne-Jones entered Friargate and began shouting for help and throwing 'murder' in to his hollering for greater effect. It did not take long for a constable to appear and half an hour later Detective Inspector Meadowbank arrived. Since his telephone call to Sir Roger five hours ago, the inspector had been at his desk so he was able to respond to the constable's report of a murder victim being found.

Meadowbank was surprised to hear from the priest that the deceased was in fact Father Gerald Fairfax, the parish priest at Saint Wilfrid's church, the man wanted for the murder of at least two women and the abduction and rape of a third.

The inspector sat on the top step, lighting his favourite briar pipe stuffed with his usual English rub, as he looked on at the murdered priest. He had already gone through the dead man's pockets and found the phial containing what he believed to be chloroform and the chemical soaked handkerchief on the floor by the entrance to the courtyard.

A switchblade knife was also in a jacket pocket. They would be strange accoutrements for the parish priest, had the past not caught up with him. Meadowbank pondered over the scene before him, taking note of the grubby trousers and pristine long-johns around the priest's knees clearly exposing his manhood. His skull had been smashed against the wall with great force. Perhaps Father Fairfax was disturbed by a victim's lover or husband? It would take a man of considerable strength to do this to the priest, someone who was no stranger to violence and probably enjoyed it.

One name came to the inspector's mind; Mr. Ambrose. Could this mysterious man be somehow involved in the murder of Father Fairfax?

Meadowbank was back at his desk an hour later. He was typing an incident report for the chief constable to the effect that the perpetrator for the murders of Bridie Wilkies and Emily Fields was Father Gerald Fairfax, who was now a murder victim. Meadowbank rubbed his face when he read it back to himself, it did sound like a work of fiction created by Arthur Conon Doyle. His summary concluded that the evidence indicated Father Fairfax was more than likely attacked, receiving fatal injuries by a person or persons unknown while he was sexually assaulting or raping an unknown female, allowing both the victim and his assailant to flee the scene. He made no mention about the identity of a possible suspect, keeping his suspicions to himself in the event he was completely wrong. He had learnt that the hard way as a junior detective.

Satisfied, he signed all four copies, addressing the envelopes to Chief Constable Moorsom, Chief Superintendent Montague-Fox and Superintendent Malone. The original copy he put in the file marked 'Winckley Square Murders'.

Meadowbank heard the clatter of tin mugs on a metal tray, which could mean only one thing, Phoebe was making an early brew round. It had just gone eight, and there was no one else in the office when she appeared at the doorway with a tray and several steaming mugs of tea and a huge plate of one inch thick toast. He did not get the opportunity to engage in his usual teasing.

"Afore yer sez owt clever Mr. Meadowbank, I know's you've bin 'ere all neet an' I know's you've 'ad an 'ell of a neet as well. I thought yer could do wi' a strong brew t' put 'airs on yer chest, I've 'eard yer could do wi' a few".

"Yer mucky hussy, 'ave yer bin peepin'?"

They both laughed, even though Phoebe tried hard not to. She gave the inspector a wink and put the tray on his desk, balancing on numerous files and bundles of paper.

"Any 'ows, I've got some news fer thee".

"Let mi guess Phoebe, you've bin promoted t' Superintendent, because yer could do a damn site better job than t' current one".

"Mr. Malone's alreet, you just don't know 'ow t' talk t' 'im. Anyway, will you shurrup an' listen. Me an' Sergeant Thackeray are steppin' owt together, thought yer like t' know, seein' 'ow you've bin pesterin' us to fer ages".

Meadowbank jumped up, rushed round his desk and gave her a big hug. "Abowt flamin' time as well. I'm really chuffed, Ernest will d' yer proud Phoebe. 'E's a gentleman an' it's what yer deserve". Phoebe had gone quite red and both of them were close to tears.

"It's bin so long since Stan passed away, Mr. Meadowbank…".

Meadowbank was still embracing Phoebe when Station Sergeant Thackeray entered the office and coughed. It was Meadowbank's turn to blush, as he looked over Phoebe's shoulder at Ernest Thackeray looking on surprised.

"Sorry t' interrupt yer sir, but Paddy Button's wife is at t' desk. Brought some breakfast for 'im, as 'e 'asn't bin 'ome fer nearly twenty four hours. D' yer know owt abowt this?"

Meadowbank nearly threw Phoebe to one side, brushing past Sergeant Thackeray as he darted from the office without saying a word to either.

35

Mr. Ambrose followed the brick path that ran along one side of the uncut lawn, heading towards the direction of the screams. He held a boiled ham shank in his left hand. As he reached the yew trees at the bottom of the garden he became more cautious, cursing as he clumsily kicked a flask in the undergrowth. Stopping to pick it up, he unscrewed the top and smiled as steam from the hot tea escaped. Steering his way through the low hanging branches he heard the disturbing sound of ravenous feasting taking place.

The hyena had its back to Mr. Ambrose as it bent over Paddy Button, turning to give him a snarling warning, showing off those bone-crushing teeth, its muzzle covered in blood. He had removed the bandage from the animal's chest a few days ago without any commotion, so Mr. Ambrose was confident he had gained the hyena's trust.

"LEAVE!" He shouted, signalling with his right arm.

"LEAVE!" He repeated.

With its head low, it continued to snarl at Mr. Ambrose, as if daring him to approach its kill.

He waved the cooked ham towards the animal, which immediately reacted to the scent, sniffing the air loudly. He tossed the meat several yards away from the hyena and it followed eagerly. Mr.

Ambrose approached the body, wincing at the wound to the neck which seemed to have removed the head from the rest of the body. There was so much clotted-blood and torn tissue it was hard to tell for certain, but the protruding white bone of the fractured vertebrae glistening in the morning sun should have helped him. The holstered gun aroused his suspicions, which were soon confirmed when he searched the pockets and found a wallet displaying an identity card:

This is to certify that Patrick Joseph Button holds the rank of Detective Constable 169 in Preston Borough Police. This is the Warrant and Authority for executing the duties of his office. Signed: Major Francis Gore Little, Chief Constable.

He removed the holstered revolver and together with the wallet and warrant card he returned to the house, leaving the police officer where he lay and the hyena gnawing on the ham joint.

Auntie Vena was sat on a wooden chair under cover of the verandah, looking across the garden as a gardener would do after a successful day's toil and cultivation. She watched Mr. Ambrose emerge from the yew trees and follow the brick path to the house.

"Well?"

"It is not good news ma'am. He is a copper, a dead copper now, but still a copper".

"Who killed him? You or the animal?"

"He was already dead when I found him".

"By copper, I assume you mean a police officer? And where there is one police officer, there will always be another. What was he doing here? That is the question Mr. Ambrose and what do they know?"

He handed her the wallet and warrant card.

"Do you want me to bury him, ma'am?"

"It may be a good idea to do so, Mr. Ambrose. We could get more visitors looking for Detective Constable 169".

"Evergreen Bartlett will be calling in twenty four hours. I should be able to deter further visitors till then ma'am".

"Do you trust Evergreen?"

"Not for a second, but he would not dare double-cross you ma'am. He knows you are a Demdike and what you are capable of".

"He may know I am a Demdike, but he has no idea of what I am capable of Mr. Ambrose", she said with no arrogance. "How is our other house guest by the way?"

"She's in the stables trussed up like a chicken ready for roasting, ma'am".

"Excellent but don't do anything silly. After Hallow's Eve the harlot will be yours to keep".

A sound of purring caught her attention as the one-eyed black cat rubbed itself against the chair leg, its tail held high and whiskers forward.

"This cat is a grimalkin Mr. Ambrose. Do you know what that means?"

He looked at the cat, its head and coat slick with something red and viscous, then he shuddered realising the cat was covered in blood, as if it had been rolling in gore.

"No ma'am, I've never heard of that word before".

Sounding unusually melancholy she said, "There is so much you do not know about the Craft, perhaps I should have been more inclusive and educated you in the ways of the Demdikes. Anyway, a grimalkin is a companion. He is my companion and guardian". She stroked the cat, oblivious to the blood smearing her hand. "He is more than three hundred years old, can you believe that?"

Mr. Ambrose was uncomfortable with the direction the conversation was going.

"Would you like a drink ma'am?" He wanted to change the subject.

"A good suggestion, have one yourself and bring the bottle".

He shivered again as he watched the cat jump on to her lap and begin washing its fur, its pink tongue licking off gobbets of congealed blood.

He hurried into the house.

"What to do my friend, what to do?' She said to the grimalkin. The cat paused its grooming and opened its mouth, as if silently meowing, showing blood stained teeth.

"Hmm! You could be right. And what of Mr. Ambrose and the brats?"

The cat once again moved its mouth.

"You have never him liked have you? But for the time being then, he does have his uses I know.

The brats though, we may no longer need them. What's that?"

"No, I do not need them alive. Living would be preferable, but I have done this before without a pentangle, just as I awoke Meg Shelton a few weeks ago. It would be easier I agree, to raise so many, but I am the necromancer and have the power to free my mother, grandmother and the others from their sleep".

The grimalkin gave the witch a look of adoration.

"Thank you and you are right of course, we will be unstoppable".

As the one-eyed cat preened itself, Auntie Vena licked the coagulated blood from her fingers.

36

The young constable had run from Fishergate Hill and was breathless when he reached the C.I.D. office.

"Sir, it's Miss Babbitt. She's bin taken", he blurted out to the detective inspector.

"What?"

"T' front door an' door t' 'er room 'ave both bin forced. She ain't there an' there's stuff all over t' place".

"Come wi' me lad. We're goin' t' speak t' neighbours. Sam, can yer organise a wagon t' tek us back there?" He may have sounded calm under the circumstances, but he feared the worse and knew who was behind this.

Two hours later the C.I.D. office was full of police personnel. Meadowbank had arranged this operation before he received the news of Mary's kidnap. It added to the urgency as far as he was concerned and he put the call out for every officer to return to duty and also those who were on their day off. An officer visited home addresses with an urgent request that police personnel to attend the police station by 11am.

He had briefed the chief constable, together with his chief superintendent and superintendent, of the danger facing the people of Preston. He made no mention of the word 'supernatural' as he still was not convinced of an 'evil entity' stalking the town's streets, and even if he was, this was not the time or place to introduce stories of the living dead. He said enough to convince his senior officers that Constable Button was either being held captive at "Hoarstones' or he had been murdered on the premises, and now Mary Babbitt had been abducted and was most certainly at the house as well, and any attempt to enter would be met with deadly resistance. Before he attended the briefing he had organised, Meadowbank rang Lytham Hall; he wanted to speak with Sir Roger. Eventually he spoke to Lady Vivian who informed him that her husband was working on the estate all day and not contactable.

He thought Lady Vivian sounded anxious, but then again, that is exactly how he felt.

The Detective Inspector had already sent two detectives, Collier and Huxley, to do a furtive reconnoitre of the perimeter of 'Hoarstones', but not to enter the premises or grounds under any circumstances. Both detectives were armed.

Chief Constable Major Little had persuaded the commanding officer at Fulwood Barracks, General Sir Richard Thomas Farren, to provide three sharp-shooters from the 1st Battalion, The Loyal North Lancashire Regiment.

Preston Borough Police Service had been mobilised like never before and the chief constable had put Inspector Meadowbank in operational charge, much to the visible chagrin of Superintendent Malone.

"Gentlemen, thank you for comin'". Meadowbank raised his voice for those at the back of the parade room, aware that Superintendent Malone had moved next to him. "This will be a short briefin', but you'll know what yer need t'know. Sometime in t' last twenty four hours, D.C. Paddy Button has gone missin' while engaged on 'ouse t' 'ouse enquiries on Moor Park Avenue. I've received information that t' occupants of an address Paddy was payin' attention to, namely 'Hoarstones', are implicated in an outstandin' murder an' three serious assaults in t' town. They are also plannin' or preparin' t' commit a serious crime at a stately 'ome in Lytham, roughly a dozen miles away. I believe these two suspects, an' there may be more, will resist arrest at any cost. Yer lookin' fer an elderly woman called Vena Demdike an' a giant of a man known only as Mr. Ambrose or Ambrose. We also believe Ambrose is responsible for t' kidnap of a woman called Mary Babbitt an' think she is bein' kept ont' premises as well. If you are confronted bi someone you suspect t' bi either Vena Demdike or Ambrose, for your own protection you must shoot first an' ask questions later...".

"What Inspector Meadowbank is saying", interjected Superintendent Malone, "Is simply use common sense. You cannot enter a house and start shooting the occupants at random".

"Thank you sir fer clearin' that up for mi. I was about t' say that two of mi detectives are already down there, 'avin' a look around, an' I've recently bin told that Paddy's 'aversack 'as bin found in t' ginnel at rear o' these premises. But there is no sign of 'is service revolver, so we must assume an occupant of that address 'as possession of Paddy's Webley and ammunition. They should now bi regarded as armed an' dangerous. Any questions afore wi get crackin'?"

As the assembled officers began to file out to where a number of transport wagons were waiting outside the station, Superintendent Malone turned to Meadowbank.

"Why was I not informed about Constable Button's haversack being found and the loss of a firearm? And what's this about a woman being kidnapped and held at the premises?"

"Yer wern't 'ere when I got t' messages". He gave the thumbs up to Sergeant Huggins who was waiting by the door. "This a fast developin' situation sir an' I 'ave t' bi able t' mek decisions wi' out worryin' abowt reportin' t' you. And as operational leader that is what I'm doin'".

"You may still be basking in the glory of the Ripper case, but do not think you can undermine my authority. You are running this show today, tomorrow you will not be, that I guarantee. I am your senior officer and you report to me, understood? And never put on another performance like you just did at my expense".

Meadowbank chose his words carefully. "I've got some news for yer Superintendent. This is not abowt me or you or yer bloody superiority, it's abowt findin' Paddy Button and Mary Babbitt alive

242

and if yer want t' know what's goin' on, do some bloody police work fer a change".

Not waiting for a reply, Meadowbank pushed past his superintendent and left the office with Huggins, their mounts, Bernadette and Floss already prepared and tethered in the stable yard by Young Ted.

Superintendent Malone had never been spoken to like that in his entire military or police career. Bristling with rage he hurried to his office, put on his greatcoat and cap and from the bottom drawer of his desk took out a leather holster and ammunition belt, removing the Colt .455 New Service Revolver. He breeched the sidearm, loaded the six chambers, re-holstered the weapon, then rushed downstairs, managing to scramble unceremoniously into the last open wagon trundling towards Lancaster Road.

The wagons rendezvoused at the north end of Moor Park Avenue. There were twenty five police officers and three military personnel. He sent twelve men, three carrying ladders and one sharp-shooter, to the rear of the property, where D.C. Huxley was waiting. The rest followed him to the main gates, meeting D.C. Collier, who had been keeping the house under observations from nearby. Meadowbank, holding the reins, walked Bernadette along Moor Park Avenue and in his free hand he held a length of heavy chain.

'Hoarstones' was its usual quiet self. Mr. Ambrose was in the stables hitching the two mares to the landau. He had given the four brats hot milk laced with a sleeping potion. That would keep them in a deep slumber for twenty four hours, even though Auntie Vena had decided they would not form part of the evening's ritual. But the blood of a virgin, no matter how young, could never be overestimated so Evergreen would transport them as arranged. Auntie Vena was getting restless, pacing the drawing room with an unease not experienced since entering Victor Von Frankenstein's laboratory. And where was the grimalkin?

The black cat was sitting in a tree, overlooking a mound of earth where Mr. Ambrose only yesterday filled in a large hole, but more importantly, the cat was watching the activity in the narrow road beyond the property.

Ladders had been placed against the wall and police officers began to climb over and jump into the long grass of the garden. The cat had seen enough and ran back to the house, ignoring the hyena laid in the undergrowth near to the yew trees, listening with interest to the sound of men whispering instructions and quietly spreading themselves in a line across the garden.

The black cat darted past the cooling cauldron under the verandah and through the open kitchen door. Auntie Vena was filling her tumbler when the cat jumped on to the sideboard.

She was immediately aware something was wrong.

The cat opened its mouth, which could have easily been mistaken for a yawn, but caused Auntie Vena to move with more haste than normal as she headed to the stables.

"Mr. Ambrose, we have a gathering of police officers in the garden and they intend entering the house. Stop them please".

Such an event to defend the house against intruders had been planned for and Mr. Ambrose knew exactly what action to take. He opened a large broom cupboard near the stalls which instead of housing brushes and bessums, stored a selection of rifles and handguns. From the armoury he chose a Lee Enfield rifle and a two barrelled Gardner machine gun, ready assembled on a tripod. It was heavy, but he soon had it positioned under the verandah, loaded and aimed across the garden.

The police line was cautious, moving slowly with weapons drawn, they had barely passed the dense line of yew trees, unaware they were being watched by a male striped hyena, normally shy and nocturnal.

Auntie Vena checked the front of the house from her bedroom window. As she moved the heavy curtain aside, the crash from beyond startled her as the iron gates, with chains wrapped round them and attached to Bernadette's harness were swiftly pulled off their hinges with a crash that shook the ground, and a small army of police officers rushed over the fallen ironwork, lead by Meadowbank.

How could this be happening?

But Auntie Vena knew what to do.

The Gardner machine gun, capable of firing five hundred rounds a minute, burst into life as Mr. Ambrose swept the two connected barrels from left to right and back, never taking his finger of the trigger. The noise was deafening to Mr. Ambrose and terrifying and deadly to the officers with no shelter or protection from the barrage of bullets. They did not have a chance and many were killed instantly, including one of the sharp-shooters from the Loyal North Lancashire Regiment. The surviving police officers had thrown themselves to the ground, the long grass hiding them, then Mr. Ambrose stopped to reload, allowing the smoke from burning gunpowder and the choking stink of cordite to dissipate under the glass roof.

During the relative quiet, the hyena seized its chance, the smell of blood saturating the air and the helpless screams of the dying driving the deranged beast into the open. As if stalking a herd of wildebeest, it kept low to the ground seeking the weakest amongst the mayhem and confusion; its large grey pointed ears and black nose soon detected its prey and moved silently through the shrubbery. The uniformed constable was close to death from two bullets lodged in his stomach, and as he lay helpless, facedown in the wet grass, he felt something grab his left foot, dragging him quickly under cover of the overhanging yew trees.

Others took advantage from the pause of the machine-gun fusillade and returned fire. Some shots were aimed, some completely random, but enough bullets ricocheted off the brickwork around Mr. Ambrose to make him dive for cover. Several constables, all recent recruits to the borough and veterans of the First Boer War, suddenly rose from the long grass as one and charged towards the house, firing their automatic Lee Enfield rifles on the run as they were trained to do, giving the enemy no opportunity to re-engage. Mr. Ambrose, a fighter who only used his fists and knives, had never encountered gunfire exchange before and crawled into the house as shattered window panes, brick dust and mortar showered over him. He quickly dragged a heavy Welsh dresser across the terracotta tiles to barricade the door. The charge along the rear garden continued and the surviving six officers, including D.C. Huxley, made it to the verandah, pressing themselves against the brickwork. Constable Herbert, a former infantry corporal, took command. Kicking the Gardner machine gun into a bed of nettles, he tried the kitchen door.

Bullets immediately smashed through the wood panels, forcing the constable to dash to one side.

Meadowbank had a haversack slung across one shoulder, it was similar to the one worn by D.C. Button, but the inspector's contained a couple of sticks of dynamite. The gunfight taking place at the rear of the house sounded like the battle of Armageddon and he could only guess at the chaos ensuing. As the inspector approached the double front doors he reached into the haversack, pulled out a red stick of explosive, lit the short fuse with a safety match and hurled it towards the doors, screaming, "Dynamite! Get down".

At that moment, Superintendent Malone entered the driveway and in disbelief shouted, "Meadowbank, have you gone mad?"

His colleagues flung themselves left and right as the oak doors erupted with a huge flash and explosion, showering the front of the house in splinters and chunks of oak, the blast knocking the superintendent onto his back.

Meadowbank got to his feet and brandishing his revolver, rushed inside the house called 'Hoarstones' with Huggins not far behind. It felt unnaturally cold and dark, every window hidden behind a heavy curtain and there was a stomach turning stench, a stench of decay and putrefaction causing Meadowbank to raise a hand to his mouth to stop him puking. As other officers piled in behind them, the inspector ordered the curtains be opened and the two sharp-shooters position themselves either side of the house. The rest split into four-man teams to search the house from top to bottom. Three nervous constables stayed in the driveway, with no idea what the hell was happening, and one of them calming Bernadette, at the same time unhitching the chain.

Auntie Vena glided downstairs like a shadow to the stables, effortlessly pulling herself into the driver's seat of her landau and the black cat jumped next to her, as if setting off for a day at Blackpool beach. The two Thoroughbred mares sensing the urgency noisily stomped their iron shod hooves on the stone floor, whinnying and feistily nodding their heads, foam flecking at their mouth bits. With a flick of the reins the horses surged forward, the stable doors smoothly opening before them as the horse and carriage rushed onto the driveway like a chariot entering the Roman Coliseum. The horses leapt over the fallen iron gates and Superintendent Malone would swear the horses and carriage were off the ground, flying, as they passed him.

With both hands gripping the Webley revolver, Meadowbank pointed the gun to his front, entering the dark drawing room, the laden coal fire giving off a near unbearable heat in contrast to the icy chill of the hallway. At the same time Mr. Ambrose, out of breath, hurried into the drawing room from the kitchen and both men froze at the sight of each other. Meadowbank recognised him instantly.

37

Before the procession arrived at the clearing, John Isles met Sir Roger and confirmed the area was safe. Sir Roger received this information with caution, after all it was Halloween, a time each year he felt trepidation, and today brought foreboding. He would finish the undertaking his ancestor and namesake started nearly three centuries ago. Sir Roger had been unable to find any recorded entry of a Vena Demdike in the volumes of handwritten parish records of births, marriages and deaths, for any of the villages around the Forest of Pendle, but concluded she must be a near descendant of Old Mother Demdike, the figure head and most powerful of the Lancashire Witches.

One thing he was now certain of, there were two Demdikes buried in Witch Wood, along with James and Alison Device, Old Chattox and her daughters Elizabeth and Anne, Alice Nutter and Katherine Hewitt. And this Halloween, Vena Demdike was to resurrect them all. He intended to stop that from happening.

The six grave-diggers inspected the nine mounds and agreed that there had already been a partial excavation of the graves before they had been refilled, leaving neat mounds of earth. Sir Roger split half the men into nine teams overseen by the grave-diggers, the remaining men stood guard around the site. After half an hour of digging the news was not good.

"They are all buried at least ten feet deep. It will take longer, even with ropes. Whoever dug these holes knew what they were doing", the head grave-digger from Saint Cuthbert's informed Sir Roger. "If they knew what they were doing, these sleeping monsters would have been burned at the stake centuries ago". He checked his pocket watch. "It's ten o'clock, so we have eight hours of daylight to finish this, we need to press on".

Several of the farm labourers were ex-navvies and even though they were getting on in years, they could still work a spade or shovel with impressive results. Their eagerness to dig out the coffins was simply a reflection of their motives, the sooner they got the job done, the sooner they could get to the ale-house, their favourite being The Trawl Boat Inn on Heyhouses Lane, as it was on the edge of the marsh away from the townsfolk.

After a few hours all nine coffins were exposed at the bottom of deep holes. Sir Roger looked at each one, his heart racing as if driven by a steam engine, sweat feeling clammy under his silk shirt and woollen jacket. Ladders had been lowered into each hole, resting on the coffin lid, allowing two men to descend into each grave and feed a rope under both ends of the coffin. Sir Roger decided to exhume the coffins one at a time and as the men climbed out of the first grave and removed the ladder, he gave a nod for them to start pulling the ropes. Eight men heaved on the four lengths of rope and almost immediately the coffin began to rise, loose dirt dropping noisily onto the lid as if attempting to warn the occupant what was afoot.

As the coffin base was more or less level with the ground, four eight-foot poles were manoeuvred underneath. The coffin was now resting on the lengths of wood and Sir Roger could only stare at the wooden casket, fully exposed to daylight for the first time in nearly three hundred years.

It was a similar style to Meg Shelton's box, a pauper's casket of rough sawn planks nailed together and several fixed across the length, forming a lid. One of the diggers remarked that it seemed solid for something that had been in the ground so long. The wood had discoloured to a seasoned brown, there were no damp patches, but in the gaps between the planks, insects and worms emerged at the sudden intrusion. At another signal from Sir Roger, the coffin was dragged onto solid ground and a labourer brandishing a crow-bar began prising the inch thick planks at one end. The four-inch nails showed no evidence of rust or deterioration, screeching as the wood was forced apart. He worked his way around the oblong box, loosening the outer planks then grabbing an edge, he gave a sudden tug, pulling free the first length of wood, throwing it to one side. The remaining three pieces came away with less effort, revealing the body of a man.

"Good God! It's not possible", exclaimed Sir Roger. "That must be the body of James Device. It looks like he was buried three weeks ago, not three centuries ago".

The corpse of James Device had not decomposed at all. With his hands and long fingernails across his chest, eyes closed and a full head of hair, shoulder length as if it was still growing, the corpse looked anything but dead. His skin was like albumen, there were no sores, no weeping pustules, no desiccated cadaver or even crumbling bones, but a man in hibernation. The six professional grave-diggers and their former navvie counterparts exchanged nervous glances. Exhumed corpses do not look like that, and the notion of visiting The Trawl Boat Inn immediately disappeared. The unease amongst the men was palpable and spreading, the mutterings of disbelief getting louder, many blessing themselves with the sign of the cross and quite a few coming to the decision that there was a need to leave this makeshift graveyard immediately.

Sir Roger had to act fast to keep his men in a mind to disinter the remaining eight coffins.
With his good arm he picked up one of the tin cans of paraffin, sloshing the liquid over James Device, placing two faggots of branches on top of the body then lit a safety match, tossing it onto the pyre. There was a whoosh as the paraffin ignited, the dry kindling erupting into flames and seconds later James Device sat bolt upright, screaming, with his burning arms and hands, charred and blistered, holding the edge of the coffin he heaved himself to his feet attempting to climb out. John Isles rushed forward with a pitchfork and thrust it through the

253

flames, forcing the burning James Device back into the inferno. A hundred men watched in silence, witnessing the impossible, as thick smoke and the stench of burning flesh wafted across the clearing, the sorcerer in the coffin no longer visible within the flames.

Sir Roger called out, "You have seen what we are up against. There are eight more of these creatures, the living dead, the undead, monsters, call them what you will, but after midnight tonight on Halloween, these things will rise and walk the earth to do the work of the devil. We must destroy them. I cannot do it on my own, I need your help. Are you with me?"

There was a near unanimous cry of "Yes" and raising of clench fists as Sir Roger walked to the next grave and the gamekeeper removed the pitchfork from the smouldering remains.

38

Mr. Ambrose reacted quicker than Meadowbank. Reaching inside his jacket, he pulled out a throwing knife and in one movement slung it across the room, the razor sharp blade embedding in Sergeant Huggin's chest. The police officer staggered back, dropping his pistol as he crashed against the wall.

"Sam!" Meadowbank cried, firing off two rounds, but Mr. Ambrose had already made it to the cellar door, wrenching it open.

Huggins was still breathing, eyes open, his chest heaving as he made slow deep gasps.

"Albert, get t' bastard for mi". He said it as if it was a dying wish.

"Don't worry about that. 'E's as good as dead". Meadowbank then called over his shoulder. "Wi need a doctor in 'ere quick".

Superintendent Malone entered the drawing room, followed by several constables.
He knelt by the sergeant and gave Meadowbank a worried look. There was banging on the door blocked by the Welsh dresser and D.C. Huxley was looking through the window. Three constables shoved the dresser to one side, opening the door onto the verandah.

Doctor Bayers pushed his way in to the room. "Doc, down 'ere. It's Sam, 'e's in a bad way".

Meadowbank shouted. He and the superintendent moved away as Archie Bayers took charge.

"Ambrose went behind that door sir". Meadowbank said to his superintendent. "I suspect it leads t' cellar".

Superintendent Malone did not reply, he was distracted. Looking through the open door and across the garden he caught sight of the dead officers lying in the long grass.

"Good God! What the hell are we dealing with?" he said to Ned Huxley who was standing by the door. "Is there anyone alive out there?"

"Six of us made it, seven are dead sir", Ned Huxley replied quietly.

The superintendent walked onto the verandah and as he tried to count the fallen in disbelief, he did not see the hyena dash through the undergrowth towards the house. Meadowbank sent D.C. Huxley and the five constables to assist with the search upstairs for Detective Constable Button and Mary Babbitt, leaving the superintendent alone. The crazed animal was striding faster and with its head low it locked its sights on the lone figure standing on the verandah. The hyena appeared from nowhere as it raced up the steps, snarling, teeth bared and eyes narrowed, it was seconds from striking.

Already it had targeted major blood vessels around the neck, its favourite point of attack.

Superintendent Malone saw it too late. Transfixed with terror he could only watch the beast leaping towards him, the firearm he held useless by his side.

Two shots, deafening under the glass roof, blasted behind the superintendent. Meadowbank, stood with legs shoulder width apart, arms outstretched holding the Webley service revolver in both hands, took aim as he pulled the trigger twice, sending two rounds travelling at six hundred and twenty feet per second into the head of the hyena, killing it instantly. The animal collapsed at the feet of Superintendent Malone, its head obliterated. The ashen officer turned towards Meadowbank, acknowledging him with a nod of the head. He was splattered with fur, flesh and bones.

"Sir, are you okay?"

He nodded his head again.

"I'm going after Ambrose. Sam is on his way to hospital, so I need back up. Can you do it sir?"

The superintendent exhaled loudly, as he looked at the dead hyena and what was left of its head resting on his right boot.

"Lead the way Inspector". He did not sound convincing.

The black painted wooden cellar door opened outwards and Superintendent Malone stood to one side, pointing his revolver at the ever widening gap. Meadowbank reloaded his side-arm and was the first to enter the darkness waiting for them.

Stone steps descended, but it was impossible to see where they ended or what was beyond. The inspector produced his flashlight and found a candle-lamp hanging from the ceiling. Meadowbank lit the candle and handed the lantern to Superintendent Malone and together they made the descent, both of them aware of the unmistakable smell of human waste breezing over them, as the stench headed for the open door.

On reaching the bottom of the steps, Meadowbank found another lantern fixed to the wall and lit that. The curved whitewashed ceiling was high enough for the inspector to stand upright and the bare brick walls made the six-foot wide passageway seem narrower. It felt cold and damp. The passageway opened out to a room-sized area and as the torch beam swept across the right hand wall, rows of metal bars from floor to ceiling were revealed.

The superintendent moved forwards with the lantern, illuminating six gaol cells.

"Bloody 'ell! These are dungeons". Meadowbank exclaimed, and shone his flash light through the bars. In the corner of the first cell, a young girl was curled up on a wooden bed. She seemed to be asleep and did not respond when the light hit her face. The cell measured no more than six foot square, the stone floor was strewn with straw and two metal buckets were pushed against the wall. These were makeshift toilets and where the stink was coming from.

Meadowbank tugged at the locked gate.

"Oy, love. We're police officers", he called out.

"I suspect she will be Mary Scott, the missing lass from the Shambles", offered Superintendent Malone.

Meadowbank agreed, shouting, "Mary!, Mary!"

There was no movement from the girl. The inspector and superintendent exchanged a worried look. They moved to the next cell and it was identical, but a boy, who could not have been older than eleven was laid on his back on a wooden bed. They did not recognise Arnold Swann, the butcher's son. He too, appeared to be asleep, confirmed by his gentle breathing. There was no bedding and he was still wearing the same clothes as when he was kidnapped two weeks earlier. One of the two buckets by the wall was overflowing.

The next two cells each contained a young boy, Gilbert Randall and Talbot Webb, in equally squalid confinement. Not one of the four children moved when Meadowbank attempted to wake them.

The last two cells were empty, which brought little relief to the officers. More beams of flashlight approached from the steps, accompanied by voices echoing along the passageway. Meadowbank was glad to see D.C. Huxley and four uniformed constables.

"Ned, you lads, we need doctors down 'ere urgently an' locksmiths. We've found t' four kids, they seem t' bi unconscious. Get some lightin' down 'ere as well. I'm going after Ambrose. What are you doin' sir? Stopping 'ere till 'elp arrives?"

"No Inspector, I'm coming with you. We still need to find Constable Button".

"And Mary Babbitt". Meadowbank added quickly.

They carried on through the cellar, searching every nook and dark corner in the event Mr. Ambrose was waiting in ambush. They passed the coal bunker with a man-hole cover allowing slivers of daylight to pierce the gloom and then arrived at another set of steps going up. This was a wooden staircase and had obviously been built recently.

Meadowbank went first, still pointing his gun forward and the superintendent climbed the steps sideways, covering the rear, should someone charge at them from a hiding place. The door at the top was unlocked and as the inspector opened it slowly, he heard movement beyond and the noise of an engine start up. He shoved the door open, finding himself in a stable block with smoke swirling around and the engine noise seeming to accelerate as a horseless carriage drove from the stables. He chased after it, with the superintendent close behind, the vehicle crossing the fallen iron gates without any difficulty, then turning right onto Moor Park Avenue.

The horseless carriage, a Daimler, had picked up speed along the arrow straight avenue leaving white smoke trailing behind, but Meadowbank was able to recognise the driver.

He took aim and fired three shots with his handgun, without any realistic hope of hitting a target moving away at twenty miles per hour, obscured by exhaust fumes. He then spotted one of the sharp-shooters from the Lancashire Regiment, who had run towards the gunfire.

"Corporal, the man driving that horseless carriage is wanted for murder. I am authorising you to shoot to kill. Can you do it from 'ere?"

The corporal, without replying to the inspector, immediately took aim with his Lee-Enfield rifle fitted with a telescopic sight. He adjusted the magnification of the scope as the open top Daimler approached the junction with Deepdale Road.

Meadowbank held his breath he knew within seconds the carriage would disappear from view.

The corporal, a veteran of the First Boer War, held the rifle as he had been trained, leaning forward on his left leg to absorb the recoil and to keep the rifle steady. He pulled the trigger once, then looked up as he watched the Daimler swerve to the left onto the grassland of Moor Park, narrowly avoiding colliding with a tree before it came to a stop.

The inspector, superintendent and corporal stood in a group, watching the Daimler carriage remain motionless several hundred yards away, with the driver slumped forward onto the steering wheel.

"Nice shot Corporal. Looks like you've got 'im", Meadowbank said with relief.

"I know I definitely hit him sir", he paused as he peered through the telescopic sight. "But I don't think it has stopped him, he's still moving, whoever he is".

As if to confirm this, the Daimler lurched forward, accelerating erratically across the grassy terrain towards Fulwood. The sharp-shooter took aim again and fired. He brought his rifle down and shook his head. "Missed! It's no good. Too many trees for a clear shot".

With his right arm Mr. Ambrose kept control of the Daimler horseless carriage as it pitched across the parkland, despite the bullet lodged in his back.

He knew his injury was critical. Fighting the pain he had one thought, get to the graves, Auntie Vena needed him. He manoeuvred the vehicle onto Blackpool Road, pushed the accelerator pedal as far as it would go and hoped a full tank of fuel would to get him to Lytham.

"We cannot let him escape. I must organise a manhunt immediately", Superintendent Malone said anxiously, looking round for officers to deploy.

"No need sir. I know where Ambrose and Vena Demdike are 'eading". Meadowbank replied with confidence.

"And where is that?"

"Lytham 'all. They 'ave unfinished business there an' I suspect that's where we'll find Mary an' Paddy. At least I 'ope so, an' Sir Roger will need all t' 'elp 'e can get".

"Well let's crack on Inspector".

"Can you 'andle an 'orse at speed?"

"That is a not question you need ask of me. I trained as a Dragoon".

"In that case sir, you can tek Sam's 'orse, Floss. She can be an' 'andful, but she's a big strong un".

As they hurried towards the horses, Meadowbank turned to the sharp-shooter.

"Corporal, tell my lads we've gone t' Lytham t' carry on with t' search fer Paddy and Mary. An' tell Detective Ned 'uxley, he's now in charge".

39

The black landau thundered along Blackpool Road, the two Thoroughbred mares galloping like never before. Auntie Vena held the reins equal to any accomplished coach driver, the black cloak she wore billowing behind her, resembling a chasing banshee. The grimalkin, sitting next to the witch, dug its claws into the leather seat.

As the carriage approached the turnpike at The Lea Inn, the gates were closed and the turnpike warden looked alarmed at the speed of the oncoming carriage and fury of the horses as they got nearer. Clearly they would not stop in time.

The warden dived to one side as the horses leapt over the four foot high gate, pulling the landau over the barrier with them. He laid on the ground, breathless, watching the carriage career and glide along the tarmacadam road taking the left fork following the Clifton Marsh Road.

Auntie Vena was changing. Her once distinguished white hair, pulled back into a tight bun had dropped forward, no longer strands of hair, but sheafs, like straw, dancing in the wind. The mask she had used for so long was disappearing more with each mile nearer to the graves she travelled. A ridge of excrescence protuberances framed her face, and hard and crustated warts on her jutting chin and nose displayed coarse bristles. Her hands clutching the reins were once again gnarled and ancient as if arthritic, and her eyes for so long an alluring steely blue, turned green and reptilian. As the sun approached the horizon where the Ribble estuary met the darkening sky, the witch cracked the reins, spurring on the two mares, and the grimalkin leant into the wind, ears back, giving the witch an occasional look as if urging her on.

The carriage sped through the villages of Freckleton and Warton, approaching the parish boundary of Lytham: around the same time Mr. Ambrose approached The Lea Inn turnpike. The warden, shaken by witnessing a large carriage fly over the turnpike gate, now believing it was a phantom horse and carriage, had dragged Dick, his protesting subordinate, from his refreshment break in the pub, and both men stood in front of the closed gate watching a horseless carriage with smoke billowing from the exhaust, stop a few yards away. Mr. Ambrose stepped from the vehicle and without acknowledging the two gatekeepers, walked towards the gate.

"Oy! You. What d' yer think yer doin'? It's a tanner t' open t' gate", shouted Basil the senior warden holding aloft a glowing red lantern.

Mr. Ambrose unlatched the handle, and with a single push, the heavy gate swung silently open. The exertion making him gasp, and he ignored the bloody palm print he left on the white painted gate. The two wardens looked at each other in disbelief. "Who does this big oaf think 'e is?" Basil said to Dick, his number two. They approached Mr.

Ambrose who was now heading back to the Daimler carriage.

"Ey! What t' 'ell are yer playin' at? There is no right o' free passage along this road, yer 'ave t' pay six pennies, so pay up or we'll 'ave t' law onto yers", Basil called out, still marching towards the man, accompanied by Dick.

He pulled a revolver from a shoulder holster and pointed it at the two wardens.

"Whooaa! There's no need for that, is there?" Basil protested, as both men immediately put their arms in the air, but Basil had more to say. "Now listen 'ere you. You cannot go round behavin' like this, you 'ave a duty t' pay the toll an' if I wer ten years younger I'd thrash a flamin' tanner out of yer".

Mr. Ambrose fired a shot over their shoulders, smashing a window in the toll house, and both ducked instinctively.

"I haven't got any money, okay?" Mr. Ambrose informed them quietly.

"Well why didn't yer say so int' first place then? I'll give yers an IOU for t' next time yer passin' through", said Basil, just wishing this mad man would go away as soon as possible. "In fact, forget the IOU, you just carry on yer journey compliments of The Lea Gate Turnpike Company".

Mr. Ambrose kept the gun pointing at the two wardens as he got back behind the steering wheel then accelerated along Blackpool Road, leaving the gatekeepers waving away the choking exhaust smoke.

"Dick, this never 'appened, alright? You know I 'ate doin' paperwork".

His number two started to walk back to the inn.

"Where d' ya think you're goin'?"

"Back t' mi pint".

"Oh no yer not. You can pull that gate to fer a start and then you can stay 'ere wi me, in case that nutter decides to come back".

A few minutes later the sound of galloping horses approaching the turnpike from Preston, spurred Basil into action.

"Right, leave this t' me. I'll sort 'em out", he said confidently to Dick.

His number two was quite happy with this arrangement and remained where he was, hands in pockets, as his boss strode to the front of the gate, adopting a stance which he had found successful over the years: feet apart, right hand held above the head, palm of the hand facing forward accompanied with the command "Stop", and waving the lantern from side to side with his other hand.

Basil felt he needed to regain his credibility in the eyes of his less senior gatekeeper and intended to demonstrate a text book example of collecting tolls. He again called out. "Stop", adding, "Present yourselves".

The two horsemen pulled their glistening horses up a few yards from the man blocking their way.

"What is the meaning of this? Can you not see I am a police officer?" Superintendent Malone protested.

"Police must pay the toll like everyone else. That's six pence each, a shilling altogether".

The superintendent looked across at Meadowbank as if he was hearing things. The inspector shrugged his shoulders.

"We are both senior police officers, I am wearing a superintendent's uniform for Christ's sake! We are on official business and you are wilfully obstructing us in the execution of our duty. Now open that bloody gate immediately".

"Do you have written authority from a chief police officer, exempting you from the toll charge?"

"I am a chief police officer you idiot and we are in pursuit of a criminal. I am not going to ask you again, open that gate now".

Meadowbank turned Bernadette around, walked the horse back a hundred feet, then turning to face the warden he jabbed Bernadette with his heels causing her to rear up, before the inspector urged her on. She was soon at full gallop and jumped the gate as if rider and horse were on the final hurdle of the Grand National. The superintendent was impressed and decided to do the same. Even if he was not sure about his own ability to stay in the saddle, he was certain Floss would get them both over. Basil and Dick watched as another horse and rider leapt the gate without paying the toll. Basil said wearily, "Go an' finish yer pint, an' this never 'appened either".

40

She was no longer Auntie Vena.

The witch had returned to what she always was, a Demdike, The Necromancer, Queen of All Cunning Folk and Sorceress of the Unknown Realms of Darkness. The witch stood in the driver's footwell, balancing without any difficulty, snapping the reins as horses and carriage hurtled nearer to Witch Wood. The smell of the Demdikes was stronger, it filled the air and she knew that the only two coffins she wanted had been uprooted and the witch finder was with them. The witch had morphed, like an amniotic reptile shedding skin. She had cast her mortal being. Now eight feet tall, and hideous she bellowed, with rage into the rushing wind, "Noooo!". No more woollen tartan skirts, cashmere sweaters or polished brogues; instead foul black ankle length attire billowed, exposing three long toes with ink coloured talons, covered in grey horny scales up to her ankles as she demanded more from her horses.

The landau approached the driveway to Lytham Hall. The two huge iron gates were locked with a dozen armed men stood behind, guarding the entrance. Suddenly the ornate gates flew high into the darkening sky, with a screech of rupturing metal, as if a hurricane had passed through. The guards ran for cover as the carriage streaked past.

Some of them had the presence of mind to discharge their weapons at the intruder, but most looked to the sky waiting for the heavy gates to come crashing down, but they had disappeared into the night completely.

The witch fixed her dark green eyes, the colour of pondweed, on the meandering driveway in front, thrusting her hooked nose and her jutting chin into the turbulence. She knew she was very close.

Didier Pascall and his platoon of mercenaries heard the gunshot coming from the gatehouse. He walked down the steps of the great hall, gripping a double barrelled shotgun and called out to those around him.

"Messieurs, I think you are about to earn your money".

At least fifty men lined the tarmacadam drive at the front of the hall, a formidable group, armed and ready, with some battle hardened veterans feeling unusually nervous. The Frenchman stood at the forefront, and already he was aiming his shotgun towards the bend in the driveway.

The black landau appeared from the slight bend as the Hall came into view, pristine white railings either side, and the Frenchman fired the first shot, followed by a fusillade of gunfire bombarding the horses and carriage.

The witch soared upwards and hovering like a raptor seeking prey, cast her right hand down as if throwing a dice. Didier Pascall instantly exploded into nothing, vaporised, moments before his men were engulfed in a fireball. The grounds at the front of the ancient hall exploded, as if a meteorite had struck, shattering windows, melting paintwork and obliterating most of Sir Roger's hired help.

She plummeted back to the carriage, which was still charging towards Witch Wood, the two Thoroughbred mares never missing a stride as the witch landed like a circus acrobat, standing once again in the footwell. She left the reins alone, the horses needed no further encouragement, instead she whispered her thanks. She had no names for these chargers that had been with her for so long, none were necessary, they came when summoned by the Demdike. The woodland appeared in the dwindling light and the witch was ready.

* * *

The Daimler horseless carriage came to a dismal stop near to the windmill and boathouse on Lytham Green. Mr. Ambrose knew what the problem was, the contraption had run out of fuel. Even though it was early evening, the beach road was quiet and some of the facing villas, with curtains still open were already discreetly lit like it was early Christmas morning, and Southport across the estuary was an illuminated shorefront.

Mr. Ambrose was planning on stealing some other transport, so loitered nonchalantly like a Venus flytrap, knowing he was not too far from the grave site.

The injury from the bullet wound was becoming worse by the minute and many men would have curled up and died from the pain, a pain that only a surgeon with a scalpel and plenty of morphine could help relieve. Leaning against the Daimler he waited, closing his eyes and folding his arms, gripping D.C. Button's revolver, and ignoring the muffled groans coming from the rear seats.

Several minutes later Meadowbank and Superintendent Malone brought their horses to a stop a good distance from the horseless carriage. They could see Mr. Ambrose with his vehicle.
He was watching them.

Superintendent Malone proposed the legitimacy of shooting the fugitive in the head from here. He had a rifle and was confident he could take the shot from a hundred and fifty yards away.

"There's somert not reet about this sir. Just 'old fire, I'm goin' t' tek a look".

"You have to be the bloody hero don't you? Barge in where fools fear to tread, that's you all over Inspector".

Meadowbank held his breath for a second. "We still 'ave not found Mary or Paddy. Ambrose knows where they are. If 'e's dead we'll never find 'em. We 'aven't time t' argue abowt this sir. You're t' senior officer, your decision".

"You take a look then and I'll cover you, but it could be a trap", he said to regain authority.
The sun was disappearing for the night, silhouetting the Snowdonia mountains beyond as Meadowbank walked slowly towards the Daimler. Keeping his finger on the trigger of his revolver he was about a hundred yards away when Mr. Ambrose called out,

"That's far enough Inspector. What I want you to do now is walk back and bring your horses to me".

Meadowbank did not reply, but continued walking forwards. Mr. Ambrose reached into the rear of the Daimler, ignoring the searing pain the effort took and grabbed a handful of blonde hair, pulling Mary Babbitt to her knees on the rear seat. Her hands and feet were tied and mouth gagged.

He let go of her hair, then pointed the revolver to Mary's head. Meadowbank froze and even from where he was, could see she was terrified.

"Do as I say or sweet Mary is dead. I will not ask you again". He was struggling to speak, and released his grip to pull the gag aside, the gun still in his other hand.

He said to Mary. "Tell lover boy to bring the horses over".

Without hesitation she sank her teeth into his wrist.

"You stupid bitch". He snatched his arm away and thumbed the trigger back.

This was the only distraction Meadowbank needed. He ran towards the Daimler with his right arm extended, aiming his Webley sidearm. He fired two shots in quick succession, never missing a stride as he carried on running towards Mary.

The first shot hit Mr. Ambrose in the forehead. The bullet did not penetrate the back of his skull, instead released kinetic energy that scrambled his brain to a mush in an instant. Even though he was dead, Mr. Ambrose defied gravity and remained standing, swaying slightly, still pointing the gun at

Mary, until the second shot hit him a split second later, going straight through his neck, the force sending him toppling to the grass.

Meadowbank lifted the sobbing Mary from the carriage and, producing a knife from an ankle sheath, cut through the cord around her wrists and ankles, then held her as she collapsed into his arms. Superintendent Malone approached with the horses and examined the dead man.

"Nice work Inspector". Acknowledging Mary Babbitt he said, "You are safe now madam. Do you need a doctor?"

She shook her head.

"Mary, this doesn't end 'ere. We need t' get t' Lytham 'all an' 'elp Sir Roger. You can either ride wi' me or stay 'ere till 'elp arrives". Meadowbank hated doing this.

"You can see for yoursel' I'm still wearin' mi nightdress and it's filthy an' I've nowt on mi feet. I can't get on an 'orse wearing this. I'll 'ave t' wait 'ere". She was indignant, but too composed, too logical considering a psychopath was pointing a loaded gun to her head only a minute earlier. Then she suddenly collapsed in a swoon as her legs gave way. Meadowbank managed to grab her and laid her onto the back seat of the Daimler. He retrieved the gun from Mr. Ambrose's hand and placed it by Mary's side. More lights came on and front doors opened as residents and servants responded to the gunfire and activity a few yards away on the green. Meadowbank called out to them. "We're police officers. A woman is injured, we need help. We need blankets".

An elderly couple cautiously approached them from their three-story house. The man was wearing black trousers and braces over his collarless blue shirt, puffing on an after dinner Havana. His wife, ready to retire, was dressed in a dark pink silk dressing gown in a William Morris thistle print and matching slippers. They seemed eager to help.

"Be careful. There's a dead fugitive here at the scene. But you are quite safe, be assured of that". Superintendent Malone crossed East Beach to speak with them. "The young lady in the horseless carriage has had a terrible ordeal, a life threatening ordeal in fact and my colleague and I need to pursue another suspect without delay. Can we leave Mary with you, until more police officers and a doctor arrives?" his Irish tones emphasising the seriousness of his request.

The couple took reassurance from the superintendent's manner and uniform of rank complete with the braided cap that he was still wearing and the Lee-Enfield rifle he held. The lady in the pink dressing gown gave an exaggerated wave towards the sea-facing houses, trying to attract the attention of her maid, but other residents watching with interest took it as a signal they had been waiting for, and a stream of men, women and children crowded onto Lytham Green gathering around the Daimler machine, some just nosey neighbours, many offering assistance and hot drinks, showing genuine concern for Mary who was still out cold on the leather seat. A few of the men carried shotguns, taking up sentry positions. The sight of Mr. Ambrose's body and armed police had unnerved them.

The two officers had no time to lose and climbed back onto Bernadette and Floss, riding through the side streets as if it was the charge of the Light Brigade and onto Ballam Road, where the gatehouse was illuminated in the distance.

The work at the cleared site was taking too long, as far as Sir Roger was concerned. The lengthening shadows would soon give way to darkness and John Isles, with helpers, had made a bonfire, ready to set ablaze for when extra lighting was needed.

Extracting some of the coffins had proved more difficult than others, resulting in more digging and the removal of earth using buckets and pulleys. Seven coffins had been opened and the corpse-like occupants, dormant in peaceful slumber, were abruptly awoken with the searing heat of a conflagration within the coffin. As much as they screamed and writhed, the flames were too consuming and very quickly they were nothing but charred bones, bubbling body fats and smoking tissue fluids never found in any human body. One witch, still resembling the teenager she was on the day of her hanging and burial, managed to escape her burning coffin and stand on solid ground, despite being ablaze from head to foot. It was quick thinking by a gravedigger who used a shovel to push the shrieking witch back into the inferno.

Sir Roger looked down at the two remaining coffins. One contained an old woman, the other a younger woman. He did not know he was giving his attention to Old Mother Demdike and her daughter, Elizabeth, resting in calm repose, ignorant of the holocaust taking place around them. Eye-watering black smoke and the stink of charred rotten meat swirled throughout the clearing and many men coughed and wretched from the noxious fumes.

It was a vision of hell. Coffins blazed, pouring out more poisonous smoke, which seemed to hang within the surrounding trees, despite the sea breeze, and the screams from the once torpid witches rose and fell in volume. Even Dante in his epic poem could never have imagined such a spectacle.

The last two sleeping witches were soaked in paraffin and the tied bundles of kindling piled on top them as John Isles prepared himself to despatch the last creatures back to Hades.

An ear-splitting thunderclap, like an airborne gun powder explosion, caused everyone to look to the sky in surprise, as the clouds were not threatening rain, let alone a thunderstorm. A howling wind came from nowhere, and this was not the prevailing southerly, but a powerful wind, as if the tropics had released a wayward monsoon. Trees bent and snapped, and the last autumn leaves were sucked into the whirlwind. Sir Roger scanned the woodland around the clearing, feeling very uneasy as the gusting wind blasted his face, making breathing difficult and sending the black smoke into crazy spirals. Ignoring the sharp pain from his shoulder, he touched the howdah pistol holstered around his waist, for reassurance and then moved his hand to the Very pistol on the other side.

****

Meadowbank and the superintendent arrived at the gates to Lytham Hall, passing through the destruction at a canter, before their horses increased to a gallop for the remaining mile. The fire at the front of the hall was still raging and some of the few survivors had unrolled hosepipes attempting to keep the blaze away from the house.

It was now early evening and the night was proper. One of the men tackling the fire pointed the way to Witch Wood and where Sir Roger would be found.

Meadowbank knew both horses were exhausted and it was incredible Bernadette and Floss had got them this far, but there was no time to spare, they needed the horses to push themselves for another mile.

* * *

As the landau approached the bend at Witch Wood, where wagons and horses had been left and tethered, the witch launched herself from the carriage, allowing the Thoroughbred mares to continue their dash through the grounds.

The Demdike surged through the woodland, unleashing a cyclonic wind which Mother Nature could never produce. Thunder boomed overhead and the storm gathered strength. The witch burst into the clearing and then froze at the sight of the burning coffins.

"No! No, no, no, no…", she roared, taking in the destruction.

At the far side, she saw Sir Roger standing near the two coffins waiting to be lit. She knew instantly who he was.

"Witch-finder! Stand back from those coffins". The witch's voice boomed like the overhead thunder. She extended her right arm, pointing her index finger at Sir Roger, as if she was accusing him of a terrible crime. He immediately shot backwards with a force similar to being struck in the stomach by a discharged cannonball, his head hitting a tree stump with a worrying crack, rendering him unconscious. John Isles, witnessing Sir Roger's plight, rushed towards the coffins eager to strike a bundle of matches, when he too was lifted off his feet and catapulted headfirst into the adjacent coffin which was a raging bonfire. His clothing immediately ignited and the can of paraffin he held exploded like a bomb, the flames from the pyre engulfing him within seconds as he thrashed about on top of the already immolated witch.

The eight foot monster levitated with purpose across the clearing, pointing randomly at the fleeing workforce, each one erupting in spontaneous combustion. The witch reached the coffins and began to gently remove the faggots of wood from one in particular, until the sleeping face was visible.

"Mother, we shall soon be together. It has been too long", she croaked.

"At last, the Demdikes shall be a family again. I am putting things right mother, like you asked all those years ago. Soon we can all take revenge on the mortals".

Elizabeth Demdike did not answer, she was not expected to, the hibernation was far too deep. She was not surrounded by a silk or satin lining but rough wood, dirt and crawling subterranean life. She lay in the coffin like Morpheus, with her arms by her side, her wavy brown hair swept back from her face, and her eyes closed as if waiting for a handsome prince to arrive. There was no gentle rise and fall of her chest indicating life, but her face said otherwise. She was pale, her skin soft, unblemished, her lips still pink, the mark around her neck from the hangman's noose visible, red and raw.

The brown threadbare dress was the only one she owned, and the witch recognised it immediately and the crude boots, homemade from horse hide. She smiled, remembering the happy times at Malkin Towers and how she always looked forward to All Hallows' Eve and the gathering, playing hide and seek with the grimalkin, which always won.

She inhaled, breathing in her mother's very essence.

The witch moved to the other coffin and discarded the fuel soaked wood piled on top of her latent grandmother.

Stooping between the coffins, like an embalmer appraising clients, she knelt, tears in her eyes as she stroked the emollient faces of her dear family.

"It will soon be time", she whispered.

The inspector and superintendent arrived at the bend in the road, tethering their weary horses with the others. Both officers could taste the sulphurous smoke which seemed to be everywhere, eye-stinging, thick and choking. The path in front of them was no longer a narrow deer track. The trampling of a hundred men had widened it, but what lay before them was an avenue wide clearing of demolished trees and flattened undergrowth leading deep into the woods, as if a herd of elephant had stampeded through. The officers set off on foot in silence, following the path of destruction, and all too aware of the howling wind around them.

They hurried along the path, listening to the distant screams getting louder. Men were running towards them. The first few ran past Meadowbank and Superintendent Malone with pure terror on their faces. The inspector grabbed an arm of a man who was sprinting by.

"What t' 'ell are yer runnin' from?"

"What? You have to get away from here. It's huge, a monster from hell". He pulled his arm free and ran like his life depended it.

The police officers did not say a word to each other, instead they continued walking against the gale force wind, towards the thickening black smoke. More men, carrying weapons, ran past without any acknowledgement, as if they had not seen the officers in their eagerness to flee.

Nothing could have prepared the two officers for the carnage in the clearing. There was chaos.

Men on fire and beyond help ran blindly in all directions before sinking to the ground. Most of the coffins had burnt themselves out and the wind had stopped as suddenly as it had started, allowing the smoke to hang amongst the trees like a rancid smog. Meadowbank spotted Sir Roger, seconds before he saw the giant near to the remaining coffins.

He ran across the clearing, avoiding the burning remains littering the area like unattended campfires and quickly reached Sir Roger. He lifted the injured man's head, feeling blood on his hands. Sir Roger opened his eyes acknowledging Meadowbank. He spoke quietly. "You need to stop the witch. My gun has two silver bullets loaded. They will do the job Albert". His right hand pointed to the howdah, then he dropped his head back, trying to focus his vision and regain his breath.

Meadowbank removed the strange weapon from the holster. It looked to him like a sawn off shotgun in pistol form and it was as heavy as it appeared. A noise made him spin round and Superintendent Malone appeared next to him, crouching by a pile of logs.

"How's he doing?"

"'E needs a doctor I know that. We 'ave t' end this nightmare an' soon".

The superintendent, looking across at the monster said. "What do you want me to do?"

"Go over yonder an' kill that thing".

Before he replied, the inspector continued, "It won't be that easy sir. Just a joke".

"Bad time for jokes Inspector, in fact it looks a bad time for most things".

Meadowbank checked that the gun was loaded as Sir Roger described and saw the crude solid silver bullets in both barrels. Without another word he stood and walked towards the witch, as if crossing no man's land.

She was now planning the future with her coffin-bound mother and grandmother, unaware of Meadowbank approaching.

"Demdike. I've somert for yer".

The witch reared like a grizzly bear protecting its family. Her facial expression changed from one of calm and soothing to complete rage when she saw Meadowbank stood thirty feet away.

"I am surprised to see you still alive Inspector. Mr. Ambrose is getting careless". Her voice was rough and broken.

"'E got so careless 'e's dead. Now it's your turn", he shouted, aiming the howdah and pulling the trigger of one barrel. "Yer goin' back t' where ever yer came from".

She took to the air, hovering several feet from the ground and screamed as the one inch solid silver slug hit her squarely below her neck. Putting a hand to her throat, the witch removed the silver bullet and held it out in her hand towards the inspector, laughing without any mirth.

"Would you like this back to try again?" the witch mocked.

Meadowbank pulled the second trigger. The retort was loud and the witch caught the bullet in her other hand, crushing the two together, silver dust falling between her fingers. She let out a deep sigh, as if finding the inspector's attack nothing more than tedious shenanigans. Hovering between the coffins, the Demdike looked down at Meadowbank as a headteacher would on an errant child. Even from where he was standing Meadowbank could detect the unmistakable smell of paraffin wafting from the soaked fabric of the witch. He withdrew his service revolver and fired until the six chambers were empty and the trigger clicked and clicked.

Superintendent Malone took up a kneeling position, bringing to his shoulder a pump action shotgun he had found abandoned in the clearing and aimed at the witch's head. He fired six shots in quick succession, each time smoothly ejecting a cartridge until the smoking gun was empty like the inspector's. The witch, ignoring the bullets being absorbed into her billowing black layers of clothing and the lead shot hitting her face, pointed at the superintendent. Immediately his skin erupted into scalding blisters, his nose and mouth emitted copious fumes as his blood boiled in his veins like a witch's brew. Steaming hot blood spurted from countless fissures on his body, and he fell back shrieking, his clothes bursting into flames and his chest rupturing like an overcooked sausage.

Meadowbank watched in horror. There was no place to hide, and no time to run for cover so he charged at the cackling monster, and she waited with her arms outstretched. The witch had special plans for the police inspector and welcomed him to his death. Holding his dagger he ran like he did in his school rugby days, head up sprinting for the line with anger driving him forward. This was an anger so intense that perhaps only death could appease it. In those final yards he thought of Mary who he abandoned on The Green and Sam and Paddy, were they alive? With a yell he raised his arm, ready to plunge the dagger, when suddenly...

* * *

Sir Roger opened his eyes to a miasma of swirling black smoke above. Lifting himself up with his good arm he looked around, his head banging like a steam hammer pounding rivets. He saw a body bubbling and smouldering near to him, but Superintendent Malone was beyond recognition, and then he spotted Inspector Meadowbank facing the monstrous witch, with a dagger drawn, a scene not unlike David and Goliath. Sir Roger felt for the howdah pistol forgetting it had gone. He reached for the flare gun and pulled it from the holster, aiming it towards the witch as Meadowbank charged. The iridescent projectile's trajectory looked too high, and the witch with arms spread, waiting to encircle Meadowbank, gave a croaking chuckle watching the flare arc above her, then turned her attention once again to the inspector.

The burning magnesium fuse, responding to gravity began its rapid descent, landing in the coffin containing Elizabeth Demdike. The witch's mother, inactive for so long, bolted upright to a sitting position as her paraffin dowsed body erupted into an instant furnace.

She screamed, "Vena, Vena, help me". Her first words for nearly three centuries rose above the roar of the fire.

The witch was frantic and helpless watching her mother twist and flail in the inferno.

"Mother! Noooo!" She moved too near the flames, and the methane fumes ignited, setting alight the witch's sleeve. In panic, and as any witch would do when fire threatens, she attempted to shake the hungry flames away, forgetting that fire thrives on oxygen and moving air. The fanned flames spread along her arm and across her back, and her shoulder length hair crackled as the eager fire took hold. She hung in the air like a poisonous gas cloud, her head on fire. The witch remained silent and confused, this could not be happening. The scorching flames licked her face, her skin sizzling and even though she knew there were only two ways to kill a witch, she was a Demdike, a necromancer, immortal, born to straddle time and bring ruination to mankind.

And the time to put things right was now. The witch, immune to pain, was overwhelmed by the fire and crashed to the ground like a clumsy hen. Stumbling and staggering backwards, her vision was blinded by the smoke and flames ravaging her head and shoulders. Singeing bristles and peeling skin revealed raw flesh the colour of a cancerous liver as she lurched and tumbled towards the remaining coffin and discarded bundles of kindling. The fire consuming her was now uncontrollable. With arms ablaze and hands a molten flux and those long foul fingernails now charred stumps, she reached out. Meadowbank dashed to one side to avoid the searing heat. He watched the giant witch burn like a brazier, the flames enveloping her completely as she called to her mother a final time, the roar of the blaze silencing her cry.

"Mother, I'm so sorry. I only wanted to put this…".

The burning witch blindly toppled against her grandmother's coffin, her head a blackened skull, green eyes scorched and swivelling. Close to death she collapsed onto the combustible kindling, the faggots igniting instantly, flaring into a conflagration and while her mother's screams faded, the screams from Old Mother Demdike increased. She too reached out, desperate to embrace her granddaughter.

This old witch, who like the others had survived a hanging, defying death and time, had little chance of surviving the flames devouring her. Putrid blood hissed and spurted, grey wiry hair withered and her scalp burned readily as if made of cork. Colliquant skin shrivelled, rotting flesh ruptured and roasted, and as the fire roared, the fetid stench and black smoke, thick like burning rubber was choking, poisonous, blinding.

The minutes ticked away and Meadowbank and Sir Roger watched in silence as the hungry flames no longer being fed, subsided, revealing a glutinous mass, resembling a smoking primordial tar pit. Then all became quiet, as a cemetery should be even at Halloween.

The Demdikes were no more.

41

Thirty six hours later.

The Preston and County of Lancaster Royal Infirmary on Deepdale Road was a hive of activity. Journalists, photographers from all around the country together with the boisterous crowd of well-wishers, onlookers, the curious, the concerned and the downright morbid, and those with nothing better to do were kept away from the main entrance by numerous police officers who were becoming more belligerent by the minute as they were jostled, pushed and bombarded with questions about the survivors of 'The Halloween Massacre'. This was the headline adopted by the local and national newspapers and the readers wanted more.

Meadowbank avoided all this by using a side entrance, opened to him by a uniformed constable. He knew where he was going and took the stairs to the first floor and nodded his head to the officer sat outside a private room off the main men's ward, then nervously opened the door.

Sergeant Huggins appeared to be asleep, sat up in bed, propped by several pillows. His bare chest was heavily bandaged which in parts were blood soaked. Meadowbank sat quietly on a bedside chair and took out of his pocket a betting forecast for

Saturday's racing. With a well worn pencil he settled down to earn the fortune which kept evading him.

The inspector had nodded off after half an hour or so and on waking saw Sam looking at him, smiling.

"Bloody 'ell Sam, it's good t' see yer mate".

"You too Albert, but what t' 'ell's gone on? No one 'as told mi owt abowt anythin'".

"I called 'ere yesterday an' yer wer fast asleep. You've bin 'eavily sedated. Listen, I'll get a couple o' brews an' tell you what 'appened after I left you at 'Hoarstones'".

He came back ten minutes later carrying a tray with two mugs of strong tea and a plate of biscuits.

"Anyway, 'ow are your doin'?" Meadowbank nodded towards the bloodied bandage around Sam's chest.

"It was close, apparently, but t' knife wedged in mi ribcage. I've 'ad a few stitches, I'll bi fine".

Meadowbank talked Huggins through the few hours after the raid on 'Hoarstones'.

The total number of men killed at Lytham Hall was seventy three, with many more suffering horrific burns. The hall was saved from the blaze, thanks to the quick thinking of Didier Pascall's men. But it was the torment of some of the survivors who had seen the witch, that would go on for ever. Wounds and burns heal, even for those feeling pain beyond measure, but to witness what occurred in the clearing on the eve of Halloween exceeded the comprehension of many, and they were destined to spend the rest of their days in the care of Whittingham lunatic asylum.

Paddy Button was found buried in the garden at 'Hoarstones' and the four children, who were now attracting much of the news, were in the nearby children's ward, recovering from malnutrition, dehydration and trauma. Meadowbank started to tell his sergeant about Superintendent Malone, but dropped his head in silence after a few seconds.

"Truth is Sam, I under estimated 'im. When it mattered 'e came forward an' it cost 'im 'is life. We faced a monster beyond belief. A giant witch…" . He shook his head as if still not believing what had happened. "Ten foot tall, three 'undred year old an' sendin' lightin' bolts from 'er very 'ands! This thing was livin' amongst us an' no one knew until t' end. Christ Sam! Are there any more out there?"

"God 'elp us if there are".

" All t' graves 'ave been refilled along wi' those monster's ashes from t' coffins an' a priest gave a blessin'. Sir Roger 'as already started replantin' t' clearin' wi' trees.".

Sam let his friend carry on talking; his questions could wait.

"What wer left of t' last three witches 'as bin scooped up an' buried in t' grounds of a local church. I went t' watch an' t' priest went a bit mad wi' t' 'oly water, sprinklin' it all over t' show. Would 'ave bin easier usin' an 'ose pipe". He joked half heartedly, keeping his head down.

"Anyway are yer goin' to Malone's funeral?"

"There's not much left of t' poor bugger t' bi 'onest Sam, but yes, I will go t' 'is funeral. It's t' least I can do t' pay mi respects".

"I don't like t' speak ill of t' dead, but don't forget Albert, we all thought 'e was a complete arse'ole an' 'e was. Okay, 'e came good at t' end, but look at all t' problems Malone caused. A few days ago 'e wanted you sacked remember?"

"Yer right Sam, 'e was an arrogant sod an' I felt like twattin' 'im every time I saw 'im, but I'll not forget that 'e stayed with mi t' fight that monster when 'e didn't 'ave to, an' that says a lot abowt t' man as far as I am concerned".

"I thought yer where 'ere t' cheer me up. I'm t' one stuck in an 'ospital bed".

"I do 'ave some good news for yer. You've bin recommended fer t' Kings Police Medal fer gallantry along wi' Ned Huxley an' some of t' other uniform lads. It's well deserved Sam. Congratulations".

Huggins was embarrassed. When so many of his colleagues had died the last thing he wanted was to be singled out for an act of bravery. He knew he did not deserve the recognition, when others did.
He changed the subject quickly.

"What about you an' Mary. Are yer steppin' out yet?'.

It was Meadowbank's turn to feel uncomfortable as he fidgeted on the chair, doing his best to avoid eye contact.

"Yeah, thing's are good wi' Mary, an' I've spent' a bit o' time at 'er lodgings past day or so". He sat upright, his eyes brimming with tears as he looked at his friend.

"She went through 'ell wi' that maniac Ambrose, but somehow she's put it behind 'er. She's an amazin' woman Sam, an' I don't mind tellin' yer that, an' it feels reet bein' with 'er, if yer know what I mean".

Sam nodded, smiling. He was pleased for his mate.

"Strange thing is though, she's taken in a stray cat, black as soot it is, wi' one eye. I'm certain it's t' same one that came in t' mi room a few days ago . It seems friendly enough, an' follows Mary everywhere. Talk about coincidence, eh?".

Printed in Great Britain
by Amazon